Deborah Carr, *USA Today*-bestselling author of *The Poppy Field*, lives on the island of Jersey in the Channel Islands with her husband and three rescue dogs. *An Island at War* is set on the island during the Occupation when Jersey was occupied by the Nazi forces from 1940–1945.

Her Mrs Boots series is inspired by another Jersey woman, Florence Boot, the woman behind the Boots (Walgreens Boots Alliance) empire. Her debut First World War romance, *Broken Faces*, was runner-up in the 2012 Good Housekeeping Novel Writing Competition and *Good Housekeeping* magazine described her as 'one to watch'.

Keep up to date with Deborah's books by subscribing to her newsletter: deborahcarr.org/newsletter.

www.deborahcarr.org

twitter.com/DebsCarr
facebook.com/DeborahCarrAuthor
instagram.com/ofbooksandbeaches
pinterest.com/deborahcarr
bookbub.com/profile/deborah-carr

D0028336

Also by Deborah Carr

The Mrs Boots Series

Mrs Boots

Mrs Boots of Pelham Street

Mrs Boots Goes to War

Standalones

The Poppy Field

AN ISLAND AT WAR

DEBORAH CARR

One More Chapter
a division of HarperCollins*Publishers* Ltd
1 London Bridge Street
London SE1 9GF
www.harpercollins.co.uk
HarperCollins*Publishers*
1st Floor, Watermarque Building, Ringsend Road
Dublin 4, Ireland

This paperback edition 2021
First published in Great Britain in ebook format
by HarperCollins*Publishers* 2021

3

A catalogue record of this book is available from the British Library

PB ISBN: 978-0-00-843630-8
TPB ISBN: 978-0-00-850578-3

This novel is entirely a work of fiction. The names, characters and incidents portrayed in it are the work of the author's imagination. Any resemblance to actual persons, living or dead, events or localities is entirely coincidental.

Printed and bound in the UK using 100% Renewable Electricity
by CPI Group (UK) Ltd

To all the Channel Islanders who lived through the Occupation years and especially to those here in Jersey

War Cabinet decision is that the Island of Jersey is to be demilitarised. Further instructions regarding the Governor will follow.

The Channel Islands will not, repeat, not be defended against external invasion by sea or air.

Official communications received by The Lieutenant Governor of Jersey, Major General Harrison on 19th of June 1940

Prologue

28 JUNE 1940

Philippe Le Maistre flinched as he heard a distant boom. It sounded closer than the recent bombs the Germans had been dropping on St Malo. He checked that the rope holding the wooden boxes filled with his recently dug Jersey Royal potatoes was still secure. It was a warm evening and he had been queuing on the Albert Quay for several hours and was now fifth in line to unload his precious cargo. He couldn't help thinking about the exhausted Canadian soldiers he had helped rescue from St Malo on his friend's boat a couple of weeks before. They had been traumatised by the speed at which the Germans had forced them from Dunkirk cornering them in the walled town with only the sea as their escape.

'They are unstoppable,' a young Lieutenant insisted as he was helped aboard the boat, close to tears. 'Save your family while you still have a chance.'

The sound of plane engines disturbed his thoughts. He looked up towards Mount Bingham, shading his eyes against the bright sunlight. Phillippe's mouth dried as he noticed the black crosses on the underside of the wings. What did they want this time?

'It's a bloody Heinkel!' he heard Chas Vatel bellow. 'No, two of them. Hell, there's three of the buggers. What are the Jerries doing now? Don't they know St Malo's that way?' He waved his hands towards the Channel.

Philippe's heart pounded in shock. He couldn't tear his eyes from the approaching planes. He willed them to be doing reconnaissance, as others had done in the preceding weeks. These were flying very low though. He guessed they were no more than two hundred feet above where he was standing.

Philippe gasped to see something small and dark drop on Mount Bingham. The dull thud of the bomb as it landed was immediately followed by aloud crash as two further bombs smashed into houses on the large hill, sending masonry spilling down on to the nearby road. The men cast their eyes in the direction of the explosions. Then two more fell on Fort Regent, the Napoleonic fortress with its commanding position high over the harbours below. 'B-Bombs!' he shouted, the sound of his voice obliterated by more loud ear-splitting booms. 'Everyone get down, now!'

A bomb exploded on the old harbour less than a mile away sending sharp pieces of granite a hundred feet into the air. Others hit small boats, setting them on fire shooting debris and plumes of thick black smoke high into the St Helier sky. Philippe ducked, his trembling hands covering his head.

'Blimey, that was close!' Chas shouted. 'You all right, Philippe, mate?'

Philippe nodded, unable to speak.

He stared as flames leapt up through the hole in the wood store in Commercial Buildings on the quay. Is this what we have to look forward to? he wondered, barely able to take in what he'd just witnessed. Thank God his dear wife Marie hadn't lived long enough to have to face this nightmare.

Philippe took a deep breath trying to compose himself. It wouldn't do to let himself down in front of others. He studied the row of trucks in front and behind him. None of the other thirty or so men seemed to be moving, so he would have to stay and hope that the dockers unloaded his truck soon.

He walked around the front of his truck and pulled open the door. He had a flask of tea in there, maybe it would help calm him. He lifted it to go and offer some to those nearest to him, when the sound of the plane engines increased.

'They're coming back!' Chas bellowed.

Everyone followed the familiar sound of the bombers and Philippe noticed to his horror that they were racing towards them across St Aubin's Bay, landing a direct hit on the row of granite buildings lining the road next to the old harbour.

Within seconds, the Heinkels opened fire on the lined-up lorries and men as they flew the length of the Albert Pier towards the town. Bullets strafed the parked vehicles, their drivers and dockers open targets with no possible chance of escape.

Shards of granite exploded from the promenade wall running alongside them, piercing the men's flesh as they ran for cover.

Acrid smoke-filled Philippe's nostrils. He didn't like his odds. He tried to ignore the screams from injured men along the pier. Then, covering his mouth with the lapel of his jacket, Philippe took a deep breath and ran as fast as he could towards the closest crane leg, where others were sheltering.

Just before he reached them, a searing pain pierced his side and back as several bullets hit their target. Philippe knew that this was it. The Nazis were here. They were invading his beloved island. The girls. His precious daughters. Who would protect his eldest daughter Estelle now? If only he had sent her to England with little Rosie and not insisted she stay on the island to help on the farm. He had let them down. His last promise to his beloved Marie had been to protect their babies, and he had failed her.

'Forgive me,' he whispered, as everything went black.

ONE

Estelle

E stelle held her little sister's hand tightly in one hand, her small cardboard case in the other as the crowds jostled pushing to board the SS *Shepperton Ferry*. She hated being parted from Rosie, but the thought of her sister staying and having to face the Germans if they did invade like everyone expected was far more terrifying.

'I'm scared, Essie.'

Estelle stared down at the large brown eyes that reminded her so much of their beautiful mum. Only she had been lucky enough to know Mum's love. She coughed to clear her throat and push away the memory of the day twelve years ago when her sister was born. Estelle had been barely seven, but Dad had needed her to be strong and help look after her new baby sister, while he and her grandmother made arrangements for the funeral. She had welcomed having someone to cuddle during those heart-breaking weeks after her mum's unexpected death. She

5

could barely remember a time when Rosie had not been around following her everywhere since then.

'Don't be,' Estelle said. 'You've got to be strong. We all do. Anyway, you'll be safer staying at Aunt Muriel's in London. She'll take care of you.'

Since her mother's death, Gran had been Rosie's mother figure and now Estelle knew that however difficult it might be for her to ensure Rosie was evacuated to the mainland, it was something that she needed to do.

'But I don't remember her. Do you?'

'You must do, she was only here a few years ago. Don't you remember going swimming with her at Havre des Pas bathing pool? She treated us to one of Smith's ice creams that day, too. You know, the boy on the bicycle with the cooler on the front?'

Rosie shook her head, her usually smiling mouth sulky. 'I don't want to go away, I want to stay here with you, Gran and Daddy.'

'I know you do.'

'I wish you were coming with me,' Rosie added her chin beginning to wobble.

'So do I.' Estelle lowered the case to the ground and gave her sister a tight hug. 'I'll tell you what, when this is all over we'll plan a family holiday somewhere.'

'Do you promise?'

'Yes… but you know I need to stay here with Dad and Gran to help them at the farm until that time comes.' She needed to distract Rosie somehow. 'Now, where's your gas mask?'

Rosie pointed to her shoulder indicating the string attached to the box hanging slightly behind her back.

'Good. You mustn't lose it.'

'I won't,' she mumbled. 'Is Aunt Muriel nice?'

'Very, and she's great fun, too.' Estelle pictured her mother's sister. They looked so similar, although their lives had been very different. Her mother had come to live in Jersey when she married their dad whereas Muriel enjoyed a more glamorous life as a manager in a smart clothes shop in London. 'Look, don't worry. You'll remember her when you see her again. I know you will.'

'But why is Daddy making me go? I promised him I'd help more if he let me stay at home.'

Estelle's heart ached to hear her sister voicing her own thoughts. 'He wants you to be safe. You've heard the sound of bombing from St Malo, haven't you?' Rosie nodded miserably. 'And I heard Dad speaking with Gran about some of the things the Canadian soldiers told him they'd witnessed after he helped rescue them.'

'You mean those men he saved who had escaped from Dunkirk?'

'Yes, that's right. Quite a few of them managed to get as far as St Malo, but there was nowhere else for them to go once they'd got that far.'

'And he doesn't want that to happen to us?'

Estelle sighed. 'No, and I think he worries about us being stuck here if the Germans come and the same thing happens.'

Rosie's hand squeezed hers a little tighter. 'I hope it won't.'

So did she. Part of her wished she was going with Rosie, but she was nineteen now and needed at home. Her sister was going to have to find a way to cope without her.

Estelle spotted one of her old school friends. It made her feel a little better to know that someone she knew well was also being evacuated to England. Estelle opened her mouth to call to her.

'Janine!' she shouted, relieved when the girl turned and after scanning over the heads of the others in the crowd saw her. Estelle picked up Rosie's case. 'Come on, Rosie,' she said, pulling her sister passed the hot, sweaty bodies pressed against each other waiting to board. She ignored Rosie's grumblings and kept going until she reached her friend. 'Are you going to England on this boat?'

'Yes,' Janine said, somehow looking cool and not as stressed as the rest of them. 'I'd rather stay here and take my chances, but my Mum has arranged for me to stay with a cousin for the duration in Southampton. Hopefully, it won't be for too long. You?'

'I've got to stay here,' Estelle said thinking of her plans to enrol in art college. She had wanted to be a dress designer for as long as she could remember ever since falling in love with films at the pictures. She couldn't see that happening any time soon. Not now. 'My little sister Rosie's going. You remember Rosie, don't you?'

Janine's eyes followed the line of Estelle's arm until she saw Rosie. 'Ah, there you are, Rosie. I didn't see you standing there behind your sister. Don't look so worried, it'll be fine. You'll see. Think of it as an adventure.'

Rosie mumbled something Estelle couldn't hear over the anxious voices around them.

'Rosie's travelling alone?'

Estelle explained that Rosie was supposed to have gone to her school to meet up with her teachers and schoolfriends. 'I think she was hoping that if we came straight here she could persuade me to give in and either go with her, or let her come home to the farm with me.'

'I don't like Mrs Gilcrest,' Rosie grumbled. 'And I don't want to go all the way to England with her. Anyway, I'm sure it wouldn't be so bad if Estelle let me stay here.'

Estelle pulled a face at Janine. 'As you can see, it's been a bit of a battle this morning.' She turned her attention to her sister. 'We've been through this, Rosie.' She was finding it difficult to keep her emotions in check. It was painful enough parting from her sister for the first time, especially when she didn't know how long it would be for, but this was almost too much for her.

She usually gave in to Rosie, but this time she had no choice and had to remain firm. She reached out and brushed Rosie's messy fringe away from her warm forehead. 'You know Dad was the one who decided this and he's only doing it because he wants you to be safe. We must do what he asks. Sometimes we have to do the right thing, even if we'd rather not.'

Rosie didn't look convinced. 'But surely, if it's dangerous for me to remain here, then you should be coming with me?'

Estelle closed her eyes, trying to contain her frustration. 'You know he needs my help on the farm with all the boys away fighting. Now, please stop making such a fuss, it won't change anything, only make this harder for us both.'

Janine rested a hand on Estelle's shoulder. 'Has Rosie got someone to stay with when she gets to Weymouth?'

'Our Aunt Muriel. She's going to meet her off the boat and take her back to her flat in London.'

'Well, then, I'll take care of Rosie while we're on the ferry.' Janine bent so her face was level with Rosie's. 'Would that be all right with you?'

Rosie looked from Janine to Estelle and after a moment's thought shrugged. 'Yes, if you like.'

It was a success, of sorts. Estelle's shoulders relaxed slightly. 'Thank you.'

'No problem.' Janine smiled at her. 'Rosie and I will be in Weymouth in a few hours and I promise I won't leave her until I know she's safe with your auntie.'

It was more than Estelle had hoped for and she was hugely grateful to her friend. 'I really appreciate your help, it's very kind of you.'

A whistle sounded, silencing most of the voices on the pier. 'Five minutes until boarding closes.' A chorus of gasps and panicked voices filled the air. 'We need to leave in fifteen minutes if we're to catch the tide.'

'That's it,' the woman next to Estelle said, pushing passed her. 'I'm not going.'

Estelle felt Rosie's hand tense in hers. 'Come along,' she said, picking up her sister's small case and pushing her way through the throngs of people waiting by the ship to the gangway. Janine followed closely behind, bringing up the rear so Rosie had no choice but to keep moving forward.

Rosie continued to badger her with reasons why she should go with her back to the farm, but Estelle did her best to take little notice. Eventually they reached the front of the queue.

'Tickets,' demanded a flustered officer, putting his arm out in front of Estelle to stop her stepping on to the gangplank.

She had been hoping to sneak onboard with her sister and find the best place for Rosie to wave goodbye, but that looked as if it wasn't going to happen now. She took Rosie's ticket from her pocket and held it in front of his face.

'There's only one.' He gave her a knowing look and Estelle assumed she wasn't the first person today to have tried this tactic. She had been dreading this bit. 'It's for my younger sister. I'm dropping her off. I just want to make sure she's settled on the boat. Then I promise I'll get straight off again.'

'No, you won't love.'

She tried not to panic. 'But you don't understand—'

He shook his head, wearily. 'No love, it's you that doesn't understand. If I let you on, then I'd have to let half that lot on, too.' He nodded in the direction of the crowd behind Estelle and she glanced over her shoulder. Her heart plummeted. She would have to say her goodbyes to Rosie here, and quickly.

'Fine. Here's her ticket, then,' she said, handing it over, and turning to Rosie. 'I'm going to have to leave you here, I'm afraid.'

Rosie's face crumpled and her eyes filled with tears. 'What? No, you can't.'

'Be good for Janine and give my love to Aunt Muriel,' Estelle said, her voice cracking with emotion. She crouched down and pulled Rosie into a tight hug breathing in the familiar scent of the shampoo she had used to wash her hair.

'Please don't leave me, Essie. Please.' Estelle braced herself for what she was about to do and then gently pushing her away, handed Rosie her case. 'Go with Janine. It'll be fine, I promise you.'

'You don't know that.' She burst into tears.

It was true, Estelle thought, she had no idea whether or not Rosie's voyage to Weymouth would be fine. She felt sick to think of recent reports about boats travelling from the Channel Islands to the mainland needing to zigzag to avoid being hit by German fighter planes. The thought that her sister might not even make it to the other side of the Channel terrified her, especially as she was the one now forcing her to go.

'Don't make me go, *pleeease*,' Rosie sobbed.

Estelle only just managed to hold back her own tears. Her heart felt like someone was tearing it out of her chest. She gave Janine a pleading look, relieved when her friend quickly handed her ticket to the officer and put her arm comfortingly around Rosie's shoulders.

Rosie shrugged her off. 'Don't touch me. You're not my sister.'

Aware that she had no time left to delay, Estelle stepped away from them. 'I'm sorry,' she said, tears catching in her throat. 'I have no choice.'

'Come along,' Janine said. 'There's a good girl. Let's go

and find somewhere to wave to Estelle.' Rosie went to argue, but Janine simply pulled her away from Estelle and on to gangplank. Seconds later, they were stepping on to the boat, with Rosie staring tearfully over her shoulder at Estelle.

Estelle gave her sister a wave and forced a smile.

'Off you go now, Miss,' the officer said. 'You're holding everyone up.'

She mouthed a thank-you to Janine and turning, hurried away, trying her best not to be swayed by Rosie's shouts pleading for her to take her home.

She needed to find somewhere to wave to her sister. It took a few minutes to wend her way through the throng of people and up the granite steps at the side of the promenade. Estelle scanned the passengers on the deck frantically hoping to find Rosie, relieved to see her sister and friend standing by the railings searching the crowd for her.

'Over here, Rosie!' she shouted. When they didn't hear her, Estelle pulled her handkerchief from her pocket and waved it in the air. She groaned with relief when Janine spotted her and pointed in her direction for Rosie.

A short while later, Estelle saw the dockers moving the gangway away from the boat and then lifting the ropes off the large iron bollard. As the ferry slowly began to move away from the harbour wall, Estelle's chest ached.

'I'll see you soon, Rosie. Give Aunt Muriel my love.' She doubted her sister could actually hear her over all the other shouts between friends and families, but she had at least to try to say some final words to her.

Rosie brushed away tears with her fingers and then waved her arms over her head, giving Estelle a half-smile. Estelle could see her sister was trying her best to be brave and it broke her heart even more that she wouldn't be there for her. She hoped desperately that Rosie would be safe in London and would find a way to cope without her.

'Bye, Rosie!' she shouted carrying on waving until she was certain her sister couldn't see her any more. Estelle stood in a numbed silence watching the boat slowly cross St Aubin's Bay.

Everything had been so chaotic over the past few days that she hadn't had a second to think about what it truly meant for them all. Now that Rosie was being taken further and further away from her, Estelle wasn't sure how she was going to face the uncertainty of what the future held for those left behind. So many families being parted and her chance of attending art college in London vanishing. She was sure about one thing though, as the ferry moved further towards the headland at Noirmont, she would never forgive the Germans for splitting her family up like this. Never.

TWO

Estelle

28 JUNE 1940

E stelle sat and forced herself to eat the beef stew Gran had made for their supper. She usually loved her grandmother's stews but this evening it tasted like cardboard. She chewed another mouthful, hoping that if she did it enough she might be able to swallow it a little easier.

She faced her grandmother across the pine kitchen table and wondered if she was finding it as difficult being in the farmhouse without Rosie's noisy chatter. Gran stared out of the window as she ate silently. She had been quieter this past week since Rosie had been evacuated and Estelle could see she was trying to put on a brave face. 'Grace and dignity are the most important things you have to remember, Estelle,' she was fond of saying. 'Remember, one day, you will look back on this and will be glad that you acted in a dignified way.'

Estelle swallowed another mouthful of her supper and, unable to keep her thoughts to herself any longer, asked, 'Don't you find it too quiet with Rosie gone, Gran?'

'I do,' her grandmother replied. 'It's not the same without her chirping about the place, asking questions. I even miss her messy room, which I was constantly telling her to tidy up. You must be missing your sister very much.'

It felt good to admit her feelings. 'I still can't shake off how upset she was the last time I saw her. I feel so guilty making her go when she didn't want to.'

'Nonsense. You were only doing your father's bidding.'

Estelle wasn't sure her father had been right to force Rosie to leave. 'Do you think it was best for her to go?'

Her grandmother shrugged. 'We won't know that until after this is all over. Who knows what's going to happen to us here, or to her and Muriel in London? We just have to trust that we will all survive what's coming.'

Estelle shivered, despite it being a warm evening. The only good thing to have happened recently was her sweetheart, Gerard, being allowed to return to the island: with the ever-increasing threat of war reaching the Channel Islands, all the young lads who had signed up had been given some leave to see their families. He hadn't finished his basic training yet. In fact, he had barely had time to start. She felt a little comforted knowing Gerard was here, even if only for a few days, especially having heard – and then seen – German planes flying overhead earlier in the day. They had been flying low over the island and someone had said it was reconnaissance. Estelle hadn't taken too much notice and presumed they were just making their presence felt before flying on to France. The coast was close enough for her to be able to see from her bedroom window, so that was an obvious possibility.

Recently, the German Army had marched across the Continent, taking everything in its path, or so it seemed. Were they next? Estelle wondered, her stomach clenching in fear. Like everyone else on the island, she had heard terrifying stories about the atrocities and suffering inflicted on people by the Nazis. She prayed that the rumours of them invading the islands were just that.

The mantle clock chimed eight and Estelle wondered where her father was. Having delayed their supper for him, his absence was another reason she was finding it hard to enjoy her food. On days like these, when he took his spuds down to the docks, he always ended up in lengthy queues, but he was usually back by now and she wondered what was keeping him so long.

Estelle's thoughts were distracted by the sound of a truck coming up the drive. 'That sounds like Gerard,' she said, recognising the noisy engine. It would be a relief to see his smiling face.

'What's he doing here at this time?' Gran grumbled. 'Go and let him in but he's going to have to wait until we've finished eating before you two can wander off outside. And no getting up to any funny business, mind you.'

Estelle placed her cutlery down on her plate and rushed to the back door to welcome him— her smile vanishing immediately when she saw his ashen face.

'Whatever's the matter?' She asked, stepping forward and placing her hands either side of his face. 'Has something happened?'

He leant forward and kissed her lightly on the cheek,

before taking her by the hand. 'Is your grandmother around?'

'We're still eating,' Gran called. 'Come in, Gerard, take a seat. We won't be long now.'

Estelle led him into the kitchen, her heart racing, concerned to feel how clammy his strong hand was in her own. Something was wrong, but what?

'We would have finished by now,' Gran continued, 'but we were late starting, waiting for Estelle's father to come home. He must have been delayed down at the docks again.'

Estelle indicated for Gerard to take a seat opposite her grandmother before sitting back down at her own place. When he didn't make a move to sit, she felt a sense of dread well up inside her.

'Gerard? Why are you here?' she asked, instinctively fearful about hearing his answer. She'd never seen him so quiet or humourless and they'd known each other since primary school. She could see he was struggling to speak. 'Gerard?'

'Is it your dad?' Estelle asked, moving in her chair to stand back up to comfort him.

He put out his hand, motioning for her to remain seated. 'No, please, don't get up. Something has happened,' he replied, his voice shaky. 'Something dreadful.'

'Has your father had an accident on his farm?' Why couldn't Gerard just tell them?

He shook his head and cleared his throat.

'Why don't you just tell us, son?' the older woman now said, placing her knife and fork neatly on her plate and wiping her mouth on her linen napkin. 'Take a deep breath and spit it out.'

Acknowledging Estelle's grandmother for a brief moment, before returning his full attention once again to his sweetheart, Gerard did as the older woman had directed. 'I'm so sorry, Estelle, but it's not my father I've come to tell you about… it's yours.'

Estelle couldn't understand what he meant. How could her father have had an accident on the farm when he wasn't even working here today? 'No, he's not here. I told you, he went down to the docks several hours ago.'

Gran's hand stilled as she reached for her glass. 'Tell us, son.'

'German bombers flew over the docks earlier.'

'I heard them. They flew over here, too, at about six-ish.' Estelle said, confused.

Gerard walked over to her and took her hands in his. 'They bombed the docks, Estelle.'

'Bombed? Here?' She felt breathless.

'What exactly happened, Gerard,' her grandmother snapped.

'Sorry. I… It's just… well, they dropped several bombs, then flew across the island and then went back and shot at the farmers and dockers who were down at the harbour.'

Estelle leapt to her feet. 'Dad's been shot? Why didn't you say so sooner?' She snatched her hands out of his grasp and ran to the door, grabbing her coat from the hook. 'Quickly, you have to take me to see him. Is he in the hospital?' She wondered why he wasn't moving. 'Gerard. Come along. We have to go. *Now!*' She noticed him gaze from her to her gran, a strange questioning look on his face. Estelle watched her grandmother get to her feet, as if in slow motion, and move towards her.

'*No!*' Estelle shouted. 'No. Don't say it.' She pleaded for her grandmother to stop walking. If Gran didn't say what she now guessed she was about to say then it wouldn't be true.

'I think, dear girl...' her grandmother said placing one hand against Estelle's right cheek, 'that your father didn't make it.'

Estelle stared at her and then looked back towards Gerard, willing him to contradict her. 'Tell Gran she's wrong, Gerard. Tell her, please.'

He shook his head. 'There's nothing I'd like more in the world right now than to do as you ask. I'm so sorry, Estelle. Your father is dead.'

Estelle's breathing seemed to echo in her ears. She looked at the clock on the mantelpiece, its tick-tock sound suddenly echoing loudly around the room. 'Do... do you know if he suffered at all?' She prayed Gerard would say what she needed to hear.

Gently, Gerard took Estelle's coat from her before leading her back to the table. 'No, I was assured that he didn't suffer. That's something to be grateful for, isn't it?'

Estelle nodded slowly. 'Can I go and see him?'

Gerard shook his head. 'No. I'm sorry.'

'But are they sure it's Dad?'

Gerard nodded. 'Everyone knows your dad down at the docks. It was definitely him.' He bent down and hugged her. 'Three other men on the pier also lost their lives. Two others in Mulcaster Street.' He hugged her more tightly. 'He will have known nothing, Estelle. Try to take some comfort from that.'

She heard Gran's trembling voice. 'I'll make us all a strong cup of sweet tea.'

'I'm so, so sorry,' Gerard murmured. 'Your dad was like an uncle to me.'

'I know,' Estelle whispered.

'I wish I wasn't leaving you so soon. Especially now that this has happened.'

Tomorrow, he would be leaving the island to return to England to continue with his training.

Estelle replayed Gerard's words in her head. Her father was dead. She would *never see him again…*

'*Rosie?* We have to find a way to tell her what's happened,' she cried, suddenly.

Her grandmother filled the kettle and went to place it on to the range, almost dropping it when her shaking hand accidentally hit the edge.

Estelle could see she was struggling. 'Oh, Gran,' she said, sobbing as she ran over to her and into her arms. 'Whatever will we do?'

The older woman held her granddaughter tightly for a moment, before her arms dropped away and she stepped back. 'We have to be strong, Estelle. We have no other choice. I'll write a letter to Muriel tonight,' she said, having regained her composure. 'I'll ask her to break the news to Rosie. She'll be as gentle as she can.'

They had been seated for almost an hour at the dinner table, frozen in shock and grief, when Gran finally suggested that they all move into the living room. 'The seats are more comfortable in there.' She rested a hand on her granddaughter's stooped shoulder and when Estelle and Gerard agreed, she said, 'You two go and get settled and I'll make us all a fresh pot of tea.'

Estelle knew instinctively that Gran was wanting some time to herself, to control her feelings, and she didn't blame her. Quietly, she followed Gerard through the hall to the living room and switched on the light. It was cold and already seemed to feel different without her father's presence in it.

'I'll light the fire,' Gerard suggested. 'You sit down.' When she didn't speak, he took her by the shoulders and pulled her into a tight hug. 'It will be all right, I promise you,' he said quietly, his warm breath next to her ear. 'I'll do all I can to help you. You're not alone, Estelle. Remember that.'

'But you're going away, too? It's going to be just me and Gran left here and I don't think I can bear it.'

She felt him flinch. 'I wish I hadn't signed up now,' he said, kissing her forehead. 'I'd do anything to be able to look after you.'

'What if something happens to you? How would I bear it?' His face fell and she realised how selfish she was being. 'No. I'm sorry. I shouldn't have said that. You have no choice now but to return to your unit and at least you can fight and make a difference.'

He stared at her silently for a few seconds. 'I will certainly do my best.

Estelle sat down on the sofa, always liking to be nearest

the window for the best light. She watched him taking the kindling wood, lay and then light the fire.

Soon the flames crackled and Gerard added a few more small pieces of wood and coal until it caught. Gradually, the warmth from the fire seeped out into the small living room but Estelle still felt cold.

Gerard sat back on his heels and looked over his shoulder at her. 'Do you mind very much if I turn on the radio?' he asked. 'It's nine o'clock and I've taken to listening to the news each evening ever since this war began.'

'You do as you wish, lad,' Gran said, entering the room, holding a tray with three cups and saucers on it. She gave them one each, kissed Estelle on the top of her head, and sat down in her chair closest to the fire. Gerard sat next to Estelle on the sofa and Estelle wondered if it was because he wanted to sit next to her, or if he didn't like to use her father's chair on the other side of the fireplace opposite her grandmother's seat. She was glad he hadn't chosen to sit there.

The BBC announcer's clipped voice filled the room: 'The Channel Islands has been demilitarised and declared an open town.'

Estelle wasn't sure what he was saying but by the look on Gerard's face it wasn't good.

'What does he mean by demilitarised?' she asked.

'It means that the British Government has abandoned any intention of defending the islands.'

'So the rumours of invasion are turning out to be true,' her grandmother muttered.

Through the fog of her grief for her father, still so fresh, so inexplicable, Estelle felt tears slide down her cheeks. She'd lost Rosie. Her dad. And now... 'Basically, what they're saying, then, is that we're on our own.'

Gerard rubbed his face with his free hand. 'Yes, that's pretty much it.' He sighed heavily. 'It's an open invitation to invade.'

THREE

Estelle

E stelle scattered feed for the hens in the yard, while her father's Alsatian, Rebel, lay dozing in the sunshine. More planes had been flying low over the island that morning, but Estelle realised that, regardless of her grief and the uncertainty of what was to come next, the chickens and their three pigs still needed to be fed.

It was another warm, sunny day. Any other year, she would be preparing to spend the afternoon down on the beach with one of her friends, Rosie usually in tow. Today, though, she had chores to do. Responsibilities. Her grandmother depended on her. 'How are you doing?' a deep voice asked from behind her.

For a moment, she thought she had imagined Gerard's voice, but when Rebel raised his head and began wagging his tail, she realised he *must* be behind her. She spun on the heels of her work boots, accidentally dropping the rest of the feed in the process.

'I thought you'd have left by now.'

'I've managed to get a place on the boat tomorrow, so I could spend a little more time here.' He walked up to her and pulled her into his arms. 'I wouldn't leave without coming to say goodbye to you first.'

It was good to see his familiar sweet face. 'I'm glad you came. I thought you'd have too much to do before you left.'

He kissed her lightly on the mouth. 'I was, which is why I'm here later than I'd hoped.'

She wrapped her arms around his waist, breathing in his musky scent and clung to him tightly. After tomorrow, when would she see him again? She felt weary with the heartbreak of losing her father. 'My dad—'

'I know,' he soothed, stroking her hair with one hand. 'How's Rebel coping without him? He's always been very much your dad's dog, hasn't he?'

Estelle bent to stroke Rebel's silky head. 'He's been quieter since Dad didn't come home but doesn't seem too bad, thankfully. I think he's a little confused, but he's going to be all right. I'll make sure he is.'

'I know you will. He's a good dog.' He bent to ruffle the dog's fur. 'Aren't you, boy?'

'Gerard Pipon, haven't you left already? Or are you trying to miss that boat to the mainland?' Gerard stepped back from Estelle at the sound of Gran's voice.

'Hello, Mrs Woods,' he said. 'I leave tomorrow. How are you bearing up?'

She wagged her finger. 'We'll find a way to deal with everything, don't you fret about us. I know how much you respected my son-in-law, too. So, no words are needed on that score. We're just grateful it was you who came to break our sad news to us. Weren't we, Estelle?'

Estelle couldn't speak, so nodded.

'Will you be staying for something to eat?' Gran pressed her lips together, her usual determined expression on her face. 'Although I suspect your mother will be wanting you back at home with her... and I can't say I blame her, if you've only a short time left here.'

He shot a glance at Estelle. She could tell he would rather spend more time alone with her, but she was grateful for him coming to see her at all. She gave him a smile to reassure him that she understood.

'I need to go straight home,' he explained, apologetically; then hesitated, before adding, 'Would you like me to try and find someone to help you out here, now that, well, now that, um...' His voice trailed off and Estelle was relieved he hadn't said the words out loud.

'That would be kind of you,' Gran answered for both of them. 'Thank you. Estelle's a strong girl and used to help with the harvesting. We only have one more field of spuds to dig and then it'll be a little easier to manage things on the farm for a time. Estelle and I can probably cope for a couple of weeks if we can persuade some of the villagers to come and help us. But it's difficult to find someone permanent who's young and fit and who wants work labouring, now that so many of you stronger young men have joined up.'

'I'll do what I can.'

Her grandmother studied them both. 'Right, I'd better get back to the house. I've got a pie baking and don't want it to burn. Very best of luck to you, Gerard. Keep safe above all else, won't you?'

'I'll do my best, Mrs Woods. And you, too.'

They watched her cross the yard to return to the house. Then as soon as she had closed the back door behind her Gerard pulled Estelle back into his arms. 'I probably won't have time to come back and see again you before I go.' There was an urgency in his voice and he put a hand behind her head, lowering his mouth on to hers, kissing her with a passion she hadn't experienced before. It was as if he never expected to see her again. She hoped he was wrong. 'Please promise me,' he said, 'that you'll keep yourself safe. For me. Don't take any unnecessary risks.'

'I will, but you're the one who'll be fighting. In harm's way. Not me.'

'You don't know that, Estelle,' he said quietly. 'And you'll write to me?'

'You know I will.' She kissed him again not wanting to guess what dangers they both would have to face in the coming months.

The nearby church struck nine times.

'I really must go,' he said, kissing her once more. 'I'm going to miss you so much.'

'Come back to me,' she replied, her heart heavy at the thought that this was probably her last moment with him for a very long time.

Gerard hurried away, giving her one last wave as he started the truck, reversed to turn it and drove away.

Estelle watched until the dust on the drive settled. 'Stay

safe,' she whispered. Her throat caught with tears. Another goodbye. How many more were to come?

———————

The following morning, Estelle was cleaning her teeth when she heard the unmistakeable sound of a rumbling plane engine flying over the farm. She rinsed her mouth out with water and spat into the sink, quickly cleaning it. Pushing her feet into her boots, she didn't stop to tie them but ran downstairs to see what was coming, her heart pounding.

She raised her right hand to shield her eyes from the sun and looked up to see hundreds of pieces of paper floating down from the sky and above them several planes that she knew had to be the Germans. She ran forward, missing one of the leaflets but caught the next and read it. Her heart plummeted. It was an order to surrender.

She ran back into the house almost knocking into her grandmother as she was entering the kitchen from the hallway.

'Do be more careful, Estelle,' Gran scolded, steadying herself by grabbing the door frame. 'What's that you've got?'

Estelle passed the leaflet to her grandmother. 'Read this. Hundreds of them have just fallen from a plane; I watched it going over.'

'Well, that's it then. It looks like the invasion has started. Quick we need to prepare.'

Estelle thought of Gerard and how he was supposed to

be leaving the island today. 'Do you think Gerard will have time to leave, first?'

'I don't know why you keep asking me these questions, Estelle. I know as much as you do. For his mother's sake, I hope he stays here. For his, I hope he managed to leave already.'

Estelle's chest tightened and she began to panic. 'You mean we'll be isolated here? How long for, do you think?'

Gran scrunched up the leaflet in her hand and placed her hands on her hips. 'I don't have the answers. None of us do. We'll have to take it as it comes and just do the best we can with what we have.'

Later that morning, Gerard arrived at the farm on his bike, his tanned face was shiny from perspiration and he was panting. Estelle was delighted to see him so unexpectedly. 'What are you doing here?' she asked running towards him.

He almost dropped the bicycle he was riding in his rush to reach her. His face was ashen and she could see he was distressed. 'I didn't manage to find someone to help you here,' he said, taking her hands in his.

'It's fine, we'll sort something out.'

'Have you seen the leaflets?' She nodded. 'I had to come here and see you one last time. I don't know when I'll next be able to.'

'Shouldn't you be trying to leave the island rather than coming here?'

Speaking fast, he replied, 'I'm on my way now. I'm

going to do my best to persuade someone to lend me a boat.'

'What? Why?'

'The passenger boats have been cancelled, but I must get away before the Germans land. I asked my uncle, but he told me I was mad and refused.' Estelle wished he would calm down a little and not speak so fast. 'A couple of the chaps I came back here with are going to come with me. We're going to try to reach England. We can't take the chance of staying here and being stuck, probably for years.'

'Years? Don't say that.' The thought of her beautiful island being turned into a prison horrified her. More than anything, Estelle wanted to plead with him to stay in Jersey, to stay with her, but she thought of her grandmother's words and knew the best thing for him would be to find a way to return to the mainland and join his fleet in the Royal Navy.

She leant forward and gave him a quick kiss on the lips. 'Go, then. Don't waste time speaking to me. Find that boat.'

He smiled at her for the first time that morning. 'I love you. You're so brave.'

She was glad he didn't know quite how frightened she was. 'Go.' She pushed him away.

He picked up his bike and swung his leg over the saddle. Estelle watched him pedal furiously away out of the yard, raising his hand briefly in a wave. She wondered when she would see him again. *If she saw him again.*

FOUR

Rosie

R osie stared at the thick notepad in front of her. Aunt Muriel had given it to her as a present the night before.

'I know you're worried about Estelle and your family in Jersey and that you've been missing them, badly, so I wanted to buy you a diary to write in. We don't know how long this war is set to last and I thought I'd buy you the thickest notepad I could find. That way, you can keep it for writing your thoughts and everything else you want to share with your sister when you're back home again.' Rosie recalled the way her aunt had put her arm around her shoulders and given her a determined look. 'And you will be. You must remember that, especially when you're feeling down. This is a very strange time for all of us, but it will pass. I promise you it will and you'll be back at the farm in your old bedroom once again.'

Rosie had hugged her aunt, grateful for her thoughtfulness and her words of encouragement. Now, she was sitting, fountain pen in hand and a blank page in front of her with no idea what to write.

She wanted nothing more than to talk to Estelle. So that's what she would do:

Dear Essie,

Is it really true? Daddy's been killed? In Jersey, of all places. We keep hearing on the wireless that the island was bombed and that the Nazis have invaded and it all seems like someone's made a terrible mistake. I wish I could see you and you would give me one of your hugs and tell me that it had all been a bad dream, but I know that's not possible because this is our lives right now.

Big, fat salty tears splashed on the crisp paper as Rosie tried to put her thoughts into writing. The ink smudged in several places but she was too heartbroken to care, and continued writing:

I wish I hadn't told Daddy that I hated him before I left home. It was the last thing I ever said to him. I didn't hate him, Essie. I loved him. I only said what I did because I was cross with him for sending me away. It's the Nazis I hate. It's their fault I'm here and not at home.

I wish I could cuddle Rebel. He's going to miss Daddy as much as we will. Oh, Essie, I'm so scared about what's going to happen to us all. What if I can never come home? How will you and Gran look after everything on the farm by yourselves? It upsets me to think that I'll never be hugged by Daddy again, or hear him grumbling about his spuds, or how little he got for them when he sold them.

Everything's changed and nothing makes sense any more. I know I'm feeling sorry for myself and Gran would tell me off for it and that I should think myself lucky to be staying at Aunt Muriel's. You were right about her, Essie. She's very kind and told me about what happened to Daddy very gently. She said that one day I'll be able to think about him without crying.

Not today though.

FIVE

Estelle

2 JULY 1940

E stelle couldn't bear to go far from the farm in the first few days after her father's death. Most of her news was gleaned from neighbours or visiting the parish shops in St Ouen's village and especially from Mr Gibault's store. The Germans had arrived at the airport the day before but, so far, she was yet to see one in the flesh. Alone, on the farm, digging the last field of potatoes, with the summer sun warming her skin, it was almost as if nothing had happened.

'I've heard that those Jerries have already got their flag up at Fort Regent for everyone to see,' Violet Le Marrec, her grandmother's closest friend and one of their nearest neighbours, said when Estelle opened the shop door for her as she went to leave. The older woman saw her and reached out to rest a hand on Estelle's arm. 'No one knows what to expect, do they?'

Estelle shook her head. 'No, we don't.'

'I thought I'd pop in to see your gran on my way home, lovey. Do you think she'll be up for a visit?'

Estelle knew that seeing Mrs Le Marrec would be the perfect tonic for her grandmother. 'Gran's always happy to see you. She hasn't been off the farm since we were invaded and I'm sure she would love to see that you're coping.'

It troubled her to think what they might be in for over the coming days and weeks. She didn't have to wait for long as, in the local paper that night, orders were issued by a Captain Gussek.

'I suppose this is one of the things we'll have to get used to,' Gran said as she peeled potatoes for their supper at the sink. 'Read them and tell me which apply to us.'

Estelle sat at the kitchen table and read the newspaper: 'There's fourteen different orders,' she said, then gasped. 'We're to be under curfew, Gran. From eleven in the evening until five in the morning. No one can leave their homes.'

Her grandmother cut the remaining potatoes angrily and plopped them into a pan of water and carried it over to the range. Estelle could see she was doing everything she could to hold it together and not let her anger show. 'Come on, now, Estelle, my love. Neither of us are outside before five in the morning, nor out after eleven o'clock. So that shouldn't worry us too much.'

Gran was right, Estelle supposed, but at least it had been by choice up until now. She read on, then said, 'We need to take Dad's gun and any ammunition to the Town Arsenal by noon tomorrow.' She took a deep breath, a wave of sadness washing over her. 'I don't want to have to do that.'

Her grandmother thought for a moment. 'No. That gun

was precious to your dad, but if they tell us to hand it in then I think we must. We don't want to get into trouble, do we?'

No, thought Estelle, shaking her head. 'You're right, we should do as we're told.' But she couldn't help wondering what would happen to them if they didn't.

'Tell me the rest, then,' her grandmother said, as she began shelling the peas Estelle had picked from their vegetable patch earlier.

'I'll come with you to town, tomorrow, Gran, to take in Dad's gun,' she said, then read on, fear for Gerard coursing through her as she did so. 'If Gerard is still on the island, he's going to have to report at the Commandant's Office, which, apparently, is at Town Hall, at 10 o'clock tomorrow morning.' She said a silent prayer that he had found someone to lend him a boat to escape. 'What do you think will happen to him, if he does report to the Germans?'

'It's best not to think about such things until we have to, love. Hopefully, he has managed to leave. Tell me the next one.'

'We have to make up blackout blinds for all the windows. Tonight.'

'You'll enjoy that,' her grandmother teased, throwing a pea over to Estelle, who caught it and popped it into her mouth, chewed the sweet vegetable, and swallowed.

Estelle puffed out her cheeks. 'Fine. And at least it says here that the banks and shops are remaining open, as before. But we've got to put all our clocks and watches forward one hour tonight, so we're on German time. These

Nazis aren't wasting any time changing how we do things here, are they?'

'They're not. I think it's a liberty,' Gran grumbled. 'But I'm really more concerned about Gerard and the other young men who might be stuck here now. The Germans won't want to think that there's anyone here who could retaliate, and fit young farmers would be the ones to be able to at least try and stand up to them. I never thought we'd be fighting with them again. We were always told that the last war was the war to end all wars.'

'If only that was true,' Estelle replied.

———————

The following morning, Estelle accompanied her grandmother on the bus into St Helier. They decided to try to get to Town Hall before 10 o'clock when British sailors, soldiers and any airmen on leave had been ordered to report to the Kommandant.

Once they stepped off the bus and couldn't be overheard, Gran said, 'You have to listen to me, now, Estelle.'

Unnerved, Estelle nodded. 'What is it?'

'You must remember at all times not to make eye contact with these men.' The older woman hesitated. 'In fact, if you are able to, cross over to the other side of the road to avoid them whenever you can.'

A German military car drove past them, the unmissable red-and-black insignia flapping.

'Don't speak unless spoken to and whatever you do

don't accept help from them. We're at war now, my girl. We have to be alert at all times and I couldn't live with myself if anything happened to you. Promise me you'll take care.'

'I promise, Gran.' An unease was forming in the pit of Estelle's stomach and the fear in her grandmother's eyes was one she wouldn't forget for a long time.

The crowds were getting bigger the closer they got to the centre of town and her grandmother turned to her again. 'These men are smart and may try to be friendly but they are the enemy. Never forget that.'

Estelle gave her grandmother a reassuring squeeze to her hand. 'I won't forget, I promise you.'

'Good girl.'

As they walked past Charing Cross, Estelle couldn't ignore the red-and-black flag hanging from Town Hall. The material fluttered gently in the breeze, the black swastika rippling in and out of view. She hesitated, shocked at the sight. 'I can't imagine anything being right ever again, can you Gran?'

Her grandmother didn't reply but linked her arm through Estelle's. 'We must be careful not to lose each other.'

They pushed their way through the vast crowds of people milling about, trying to find their relatives among the mostly civilian-dressed men standing solemnly between armed German guards in front of the building. The sight of Nazi uniforms, which, until now, Estelle had only seen in newsreels at the cinema, was a sobering sight. She couldn't take her eyes off a small group of soldiers watching from the top of the steps at Town Hall, their intense focus on the locals sending chills running down her spine despite the heat of the summer day.

'Keep walking,' Gran said, tugging her forward. 'And, for pity's sake, stop staring at them.'

How different St Helier was to the last time she had come here. Back then, everyone had seemed carefree as they went about their business, stopping every so often to pass the time of day with friends. Now, though, the sense of oppression was unmistakable. As Estelle studied the people around her, she saw fear in her fellow islanders' eyes. Like her, they seemed unsure how to behave.

She spotted one man, his head bent as he shrugged his wife's hand from his shoulder, arguing with her as she pleaded with him about something. Both voices were low, so Estelle couldn't hear what they were saying but, by the look of fury and defiance on the man's face, he was distressed and clearly wanted to fight back. She didn't blame him for wanting to stand up for his island; she knew Gerard would be feeling the same way. She hoped he would be careful.

Finally, managing to manoeuvre their way to the front of the pavement as close to Town Hall as possible, they stood scanning the crowd.

It was then that Estelle covered her mouth in shock, as she saw Gerard standing among the assembled men, all waiting to be registered. 'There's Gerard,' she said, pointing him out to her grandmother. She stood on tiptoes and waved her arm above her head, hoping he might see her. He looked in her direction but didn't seem to notice her. Frustrated, she took a deep breath to call out to him. 'Ger—'

Immediately, her grandmother grabbed Estelle's wrist and pulled her hand down to her side. 'What are you doing?' she hissed, her eyes wide. 'Don't draw attention to yourself like that, you silly girl.'

She just wanted Gerard to know she was there. That she was with him in some way. But she mouthed an apology to her grandmother.

'Things have changed now, lovey. Remember what I told you,' she added, keeping her voice so low that Estelle struggled to hear her. 'We're two women living alone now on an island invaded by men with more power than us, and guns.'

Estelle nodded and looked back towards Gerard. All the captive Jersey men, including her sweetheart, had their shoulders back and chins held high in proud defiance. A lump formed in her throat as she wondered what was going to happen to them. Sunlight glinted off the metal of the rifles the German soldiers confidently held in front of them.

A woman in the crowd cried out a man's name and Estelle glanced over in her direction. Her gran nudged her. 'He's seen you.'

Confused, Estelle gazed back at her gran.

'Gerard. He's trying to get your attention.'

She gasped, horrified that she might have missed the opportunity to let him know she was there for him. She turned her attention back to him, forcing a smile, wishing she could run to him and hold him, if only for a moment. Gerard looked at her and mouthed 'It's all right.'

Then, suddenly, an officer barked out an order in German and immediately the men were pushed backwards.

Estelle couldn't bear the thought that this might be the last time she saw Gerard. He gave her a sad, resigned smile.

'They're being so brave,' Gran said, her voice catching with emotion.

'They are. If only he had managed to catch his boat, after all.' Her heart ached for him. Gerard was a man used to being outside in the fields and taking daily swims in the sea. His passion for life is what she loved about him. She fervently hoped that he wouldn't be locked up in a cell somewhere, it would kill him, or at least his spirit if that were to happen.

'Poor boys,' Gran said, stoically.

She put her arm around her grandmother's shoulders and held her tightly.

They watched as the British soldiers were paraded in front of Town Hall and the newly appointed Kommandant to Jersey, Captain Gussek, before being marched away down the tree-lined street in the direction of the prison. It was heartbreaking to watch the forlorn men, their shoulders back and heads held high in defiance at being kept from fighting with their units for their country. Their war over before it had begun. Estelle knew each of them would rather be with their families or away fighting for their freedom than imprisoned on the island and powerless to do anything. She had heard that many of them, like Gerard, had also been home on leave when things took a turn for the worse. Now they were trapped here. As they all were.

They watched the men as they were led away down the road. Several of them being pushed with the butts of German rifles to keep them in line.

Estelle was lost in her own thoughts until her grandmother tapped the wicker basket hanging from the young woman's right arm to remind her that she was still carrying her father's gun and ammunition inside it.

'Come on. He's a clever, strong lad. He'll be fine. But we'd better get a move on if we're to walk to the Town Arsenal to deliver this before the queue is too long,' she whispered. 'My feet are already starting to ache, and I don't want to have to stand around for hours.'

The two women made their way along The Parade, before turning right at the top of the road when they reached Cheapside. The Town Arsenal wasn't too far but their progress was slow for all the commotion in town as locals hurriedly made preparations for their life under occupation.

'For Pity's sake,' Gran grumbled. 'Look at that dratted queue. And here's me thinking we'd be right near the front.' The line of islanders waiting to hand in their any personal arms they might have owned went right down the road.

There was nothing for it but to join the back of the queue.

Estelle was about to ask her grandmother if she wanted to entrust her with the handing in of the gun on her own, when her grandmother withdrew it from under her purse. 'Here, take this will you?' She handed her the Webley service revolver that Estelle's father had treasured since being given it by one of his cousins just after the First World War. Estelle pushed her hand back into her basket. 'Hang on a second.'

She felt the weight of her father's gun in her hand as her

grandmother took out an almost full box of ammunition and passed it over to her. 'Take these, too.' She noticed that Estelle didn't have a handbag and, removing her purse out of her basket, passed it to Estelle. 'You'd better put them in here,' she said. 'You don't want to give the Jerries the wrong idea.'

Estelle did as she was told and, taking her handkerchief from her dress pocket, shook it to unfold it, then placed the neatly ironed square of linen over the two items and waited for her grandmother to speak again.

'Wait, I think I see Violet over there.' Estelle followed her grandmother's line of vision but couldn't see anyone she recognised in the crowd of people gathering near the building. Then she spotted her. 'Mrs Le Marrec!'

Violet came over to them but her grandmother's friend looked as miserable as Estelle felt, excusing herself as she walked in front of people to reach them, shaking her head at the same time. 'What a strange day this is. I never thought I'd see the likes of what's happening. And all those boys, marched around at gunpoint. I see your Gerard didn't manage to get off the island, Estelle?'

Estelle thought back to the short glimpse she'd had of her sweetheart in the square. 'It was horrible to see Gerard like that.'

'Poor lad.' Violet and her gran swapped glances. 'You going to be long here, do you think? Or shall I wait for you and we can all catch the bus back to St Ouen together? I have to admit I don't feel as comfortable travelling home on my own with all these Jerries around now.' The three of them stared in silence at a nearby soldier who was standing guard, his rifle ready at the slightest sign of trouble.

'If you're happy for me to, I think I'll catch the next bus home with Violet, lovey,' Gran said. 'Those of us who were alive in '18 never thought we would be at war with Germany again. Seeing that dratted flag is all a bit much for me.' Gran frowned. 'You don't mind me leaving you here to do this, do you?'

Estelle shook her head and bent to kiss her grandmother's cheek. 'Not at all. Do you need me to buy anything for you while I'm in town?'

'No, It's fine. I'll see you back at the house later on. Don't stay out too long though. These are worrying times and I think it's safer to stay close to home until things settle down a bit.' She looked over at a handsome younger soldier trying to make polite conversation to a couple of girls who seemed uncertain about how to respond to him. 'At least until we get the measure of this lot.'

Estelle watched her leave and stepped forward as the queue moved towards the door. As she slowly inched forward along with the others waiting patiently.

Then, someone tapped her lightly on the shoulder. 'Estelle.'

Recognising the voice, she turned to see her old school friend Antoinette, and relaxed slightly now she was in familiar company. 'I'm so glad to see you,' Estelle said, reaching out to stroke Antoinette's baby boy's chubby cheek. 'And how is little Louis doing? He looks very bonny. Don't you sweetheart?'

Before her friend could answer, the thundering of

boots filled the air. Everyone in the queue tensed and turned to look in the direction of the road. The quiet bits of chatter that had been going on fell silent. German soldiers marched passed and as the sound of their jackboots stamping on the tarmac subsided the people standing in the queue began to breathe more easily once more.

'You're so lucky to live out of town,' Antoinette said quietly. 'My heart pounds every time I hear those damn boots stamping through the streets near our place and I can't tell you the amount of times they've woken Louis with all the noise they make.' Louis began whining and Estelle smiled at him and tried to distract him as his mother continued: 'And they're always in the shops buying everything up and acting all superior.'

Estelle had had so little contact with the Germans so far and thought again how lucky she was to live away from town. Still it riled her to think about the distress her friend was going through. 'I wish we could do something about them. Show them this is still our island. Our home,' she muttered. 'But you're coping?'

'Just about. It helps that Paul's here.'

Estelle was stunned that Antoinette's husband was on the island. 'But I thought he had joined the RAF?'

'He did but came back on leave to check up on us and got stuck here like the rest of them. I just worry about what will happen to him long-term. I mean, I can't see the Germans letting ninety-odd British soldiers wander freely around the island, can you?'

Estelle shook her head. 'I suppose not.'

'My dad says that we're buggered now the War Cabinet have demilitarised the island.'

'Don't say that. It won't help us to think that way.'

Antoinette sighed. 'But I can't help worrying that he's right.'

Estelle shrugged, unsure what she believed right now. The queue moved forward once more and Estelle was waved in the direction of one desk while Antoinette was sent to another. She glanced down at the handkerchief in her basket concealing the gun. A soldier approached her and said something. Estelle's skin crawled and her thoughts turned to her father. The way he was brutally gunned down while he was just going about his day. The German's demeanour was pleasant but nothing could detract from him being a Nazi. From being one of them. The reason Rosie had been sent away and her father was dead. A small part of Estelle wished she had the courage to use her father's gun on the young man. She looked over at several other Germans, talking and laughing as if they didn't have a care in the world. She'd like to shoot them all.

'Fräulein, you must come this way,' the soldier said politely as he indicated that it was her turn.

She walked forward.

'Who owns this firearm?'

'My father.'

'Your father did not think to surrender it himself?' An officious soldier at the desk asked.

'He couldn't.' Her heart pounded and she clenched her fists tightly as she felt a burning anger start to rise up inside her.

'And why is that?'

'Because one of your pilots shot and killed him four days ago,' she snapped, unable to help herself.

'You tell 'im, love.' An older woman cheered behind her.

'You will be silent!' The officious soldier glared at the woman, who sensibly closed her mouth but refused to stare down at the ground.

Estelle watched as the soldier made a note she couldn't decipher on the form. Without even looking up, he said, 'You may go.'

As she walked out of the Town Arsenal, Estelle suddenly remembered that her father had also owned a shotgun. She hadn't seen it for a long time but he had definitely mentioned it only the other day, before he died, and that he needed to clean it. But why hadn't her grandmother mentioned surrendering it along with the revolver. Estelle didn't like to think too much about what that precaution might be in aid of. She would have to wait and hope it wouldn't be a necessity. The last thing she or Gran needed was to be arrested for failing to surrender a firearm when the sentenced carried a prison term. How would they cope if they were separated? And what would a stay in prison even be like with the Nazis in charge?

Desperate to leave town, she hurried passed Summerland, the local clothes factory, on her way back to the bus station. She was halfway along The Parade when she saw several soldiers chatting and laughing on the opposite pavement to her. It infuriated Estelle again to see these invaders giving no thought to what they'd done. To stand and chat happily on her island's streets when Gerard and the others were locked away somewhere. When her dear father could no longer walk these same streets. How dare they? She was so filled with loathing as she peered at them from the corner of her eye that she almost slammed into another soldier in her haste.

He grabbed her by the shoulders to stop her careering into him. 'Slow down, Fräulein.'

Estelle's breath caught in her throat and she recoiled instantly at his touch. How could she have been so stupid not to pay attention? She tried to steady her breathing and not let him see how frightened she was to have come face-to-face with him.

The man stared into her eyes until his piercing gaze unnerved Estelle so much that she was forced to lower her gaze to the pavement.

'Something is wrong?' She could hear the amusement in his voice. He was enjoying her obvious discomfort.

'You will answer me.'

Estelle swallowed to moisten her dry throat and looked up at him. He wasn't as tall as most of them seemed to be and maybe a little older. His heavy brow lowered and from the look of his uniform, Estelle guessed he was an officer.

'No. I mean, thank you. Sorry… I…'

His hands dropped from her shoulders. 'Where are you going?'

She looked around at the people walking past determinedly trying not to catch her eye. Why didn't one of them help her? It occurred to her that there was nothing much anyone could do. They were probably relieved they weren't the ones in her position and she couldn't blame them for that. 'I... I am on my way to the shops... for my grandmother.'

He looked her up and down for a few seconds in silence. Then, when she didn't react, he waved her away. 'Go. You must walk, not run. It is dangerous.'

She picked up a hidden meaning behind his words but wasn't sure if he was threatening her and, if so, in what way. He stepped back to let her pass.

Estelle made sure she walked the rest of the way back, but her legs were shaking uncontrollably and her pulse was racing. Her confrontation with the Nazi, who by his superior manner she definitely knew was an officer now, had frightened her. With her grandmother's words of warning in her head, the last thing she wanted was to be noticed by an officer of the Wehrmacht, especially someone like that man. She knew a bully when she saw one.

SIX

Estelle

The next ten days were ones that Estelle knew she would never forget. The fog of grief she felt for her father hung heavy and some days it took all her strength to get out of bed in the morning. But her grandmother needed her. Rosie needed her. She had to make sure they had a home and livelihood for if, no, *when*, Rosie returned. And then there were so many new rules and regulations to get used to. Most of all, though, she was concerned for Gerard's welfare. She returned to Town Hall each day, to watch Gerard and the other island men parade, but always on the lookout for the German officer with the heavy eyebrows.

Despite her fear of the officer, Estelle always stood as close to the same place as she could to make it easier for Gerard to spot her in the crowd. There was always a crowd of the same islanders who made a point of being there each day. Even if they didn't have loved ones there.

Her mood was always low as she left Gerard behind each day but at least for the time being he was still on the island and, unbelievably, as Estelle discovered, they were able to see each other. Gerard and the other men were ordered to register at Town Hall each morning but were allowed to go back to their homes after that.

It was comforting to have Gerard with her, and even helping on the farm with the potato crop, especially on the days when her grief threatened to overwhelm her. Estelle knew that both she and Gran were doing their best to be brave but the empty space, where her father's once big personality had been the life and soul of the farm, was always on the verge of engulfing her.

Time seemed to fly by as she and Gerard worked side by side and made their plans about what they would do after the war was over. Estelle had always loved to draw and her mother's interest in fashion had passed to her daughter. She had once hoped to design clothes for one of the famous boutiques in Paris but that was an impossible dream now that her father was gone and she was the only one left who could keep the farm going. Neither she nor Gerard ever mentioned the possibility that it could take years for them to see freedom again. It was more important to remain hopeful and positive, the alternative too frightening to bear.

Ten thirty seemed to come around only too soon when Gerard would have to cycle home to be inside his parents' farmhouse by curfew at eleven o'clock and she would try to take her mind off everything by spending a couple of hours with her notepad and coloured pencils, designing dresses that she knew would never be made.

'I was so happy to discover you were still on the island,' Estelle said as she walked along the lane back to the farmhouse hand in hand with him. 'I still can't believe I get to see you. I honestly thought when you had to report to Town Hall that you would all be locked up somewhere. Or worse, sent to Europe.'

His expression changed as if he was about to say something but decided against it.

'What is it?' she asked.

'It's nothing.' Gerard shrugged off.

She studied him and realised what was going through his mind. 'I understand you're frustrated being stuck here. But I can't help being as happy as I am that I still have you here with me. Is that wrong?'

He shook his head and kissed the tip of her nose. 'No more than me feeling irritated to still be going home to the farm each day when all I want to do is get off this rock and back to my ship to do my bit.'

Gerard stopped talking and took her in his arms pulling her close. 'Kiss me again.'

She did, happily. Neither of them knew how long they had together, or if this was the way things might continue.

As she opened her eyes to look at him after their kiss, she noticed Gerard had frowned and looked serious.

'What is it? I can still see you each evening, can't I?' Her stomach felt like it had been filled with tiny butterflies and she knew he was about to tell her something she wasn't going to like.

'I've heard from a friend of Dad's that they've been working on the holiday camp in Grouville. To use it as a prison.' Estelle shivered, knowing that whatever was coming next wouldn't be good. 'Estelle, I think the next time we parade, or if we're lucky, the time after that, the Jerries will arrest us and take us there.'

'Don't say that,' she pleaded. 'Let's just enjoy right now.'

He took her hands in his. 'I'd love to, but I can't bear to think that something will happen and you'll be frightened. I want you to know that, whatever happens, I'll be all right and that I'll come back to you.'

He couldn't possibly know that, Estelle thought to herself, but simply nodded. He was strong and fit and determined when he had to be so she would just have to trust him. 'I know you will be,' she said, praying he was right.

He put one hand against her left cheek and stared deeply into her eyes. 'I want you to promise me that if I am taken away, you'll be careful and not do anything foolhardy.' She opened her mouth to argue, but he shook his head to stop her. 'We both know you think you're as strong as any man, and,' he said a glint of humour in his eyes, 'you are definitely much cleverer. But, Estelle, if something happens to me, don't try to do anything that could bring you in harm's way. Please. Promise me that you won't.'

She was desperate to argue with him because if anything was going to happen to Gerard, she'd damned well not take it lying down but wasn't going to spend what could possibly be her last evening with him quarrelling. He needed her reassurance and that's what she would give him. 'I promise,' she said, almost meaning it.

The following morning, Estelle stepped off the bus at Weighbridge, the bus station from where they could see the glistening of the sea in the harbour even if they couldn't go out to it. She was glad to be out of the steamy heat of the crowded vehicle and able to enjoy more comfortable air, cooled by the slight sea breeze that was blowing gently from the harbour. She still found it strange hearing German voices and seeing the men in their immaculate uniforms standing on what seemed to be most of the street corners. Estelle had intended crossing the road if she saw one walking towards her on the pavement, but there seemed to be so many now on the island, especially on the town streets that she would have ended up crossing the road several times each time she went somewhere, so didn't bother.

Today, Gran had given her a shopping list that included a small bag of Reckitt's Paris Blue. She swore by it, claiming that it kept the whites in her laundry from yellowing and wanted to be sure to have some at the farmhouse before things became scarce. Estelle wasn't sure why it mattered so much that their laundry stayed white but didn't like to argue. She wanted to get all her shopping out of the way before going to watch Gerard parading, so hurried along the pavement, passing the front entrance of the Pomme d'Or hotel and then along Conway Street on her way to the shop on Broad Street, careful to avoid bumping into any soldiers as best she could.

She had almost reached the shop when she saw a soldier say something to a girl she presumed to be about her age. The girl walked on in Estelle's direction unable to hide the happy smile on her face when a mealy-mouthed woman stepped out in front and knocked her shoulder into the girl's sending her stumbling backward with the force. Estelle gasped when she realised that it had been on purpose and, not liking what she was seeing, she hurried over to the girl.

'You want to watch yourself, miss.' The woman sneered before seeing Estelle. Then looking Estelle up and down, added. 'And so do you.'

Estelle was so taken aback that she couldn't speak for a moment. 'Are you all right?' she asked the girl, who looked close to tears.

'Yes, thank you.'

She watched the girl walk away, her head down, and recalled her grandmother's warning. She really did need to be very careful if she didn't want people to get the wrong idea about her.

Two soldiers were standing on either side of the entrance to the shop. Only a few months ago, she had seen men in uniforms like this on the Pathé News at the Forum and here they were now, standing on streets that were so familiar to her. The soldiers greeted her politely and then stepped back to let her enter. Estelle clenched her fists at her sides, unable to stop the flash of anger as she remembered that if it wasn't for these Nazis, her father would still be at home working on the farm. True, some seemed pleasant and well-mannered, but nothing made up for what they represented. The brutality of gunning down innocent, unarmed men. Estelle ignored them and entered the shop on Broad Street.

As she waited her turn, there was a soldier standing in front of her in the queue. She took the time to study him. They all appeared so healthy and strong and, she observed, this man was no exception, with his fair-hair and golden suntan. She had heard from her friend Antoinette that many saw Jersey as a summer holiday, a paradise island with good weather and beautiful beaches. But they weren't welcome here. This wasn't a holiday for the islanders and, again, Estelle felt a tiny flash of intense hatred. They should be made to pay for being here, for what they'd done to get here. He was standing perfectly straight, making the most of his six-feet-plus height. She wanted to distance herself from him, even if only by several inches, and took a step back straight on to someone's foot.

'*Oof!*' an older woman exclaimed. 'Watch where yer standin'.'

The soldier turned to see what was going on and Estelle, mortified to be the centre of attention, spun round and apologised to the woman. She hoped the soldier didn't realise what she had really been intending to do, but by the look of disdain on his face he knew perfectly well.

'Next, please,' called the shopkeeper in his white coat. Mr Le Blancq looked irritated with his shoppers and she didn't blame him. Who would want to spend all day serving these soldiers and nervous locals? The soldier stepped forward and asked for something she couldn't quite make out. Finally, it was her turn.

'Please can I have a Reckitt's Bag Blue? The Paris Blue one, please. He nodded, picked one up from a drawer behind the counter and told her how much it would be.

Estelle smiled and opened her purse, counted out the money and went to hand it over to him.

The shopkeeper scowled at her. 'And what am I supposed to do with that, Estelle Le Maistre?'

She looked at the coins in her hand, confused by his odd question. 'Sorry, haven't I given you enough? My grandmother said—'

'I'm not allowed to take sterling now,' he said, looking past her. 'If anyone else hasn't realised this yet, please take note.'

'Since when?' Estelle asked, following his gaze. She saw two further soldiers who had now joined the back of the queue. Lowering his voice, the shopkeeper said, 'Since these lot arrived.'

'Then how am I supposed to pay for it? Gran will be furious if I don't buy some for her today.' It was a slight exaggeration, but Estelle thought it was worth a try.

'I can only take Reichsmarks,' he repeated, his voice louder now for the soldiers near the front door to hear.

'But what if I don't have any in my purse?'

He nodded in the direction of the road outside.

'What am I supposed to do with this lot,' Estelle asked angrily as she indicated her shopping in her basket. She had several tins of beans and fruit and it was heavy.

'You can leave that with me. I'll put it behind the counter here with your Reckitt's Bag Blue and you can go to the bank and change your money for the right currency.'

'The right currency? Anyone would think we weren't in Jersey any more.' She replied, frustrated. She heard two of the Germans say something to each other and one laughed. It was all she could do not to snap at him.

'Come now. We have to abide by the rules. Now, if you want your shopping, I suggest you hurry and get to the bank and come back here before I close for lunch. I'll hold this for you under the counter in the meantime. They'll change your money for you. You should get eight Marks to the pound, so make sure you get the right amount back from the teller. Go on.'

Estelle had little choice but to do as he asked so, reluctantly, leaving her shopping items behind, she took her purse and walked out of the shop and across the road to the bank... where she saw yet another lengthy queue! This was becoming interminable. All she seemed to do these days was queue for ages, often to reach the front and discover whatever she wanted had just sold out, or that the regulations had changed and she could no longer get what she needed. She knew she was over-reacting and that everyone was in the same boat, but it didn't make it any more bearable.

After exchanging her money and finishing her shopping, Estelle ran to Town Hall in the hope she would still be in time to see Gerard parading. Unlike the previous days, though, there was no sign of the men and nothing much seemed to be happening apart from quite a few women appeared to still be waiting. Presently, she spotted Antoinette and ran up to her.

'Have I missed it? I know I'm a bit late but—' She noticed how red her friend's eyes were and suspected she knew what had happened to the men. 'Antoinette?'

Her friend wiped her nose on the back of her hand. 'They've taken them, Estelle.'

Estelle swallowed her rising panic, aware that she would be no help to her friend, or Gerard, if she became hysterical. '*Where* have they taken them?' Estelle asked as calmly as she could manage. 'Do you know?'

Antoinette began to sob. 'I don't know. I can't bear it if they hurt Paul!'

'Have you spoken to anyone about where they have been taken?'

'I tried to ask at Town Hall but they wouldn't say. And I… I was scared. There were so many of them and they were all staring at me.' Antoinette replied, tears streaming down her face.

Looking around for someone to help, Estelle took hold of her friend's hand. 'I've had enough of this. Come with me,' she said, holding Antoinette's hand reassuringly and, determinedly, walked her right up to a group of German officers who were talking close by.

The men stopped speaking as Estelle approached and one turned to her, a stern expression on his face. 'Fräulein?'

'We need to know where our men have been taken?' She demanded. 'The ones who are usually here each morning.'

There was a long pause as he considered her for a moment. Then, with a brief tilt of his head to his fellow officers, he replied: 'They have been interred.'

'Interred?' Antoinette cried out and Estelle clutched her hand even tighter.

'We need to know where they are and when we can see them. To ensure they haven't been mistreated.'

The man raised his eyebrows and she wasn't sure if it was in amusement or surprise that she had the cheek to question him.

'You will find them at the Grouville camp. You know where this is?'

'Yes. The old holiday camp there. And we'll be able to speak to them?'

'I think not, Fräulein. They are prisoners of war now.'

'Come along, Antoinette,' she said, undeterred, leading her friend away, 'we have a bus to catch.'

Estelle arrived home an hour and a half later, exhausted. She and Antoinette had been turned away before they even got to the camp and were told not to come back. However, not to be put off, she had promised Antoinette she would try again tomorrow. Now, walking up the short driveway, she discovered her grandmother hurriedly pulling on her hat and marching out of the yard. Her teeth were clenched and she looked furious.

'Where are you going, Gran?'

'Come with me and you'll see for yourself. Poor Violet Le Marrec's car is being requisitioned. She sent young Peter Bisson to cycle here and ask me to go to her house to be with her.'

Estelle had no intention of letting her grandmother and her elderly friend face the Nazis alone. She turned around and walked with her up the road and down the nearby lane towards their neighbour's home. Violet was her grandmother's closest friend and had been the first to welcome her grandmother when she first arrived on the island.

'She was there to support me when I needed to be strong and help your father look after you and your new baby sister,' she said as they hurried. 'Coming to the farm to make meals and help with washing. She was my saving grace when I lost your mother, Estelle, and I'm not going to let her down now when she needs me.'

Estelle wished she too had a good friend who lived closer to the farm with whom she could confide in. She missed her father desperately and wished that Rosie was still living at home certain that the isolation she felt since the start of the Occupation wouldn't be nearly as dreadful if they were there.

Minutes later, the two women arrived at Violet's small yard, with its granite cottage half the size of their farmhouse and a beautifully kept garden at the front. Estelle was aware of the smallholding at the back where Violet's husband had grown his own vegetables; but since his death ten years before, she had given up trying to keep everything in order and had now given over the back area to wildflowers and apple trees. It looked pretty but it occurred to Estelle that it wasn't going to be much use to the older woman if she needed extra food.

They saw two German soldiers standing in front of Violet, who looked so frail beside them. One stood closer to a motorbike and the other was holding his hand out for something. Estelle was shocked to see Violet was sobbing and clutching something to her chest.

'But this was my Harold's pride and joy. Please don't take it from me.'

She and her grandmother exchanged horrified glances and Estelle ran ahead to comfort the older woman.

'Violet, we're here. It will be all right.' Estelle reassured her, ignoring the two men pristine and imposing in their grey uniforms.

'Oh, Estelle, you dear girl. Thank you for coming.'

Gran moved and stood by Violet's other side.

'Dearest Marnie, I knew you'd come and help me,' she sniffed, before blowing her nose noisily. 'These soldiers want to take Harold's Austin 7. When he was dying, I promised to always take the very best care of it but how can I do that if they take it away?'

Estelle saw her gran's eyes narrow as she turned her attention to the soldiers with their leather gun holsters shining clearly against their uniforms. 'Now, gentlemen,' she said, an obvious sneer of sarcasm in her voice. 'Mrs Le Marrec's car is old and it's not that big. I can't see how it can be valuable to you. Why do you need it?'

They both gave her a polite nod but neither seemed to wish to speak first. Estelle thought that one of them at least appeared embarrassed by the distress his actions were so obviously causing. The other just looked peeved and irritated to be wasting his time having to wait for the old lady to acquiesce and give them what they wanted.

'This vehicle has been requisitioned by order of the Kommandant. We will be taking it from here today.'

Violet let out another sob and Estelle wished there was something she could do to help ease her pain.

'Does it have to be today?' Estelle asked. 'Couldn't Mrs Le Marrec at least be given a little time to get used to the idea of parting with the car?'

'*Nein*. Today.'

'Please don't take it from me,' Violet sobbed, her wrinkled hands clasped together as if in prayer.

Estelle suspected that once the vehicle had gone and the soldiers left her home that Violet would be easier to pacify. 'Why don't you let Gran take you inside and make you a nice cup of tea,' Estelle suggested, swapping pointed looks with her grandmother. 'You can give me the keys and I'll hand them over. That way you won't have done it yourself so you won't have broken any promises to Harold.'

Violet shook her head violently. The sour-faced soldier moved his weight from one foot to the other and Estelle could see he was becoming impatient. So far any Germans she had encountered had on the whole behaved courteously towards her but how far could they be pushed before giving in to anger and force. Deep down, Estelle felt the stirrings of how unjust this all was, but remembering her promise to Gerard, she decided not to test this soldier's temper today.

'Come along, Violet, love,' Gran said, reaching up and trying to gently take the keys from her friend's grasp. 'Estelle's right. Give her those keys and you come inside with me. I could do with a sit-down, anyhow, and you can tell me all about what happened before we arrived.' Estelle could see her gran's fingers working their way into Violet's.

Finally, without warning, the older woman let go and the keys fell on to the dusty driveway. Estelle bent to pick them up quickly before Violet had a chance to do so. 'Go inside with Gran and leave this to me.'

Violet looked from one to the other of the soldiers and then back to the more serious soldier. 'You look after that car. Do you hear me?' He gave a brisk nod. 'I'll want it back after the war in the same condition as it is now.'

Neither soldier said anything and Estelle watched as her grandmother soothed her friend and, putting an arm around her shoulders, quietly led her into the house.

Estelle waited until the front door closed and then turned to address the soldiers herself. 'Can you at least tell me if this car will be returned to her at any point?' she asked hopefully.

'It will not. It is being sent to France, Fräulein.'

'I don't think I'll tell her that,' Estelle said, almost to herself, as she handed over the car keys. 'Please leave right away. I don't want her to find you here if she does come back out.'

She watched as one of them got into the car and, after a little difficulty starting it, drove it away, closely followed by the other soldier riding the motorcycle.

Was this how things were to be from now on? Not only were they forbidden from using their own currency, but their personal possessions were being taken away. What would they be coming to collect from the farm, Estelle thought, trying not to panic.

SEVEN

Estelle

JERSEY, 13 JULY 1940

T he Grouville holiday camp had been taken over by the island's military at the beginning of the war. They had surrounded it with barbed wire and converted it into an internment camp for enemies of Britain who were working on the island already. Now, though, it seemed that those men from Germany, Italy and Austria had been released and the camp was used to imprison British military personnel, like Gerard and Paul. At least, Estelle thought, that they were keeping the men on the island – for now.

Estelle stepped off the bus in Grouville and led the ten other woman who had made the journey with her up Old Forge Lane to the old holiday-camp entrance. She was thinking back to the one time she had visited the camp with her father and sister several years before, to visit friends who were staying there on holiday, when her step faltered as she took in the dramatic change in the once lively, happy place.

Now there was an atmosphere of fear and instead of

shrieks of children's laughter she heard a deep, guttural voice bark an order. The wooden chalets remained, as did the larger wooden building where they had eaten dinner after spending a fun afternoon swimming in the pool and playing tennis on the court, but now the area was surrounded by two rows of barbed wire, one several yards behind the other that Estelle estimated to be about ten feet in height.

She noticed a few of the prisoners watching her and the other women as they hurried closer to the barbed wire in the hope of catching sight of their men. A German sentry yelled out an order to them to stop, waving them away and indicating to his rifle.

'Another day of being turned away,' one of the other women said quietly. 'We were taking a gamble coming here but at least we can see where they are.'

They began retracing their steps along the narrow lane towards the bus stop when she heard her name and turned to look back. Gerard was waving frantically to her. Delighted, she ran towards the wire to speak to him.

'*Halt!*'

She stifled a scream of frustration and she slowed to a walk, fearful that to ignore the soldier brandishing his rifle might mean that either she or maybe Gerard would be punished in some way.

'You must go. Now.'

She nodded meekly and turned as if to follow the others, who were waiting anxiously further along the road. When the soldier seemed happy that she was obeying his orders, she turned her head and saw that Gerard was watching her.

He blew her a kiss. Estelle raised her right hand to her mouth and blew him one back, desperately hoping it wouldn't be the last time she'd see him.

As the bus services had been drastically reduced the women had to wait over an hour for the next bus. No one spoke. Each lost in their own thoughts. What would her father say if he had seen all this? What would he do? Having to conform to new regulations was one thing but imprisoned in your own home, all power and freedoms taken away.

Later, as she got off the bus in town and waited to switch to another that would take her out to St Ouen, Estelle found herself drawn to the harbour and walked to the sea front watching as a German cargo boat drew slowly past Elizabeth Castle, sitting majestically close to the shore, and on through the granite walls of St Helier harbour. It was the first time she had been here. The harbour. The place where her father had been so cruelly murdered. He hadn't stood a chance she realised. The pier, where her father and the other farmers had been parked on that terrible evening, ran next to large iron cranes on the harbour wall. With a high wall to one side of them and a drop into the sea on the other she understood why in that split second he had made the decision to run and hide as far away from the parked vehicles as possible in case one of them received a direct hit.

She cursed the German pilot. What sort of coward flies the length of a pier shooting indiscriminately at men who had little chance to escape? How terrified must her dear father have been as he ran desperately towards shelter just as the fatal shot struck him? Estelle squeezed her eyes closed as tears fell silently down her cheeks, wishing there was a way to stop picturing her father's death.

She tore her gaze away from the harbour and stared out at the sea for a few moments, struck by the contrast of the beautiful view of the blue sea, with Elizabeth Castle sitting proudly on its rocky mound in the bay and the curve of the golden sandy beach stretching to the right of her, against the menacing presence of the German army.

Estelle and her grandmother now knew that her father was one of ten people who had been killed during the raid. They'd discovered a few days later that another poor soul had been killed on his way to Jersey on the lifeboat and countless others were slowly recovering from injuries caused by flying shrapnel, or bullet wounds received on that horrific day.

She was confused. She had expected to feel raw hate watching the Nazi troops land en masse, but all Estelle felt right now was the pain of her loss. The panic she felt since her father's death and not knowing how long it would be before she saw Rosie again swept over her in waves. Some days she almost managed to persuade herself that she was fine and strong enough to cope with whatever was thrown at her. On other occasions, she was so frightened of what lay ahead that it threatened to overwhelm her completely.

Estelle anxiously watched the large boat dock and more and more uniformed Germans disembark.

'What you doin' there, my love,' an elderly man she recognised as Lenny Aubert asked. 'I heard what happened to your dad.' He stared at the boat. 'Bastards.' He took off his worn cap and lowered his gaze to the ground. 'Pardon me, I shouldn't use such language in front of a young lady.'

'Thank you, but please don't apologise.' Estelle agreed with him wholeheartedly. They were bastards.

'How could they have shot those men like they did? It's not as if they had anywhere they could escape to.' He coughed up phlegm into a handkerchief he had been clutching in his hand and patted his chest. 'I've been like this since their blasted chlorine gas got me in nineteen-fifteen.'

Estelle thought of how much suffering Mr Aubert must have witnessed. 'I hate them,' she muttered. They had taken everything from her.

'Why don't you go home to your grandmother? It will do you no good hangin' about here.'

'I just wanted to see them arriving for myself.'

'I can't say I blame you for that. Unfortunately, that boat will be the first of many.' He pointed out past Elizabeth Castle. 'Look there's another coming.'

Estelle looked again at the sixteenth-century granite castle on the islet in St Aubin's Bay, where her dad had walked with her and Rosie along the causeway, careful to return before the tide came in. The summer afternoons they had spent there had been so much fun, with her dad telling them stories about how Charles II had been given refuge at the castle during the English Civil War and how the castle, named after Elizabeth I, had helped protect the island for three hundred years. But no longer. He would be heartbroken to think it was now in German hands. She turned to Mr Aubert. 'How many will there be, do you think?'

'What Jerries, or boats?'

She shrugged. 'Both.'

'There's no telling, love.' He took her by the shoulder and pulled her around to face him, his lined face etched with sadness. 'That's enough now. You're not going to feel better by staying here and watching that lot march off into town, because that's what they'll be doing next, no doubt. They've been pleasant enough so far, but that was when there was only a few of them. Now they're coming in bigger numbers, so there's no knowing how things will be from now on.'

'Will we be all right, Mr Aubert?'

'Not for a while yet, my dear. They'll be wanting to show us who's in charge now, you mark my words. Look at him over there, for example.' He pointed and Estelle followed the direction of his finger to see a German soldier fixing a sign on to one that already was positioned at the end of the road. 'We're all going to have to read flippin' German now.' Before she had a chance to answer, he added, 'You get off home now to your grandmother, she'll be needing your support. Things are only going to get worse from here on, I know it.'

As Estelle made her way towards home, she could tell her fellow islanders were putting on a brave face from the dark rings under their eyes and the way they hurried about their business. There was an air of fear, but underneath that, too, she sensed a determination to overcome what was ahead. Already most of the luxury items in the shops had been bought up by the young German soldiers, to send back to their families in Germany, apparently. Shoes and clothes were having to be strictly rationed as it was already becoming difficult to buy them and with official food rationing of butter, sugar and cooking fats and meat the previous week, life was becoming harder.

Estelle doubted she would ever get used to paying for things using Reichsmarks or seeing German signposts, or road markings in German painted above their own English ones. But she had to pull herself together. Gran needed her, now more than ever before. Even in the short time since her father's death, Estelle had been shocked by the gauntness of her grandmother's face. She had lost weight and it made her seem much older and more fragile. With Rosie in London and Gerard in the prison camp, she was all Estelle had left.

She passed through Millbrook, taking her from St Helier and into the smaller, leafier parish of St Lawrence where her grandmother occasionally went to have her hair done, then on to the green expanse of Coronation Park and the glass church with its Lalique crystal to her left, donated to the island by Lady Trent. Estelle loved that church with its crystal Jersey lilies standing guard behind the magnificent altar. She hoped the Germans didn't realise how valuable the contents of the church were, or worse, destroy it not knowing or caring how irreplaceable it was.

As the bus wound its way into the countryside and out of the island's main town, the houses became fewer and further apart and the windy roads more narrow, with thick hedges on either side. Estelle stared out of the window, wondering what was to become of the island. Her home. She always chose to sit on this side of the bus to make the most of this view especially where the houses gave way to the first of two mills in St Peter's Valley and the lush meadows began. She had loved cycling through here with Rosie sometimes, preferring it to taking the main road home. Riding through this grassy, peaceful valley was always a joy.

A German car displaying its Nazi insignia overtook the bus and Estelle was reminded once again that her sister was no longer with them and it could be a very long time before they were reunited and cycling through the enchanting countryside once more. At least she could hope to see her again, unlike her father. He was gone from their lives for ever.

Estelle could feel the raw emotion building up inside her. So many heart-breaking changes in such a short time, she'd barely had time to figure out how to deal with them. She glanced at the other passengers in the almost packed bus and decided she needed to be alone before she made a fool out of herself and gave into the tears that she was finding difficult to suppress.

She stood up and made her way to the front, asking the driver to let her off. As soon as the bus pulled away leaving her behind in the beautiful valley, she breathed in deeply. The scent of long grass, wildflowers and damp earth from the meadow nearby soothed her sadness and she spotted a herd of Jersey cows, grazing peacefully on the long grass in between dots of yellow buttercups. What she needed right now was to spend some time relishing this peaceful, sunny place that depicted all that she loved about her life before this terrible war had encroached on their island.

Walking into the sunny expanse of the meadow and listening to the bees buzzing at the flowers, Estelle couldn't help smiling for the first time in weeks. She bent to pick a daisy and gazed at the three small granite cottages up on the bank across from where she stood. Each May and early June, one of them displayed thick purple wisteria tendrils reaching across the front of the small building – like a wizened arm trying to protect it from the outside world, Estelle thought.

'You have no idea what's going on, have you?' she said out loud to the cottage, 'Neither do I.'

Estelle heard the sound of a car engine approach and, not wishing to be disturbed, sat down out of site, ignoring the damp dew seeping through her skirt. She peered through the long grass, spotting a small convoy of German vehicles, sprayed in the already recognisable Nazi grey and each with their hated red-and-black flag waving from the shiny bonnets as they drew ever nearer. She knew this small piece of paradise on the island was too good to be true. There was no escaping the Occupation.

Estelle lay back as the cars slowed, her heart pounding in case they might have seen her. It was only when they sped up again and continued on their way that she sat up, resting on her elbows and realising only then how she'd been holding her breath in fear.

She thought back to Gerard's parting kiss and how he'd hugged her so tightly she could barely breathe. She pulled a blade of grass and wrapped it around her ring finger lost in thought for a moment. Hearing footsteps, she looked to her left and came face to face with a pretty face and a big wet nose. Estelle loved the island's famous cows. She pulled a clump of grass from its roots and held it out for the nosy cow to take.

'That was close, wasn't it?' she murmured, sitting up to tidy her hair and smooth down her skirt. She noticed two cows staring inquisitively at her, no doubt wondering what she was doing in their meadow. 'It's all right, I don't want any of your grass. Carry on, ladies.'

'I'm sure they will be happy to know you are not intending to eat their lunch.'

Estelle gasped, horrified to realise she was not alone and knew without looking that despite the English being perfect the man who had just spoken to her was a German.

Estelle scrambled to her feet and quickly brushed bits of grass and dirt from her lap. 'I was just—'

'Please, do not fret,' he said, reaching out to take her elbow as she stumbled backwards. 'You are here alone?'

Estelle tried her best to hide her panic, but visibly jumped as she felt his touch. Should she lie? Did he know she was here by herself? She glanced around. If she screamed she would probably be heard by someone living nearby, but how quickly could they come to her rescue if she needed them to?

'You have no need to fear me,' he said, looking confused by her reaction and letting go of her elbow straight away.

Estelle looked at him properly and for the first time took in his deep blue eyes. Was it kindness she saw in them? Certainly not like the officer with the heavy brow. She hoped she was right. She wasn't sure what to say. All she knew was that she wanted to get away from him. Being alone in a meadow with a young German soldier was not something she wanted to be caught doing, however innocent it might be.

'I have to go,' she said, making to leave, giving him as wide a birth as possible. She tried to gauge if he minded her going but wasn't certain how to read him.

He stepped back from her. 'May I escort you home?'

She shook her head. 'I can wait for the bus.' What was he doing her, anyway? she wondered.

'But one only passed by a short while ago, I thought.'

Estelle wasn't sure if he was trying to catch her out. 'Really. I'm happy to wait. Or, I'll walk. Yes, that's what I'll do, I'll walk.'

His face softened. 'If you wish to, of course you must. I will accompany you to the roadside.'

'No, please don't. I know the way,' she said confidently, praying that no one passed them by on the road. The last thing she needed was untrue gossip being spread about her and people thinking the worst of her.

'Excuse me, Fräulein? I did not catch your name,' the soldier said as he walked with her anyway, despite what she had just said.

Why did he need to know her name? Hadn't she made it obvious enough that she did not want to have anything to do with him? She wished she could shove him, tell him and all the other German soldiers to leave her home, her island.

He was waiting for her to reply and Estelle could see she was going to have to tell him. She didn't need to upset a

German officer and end up having to bear the brunt of his annoyance, especially now when she was alone with one in a field. 'My name is Estelle. Estelle Le Maistre,' she said, eventually.

He stopped and held out his hand for her to shake it. 'And I am Captain Bauer of the Wehrmacht. I am pleased to make your acquaintance, Miss Le Maistre.'

They reached the road and Estelle noticed for the first time that a grey car with the Nazi flag was parked. She saw another man sitting in the driver's seat, staring out at her, watching.

'I will leave you to go on your way unless you have changed your mind and would like me to take you to your home?'

He looked so sincere, but who knew what was under that charm, Estelle thought, suspiciously. 'No, that won't be necessary. Thank you.'

'As you wish,' he replied, giving her a quick bow of his head. Estelle went to turn from him. 'May I give you a piece of advice, though, Miss Le Maistre.'

Estelle would rather he just let her leave, but daren't refuse him. Not, she thought, that his question had probably warranted an answer. It appeared that he was going to have his say, whether she wished to listen to it, or not. 'Yes?'

'Please refrain from coming out like you have today.'

'I don't understand. I am free to do as I wish before the curfew,' she said with a tilt of her chin.

'You should not come to places like this alone, Miss Le

Maistre. I am an honourable man, but I fear that not every man you meet will be.'

'This is my home, Captain,' she said with as much dignity as she could muster. 'My island. You and your men will not make me feel like a prisoner here.'

She turned and walked away, expecting him to order her to stop. Eventually, though, she heard the sound of car door closing and engine start as the men drove off.

EIGHT

Rosie

D*ear Essie,*
    I still find it hard to imagine life without Daddy in it,
but I am pretending that everything is the same back on the farm
and that he is still taking his boots off and leaving them near his
jacket hanging on the back of the kitchen door every evening before
supper.

I miss my bedroom and all my things, especially lying on bed
with my window open listening to the waves down on the beach
and the seagulls squawking and other birds singing in the trees.
In fact, I miss everything about the farm and Jersey. The beaches,
the cliff walks and the delicious creamy ice cream. I miss the cows
lowing in the field and hearing neighbours chatting to Gran when
they call on her late in the evening and she's trying to be polite
and not show how angry she is with them for interrupting her
knitting. I miss hearing Daddy outside early in the mornings
calling to the animals and making us giggle when he rolls his eyes
heavenward when Gran says something that irritates him. I miss

you drawing pretty dresses for me. I even miss my grumpy teacher, Mrs Gilcrest. Actually that's probably a bit of a fib. Most of all though, I miss you and lying in the long grass in the top field listening to you telling me all the plans you have to travel.

I suppose I should tell you a little about my journey here. We had to zigzag in the boat to avoid the Jerries and I was sick a couple of times, but Janine was very kind and looked after me the whole time. She stayed with me until I met Aunt Muriel and then she went on to her aunt's place in Southampton. I hope she's okay there but I hear from Aunt Muriel's friends who call that they've had a lot of bombing there.

The train journey was long and hot. The carriage was filled with people smoking and we were all cramped together. One lady was angry because Aunt Muriel insisted I had a window seat. I slept most of the way and it was a shock to wake up just as we were arriving in London. The buildings look like they need a good wash, and everything seems to have a coat of soot on it. Aunt Muriel said it's due to all the coal fires. The train station was terrifying with piercing whistles and thousands of people pushing and shoving as they rushed to get to wherever they were heading. I wanted to come straight home, but Aunt Muriel, took my hand and said this was my new home.

I still can't believe how many people there are here. Crossing a road can be very dangerous with all the cars, vans and busses rushing passed. It's such a busy, noisy place, but Aunt Muriel insists it's 'vibrant'. She loves it here and is sure that once I get over my homesickness, I'll fall in love with London too. I'm not so sure I will, but I didn't say so.

You were right, Aunt Muriel is funny and very kind. She's cleared out her box room for me and was worried that it would be too small, but I'm very comfortable there in her flat. The house is Victorian, or so she tells me and is right by a film studio, Gainsborough? I've no idea what that is, but she said they make films, so you might have heard of it. Her cooking isn't so good though and not a patch on Gran's, or even yours, but she tries hard to keep us both cheerful. She's registered me at a convent nearby in Hammersmith. They don't usually take Methodists like us, but agreed to take me because they are being charitable and lots of their pupils have been evacuated.

There's a bucket of sand and one of water on every landing in this house. I thought it was strange at first, but Aunt Muriel said that every landing has to have one in case of incendiaries. Those are bombs but we haven't seen any yet, thankfully. I hope we don't. She has a photo of her and mummy. I've seen photographs of her before when you've shown me and Daddy has that one of her on the wall in our living room, but this was one of her taken on her seventeenth birthday. Honestly, Estelle, it gave me quite a turn to see it. I didn't realise quite how like her I am. I'm so glad and it makes me feel a little more connected to her, too.

Aunt Muriel always comments on things that I do that are like Mum. Like when I flick my hair off my face with the back of my hand, that sort of thing. She has tears in her eyes sometimes when I do those things. Not that I do them on purpose, because I was only a few hours old when she died, but when I apologised to her, she said not to, that although it might upset her a little, it also brings back our mum for her and in an odd way cheers her up.

We see white trails curling and making circular patterns in the sky when we go out sometimes. It's the RAF trying to protect us from the Germans' planes and it's called a 'dog fight'. Strange, *don't you think to call something happening hundreds over feet above our heads by that name.*

Aunt Muriel's calling for me to turn out the light now and get some sleep. She can see the light under my door, so I'd better do as she asks. I'll write again tomorrow.

NINE

Estelle

27 JULY 1940

I t was another hot, sunny morning and Estelle began her chores as soon after five o'clock as she could. She thought back to a couple of years before when her dad had decided to reduce the animals at the farm and sold his herd of Jerseys that he had been building up for twenty years to a neighbouring farmer. Her grandfather had always preferred growing crops, but her father had wanted to try dairy farming to see if it was something he enjoyed more, finally deciding to go back to doing what he had known growing up.

At least now she only had to feed several chickens and the pigs. She would have liked not to register all the pigs with the German authorities but they were too big to conceal without her father's help. She had miscounted the chickens though and hoped she wouldn't be found out.

It was a strain being in charge of the farm and she still hoped to be able to bring in a couple of men or even schoolboys to help with the harvesting on the potatoes when the time came around again. Now, though, it seemed that they were going to have to grow wheat and she had no idea how to go about doing that.

She finished her work and crossed the yard to go back into the house. 'Come along, Rebel,' she shouted, looking forward to joining Gran for her cooked breakfast. It was eight o'clock and if she hurried she could be in town for nine-thirty to drop off a few potatoes and tomatoes to Antoinette before cycling on to Grouville to try to see Gerard again. It upset her that she hadn't been able to talk to him but at least she had managed to see him a few times and let him know that she had made the effort and was still thinking about him by giving him a wave and a reassuring smile.

Estelle arrived in St Helier and hid her bike behind a small bin area in Cross Street. She had no intention of letting any light-fingered soldiers steal her bicycle. With the new ban on cars, bicycles were in high demand. She was hot and clammy despite wearing her lightest cotton summer dress. As Estelle walked down the road into Conway Street and then Broad Street, she sensed tension in the air. She looked along the street and all appeared to be the same as it had been for the past few weeks. Her nerves tingled with anxiety. Something was amiss, but what. She heard a harsh voice giving an order from down by Town Hall, followed by the sounds of many footsteps and then what sounded like marching. It wasn't the usual heavy sound that the German jackboots made but something lighter.

She ran towards them, determined to find out what was

going on. They looked like civilians. Estelle joined the crowds congregating along the pavement from Town Hall to Charing Cross. 'What's happening?' she asked a few times but no one seemed to know. She pushed her way towards a German officer. 'Where are they going?' she shouted, not surprised when he ignored her plea for information.

The crowds surged forward, held back by the local police who kept trying to calm the locals.

Estelle spotted Antoinette's husband Paul among rows of men being urged onwards by several soldiers with raised weapons. He looked distraught as if he was trying to hold back his emotions. Gerard must be there somewhere, she realised. 'Can someone please tell me what's happening to them?' Estelle pleaded to anyone who would listen.

'They're going towards the harbour!' a man yelled.

A woman cried out. '*Oh, my God!* They're sending our boys away.'

Estelle spotted Gerard in a row near to the back of the prisoners. '*No!*' she yelled, her cries drowned out by others calling for their loved ones, pushing forward through the crowd to try to follow the men as they were shouted at by their German captors to keep going in the direction of the docks.

'Gerard. Gerard, over here.' She wasn't sure if he had heard her or merely sensed her presence but the next thing she knew he turned his head and saw her, a worried expression in his brown eyes.

'I love you,' he mouthed.

'I love you, too,' Estelle shouted back, tears coursing

down her hot face. She moved forward as much as she could with the crowd but soon lost him and was left praying that she would see him again.

'They're taking them to France,' someone said nearby.

'They'll be in one of those German camps before long and we've all heard what happens there,' another said.

Unable to bear listening to people's cries for their loved ones, Estelle turned and pushed her way back through the crowds. She needed to be alone, away from everyone. Not caring if anyone she knew saw her, Estelle ran up Broad Street to the town church and, finding a quiet corner on the lawn at the back of the granite building sat down and cried.

TEN

Estelle

15 SEPTEMBER 1940

E stelle switched off her father's radio. It had been six weeks now since Gerard and the other soldiers had been taken from the internment camp in Grouville and then deported to Europe as prisoners of war. She could only hope that he might be allowed to send her a message at some point to let her know he was still alive, but she didn't hold out much hope of that ever happening.

At least the islanders were allowed to listen to the wireless again. It wasn't much, but it was better than nothing. They were only supposed to listen to the German stations but Estelle and Gran relished listening to the BBC and it helped them feel less cut off from the world. Hearing voices from the mainland made Estelle feel more connected to Rosie.

But it wasn't long before the mood changed and reports were coming in on the horrifying bombing raids on London. They were calling it 'the Blitz' and the thought of her sister being sent away for her own safety and ending up somewhere far more dangerous was devastating. She couldn't help feeling angry with her dad for insisting Rosie go. She should be looking after her little sister, like she had always done.

She heard her grandmother coming down the stairs. Gran rarely came back down at night once she had retired to bed and Estelle went through to the hallway to see what was.

'Is everything all right?' she asked, anxiously. 'Can I bring you a drink or something?'

Her grandmother waved her away. She hated any fuss. 'I'm fine. I thought I was tired but, for some reason, I can't seem to fall asleep. I thought I'd come down and make myself a mug of cocoa. Would you like one?'

'Yes, please.' Estelle stepped back to let her grandmother pass and then followed her into the kitchen, leaning against the worktop, watching her she checked that the blackout blinds were fastened properly so that the nightly patrol cars wouldn't see any light escaping from the kitchen. Gran poured milk from a jug into one of their saucepans and placed it on the range to heat. Then, after taking two mugs from the dresser and placing them neatly side by side, she turned to face Estelle.

'Anyway, why are *you* still up?' she asked her granddaughter. 'Couldn't sleep, either?'

Estelle shook her head. 'I was thinking about Rosie and all that she and Aunt Muriel are probably going through. I wish they were both here with us. I know we've got the Jerries on our doorstep but at least we've only been bombed once so far.'

'Your father thought it was for the best to send Rosie though and I think it was, at the time. Back in June, the threat to Rosie felt greater here than it did in London.'

Estelle couldn't stop her mind from racing. 'Gran?'

'Yes, my love?'

'I know we're all in this together and that no one knows how long it's going to last, or what's going to happen...' Estelle realised she had no idea how to put her feelings into words that made any sense. 'That is... I feel like I've woken up and I'm living someone else's life right now...'

Her grandmother reached out and patted Estelle's right hand, giving her the courage to continue.

'Everything seems so out of control and I'm not sure how to deal with it.'

Her grandmother watched her, a thoughtful expression on her pale, lined face. 'We all feel as you do and there's nothing wrong in that. We have to find ways to cope as best we can, Estelle. When we're not busy looking after the farm, we need to concentrate on keeping an eye on our neighbours, looking out for each other, especially those living on their own or with bigger responsibilities than ours. In the last war, when I was living in London, we stepped in to take care of those devastated by the loss of loved ones, like my mother after my brothers were killed on the Front.'

'I'm so sorry, Gran. It must have been a dreadful time for you then, too.'

Gran took a sip of her drink. 'War is an ugly thing in so many ways.'

They were quiet for a moment, before her grandmother

continued, 'Most of all though, my dear, we need to remember *always* that this will pass.'

Estelle hoped so with all her heart. 'Really? You're certain it will?'

'I believe so. I have to and so must you. This vile war that keeps us imprisoned on our island and Rosie apart from us will end at some point. We will see her again. We must remember that.'

Estelle resolved to try to do her best to be positive and that they would be a family once more, albeit a smaller one. 'One day, we might even look back on this and be proud of the way we came through it,' she said, inspired to be strong whenever she could.

'That's my girl.' Her grandmother withdrew her hand and cupped her mug. 'You see? It's all about how we perceive what's being done to us.'

It was. Estelle nodded, grateful for her grandmother's uplifting and reassuring words.

'Even if it might be the end of the world as we've known it so far, my love. Things will get better. They might have to get a lot worse before that happens though and that's when we'll need to dig deep and find the strength to keep going.'

The following morning, Estelle rose early, pulled on her worn overalls that had once belonged to her father and tied her hair up in an old scarf to keep it out of her face. Then, going down to the kitchen, she ate her breakfast quietly dreading the long dark mornings that would be upon them in only a few months' time. She rubbed her lower back where it ached, relieved that she would finally finish digging up the last of the potatoes that morning. She didn't think she had ever been so weary despite falling into an exhausted sleep each night. She was relieved that David Bisson had agreed to come and help her again in the field this morning. With his help the back-breaking work could be done in half the time.

She completed the rest of her chores feeding the chickens and three pigs and looked forward to taking Rebel for a long walk. First, though, she needed to go into the village to Mr Gibault's store to collect their weekly rations.

The bell jangled as she walked in and went to stand at the back of the short queue. Two women she recognised as sisters stood in front of her and were chatting about the escape of three Frenchmen from the island two week's before. 'I heard that they used a boat and left from Rozel,' one of them said quietly.

'I heard the same thing,' the other said. 'Apparently, the poor devils only arrived on the island just before the German forces having hoped to escape from Normandy.'

'What bad luck. I'm glad they got away. If only they'd taken down a few of those Jerries before they left though. Give us a few less to deal with.' She seemed to notice Estelle standing behind them for the first time and gave her a nod.

The first of the women reached the counter. Estelle watched Mr Gibault as he waited for the woman he had been serving up until then to close the door behind her so that only the two women and Estelle were left in the shop.

'Ladies, you really need to be more careful about the things you say.'

'What do you mean?' the first one asked. 'We're only speaking the truth.'

'That's as maybe and if you want to risk ending up in prison then carry on. Don't you know that you risk being locked up for saying such things? Anyone caught trying to escape will be shot? Those men were successful but others haven't been.'

The sisters looked at each other before apologising.

'Just remember: you never who is listening. Please, be more careful in future, especially in my shop.'

The women left and he smiled at Estelle. 'Now, young lady, what can I do for you?'

Estelle opened her mouth about to speak when a teenage boy entered the shop and without bothering to close the door behind him walked right up to the counter and handed a small brown-paper bag to the shopkeeper. 'My dad said to give this to you,' he said, before turning and running out again without waiting for Mr Gibault to reply.

Mr Gibault bent to place the packet down behind the counter before clearing his throat and addressing Estelle, pointedly ignoring her enquiring look. 'Is it your rations you've come for?' he asked as if nothing had just happened.

Having taken her shopping home, Estelle fetched Rebel and went for a walk. She took the back lanes and ended up on the headland at Grosnez overlooking the Channel, the islands of Guernsey, Herm, Jethou and Sark in the distance. She thought back to when she was little, before Rosie was born, when her father occasionally brought her here and pointed out each of the other islands to her. They had been such special times, just the two of them.

She wondered about the other Channel Islands islanders and whether they were facing the same harsh realities as they were here in Jersey. She spotted a couple of German soldiers chatting several hundred yards away from her, so stepped back out of sight. Their rifles slung over their shoulders, their deep voices animated and that to her sounded mocking. They appeared so at home on the island, as if it was theirs now, which, she supposed, it was.

Rosie wouldn't recognise our island right now, Estelle thought. Not now the hated swastika flew from almost every building in town and soldiers paraded through the streets, their goose stepping noisy from their heavy jackboots.

Estelle pictured the swastika flying from Buckingham Palace, the thought making her shiver with dread. Was her life now a preview of what was going to happen on the mainland? She desperately hoped not. Then she might never see her sister again. The Germans had marched across and taken the whole of Europe and now the Channel Islands. The next stop was the mainland, unless Churchill and the British Armed Forces found a way to stop them.

Rebel moved a little too far from her and she pulled on his lead to bring him back to her hiding place. It wouldn't do to be caught here. She heard the guttural sounds of the uniformed men as they laughed at something, patting each other on the back. How she hated them.

Was this how it was to be, she wondered, a fist of fear clutching at her insides. Never to walk the St Helier streets again without coming across a German uniform, not being allowed down to the golden sands of the beaches to paddle without being given permission and having to watch for mines and barbed wire. Never·knowing freedom again? She reminded herself that she had assured her grandmother that she would try to be positive.

Right now, though, she just wished she could go back in time, just a few months to when life was happy, her father was still alive and Rosie was getting on her nerves by asking her to take her down to the beach, or the pictures. They had lived with the fear that the war might reach them on their quiet, peaceful shores, but never truly believed it actually would.

The two soldiers were coming closer, leading Estelle to crouch lower by the edge of the gorse disturbing a fat bumble bee who flew off to find a more peaceful place to work. She shaded her eyes from the glare of the sun and peered across the Channel, praying that the invaders would not reach Britain and her sister.

She loved Jersey desperately, but that was when she had every opportunity of leaving for a trip away, or to visit England, if she had wanted to, or go on the ferry to St Malo in France with her friends. Now, though, she felt isolated and was unable to leave if she chose to. She thought of Gerard and knew that if he had still been on the island and free he would find a way to fight the enemy somehow. To feel like she was at least trying to do something to undermine them. She recalled the strange incident in Mr Gibault's shop and odd whispers about small pockets of resistance and in that second decided that she was going to do what she could. The thought made her feel much better and, when she was sure the soldiers weren't looking her way, she whispered to Rebel before hurriedly making her way back to the main road.

By the time she reached the farm and strode towards the yard, there was already a grey car with its Nazi insignia parked outside her home.

ELEVEN

Estelle

JERSEY

A uniformed man, who she presumed must be the driver, was leaning against the vehicle. He spotted her and straightened immediately, no doubt frightened that she might report him to whomever was inside her home. Rebel growled at the soldier and Estelle pulled him away and broke into a run towards the house. She almost lost her footing as she saw her gran through the living-room window, looking dressed to go out, showing a German officer in through the hallway.

Estelle tried to collect herself. Her grandmother would want her to be composed and polite regardless of how flustered she might be. She took a deep breath and smoothed down her unruly hair, recalling how her gran was always telling her and Rosie to sit up straight and mind their manners growing up. Appearances mattered to Gran when they had visitors, whoever they happened to be.

Then, as calmly as she could manage, Estelle unclipped Rebel's lead, allowing him to go ahead, and walked through the front door into the hallway. She pulled the sleeves of her cotton cardigan down from her elbows and buttoned it up. Her summer dress was a little shabby, but she couldn't do anything about that now. She glanced down at her dusty, worn leather shoes and decided that this was the best she could do.

She immediately heard a deep male voice, his German accent strong, and felt how strange it was to hear in her own home, to hear any man's voice, who wasn't her father or Gerard, or one of the farmhands they'd employed before they'd all gone off to fight. Estelle stopped at the hall doorway and caught her grandmother's eye. Rebel was sitting next to her, his body so close he was touching Gran's side. Protecting her.

With barely a movement, her grandmother conveyed that she should enter. Estelle did as she expected, passing behind the officer to stand by her grandmother's side. He was standing very straight, his uniform immaculate, as they always seemed to be, and his cap under one arm. Her grandmother looked as if she was dressed to go out somewhere, wearing her hat and with her coat folded over one arm across her lap, Estelle noticed. She clearly hadn't been expecting visitors today.

The German must have heard her come into the room because he immediately stopped speaking before giving her a brief nod. With a shock, Estelle realised it was the soldier from the meadow who had warned her not to go there alone. She hadn't forgotten those eyes and the horror and indignation she had felt at what he had implied.

'This is my granddaughter, Estelle.' Her grandmother

said, looking at her. 'This is…' she didn't seem able to recall his name and looked up at the well-built young man, who seemed to be in his mid-twenties. 'Please, introduce yourself,' she said.

He turned to Estelle, and said, 'I am Captain Hans Bauer of the Wehrmacht.' He tilted his head to one side and seemed to be waiting for her to reply. 'But I believe we have already met.'

'You have?' Gran asked sharply, narrowing her eyes at the captain before giving Estelle a questioning look.

'I was out walking in St Peter's Valley. It was nothing.' Estelle replied quickly. She noticed the officer looking a little surprised.

He gave Estelle a tight smile. 'I have been explaining to your grandmother that I am to be billeted here at your farmhouse. I am told that you have a younger sister who no longer lives here and, therefore, you have a vacant room.'

Estelle did her best to hide her shock. She had heard about other families having to give up their spare rooms and how nerve-wracking it was for them to have to watch everything they said and did in their homes. To lose that place of comfort was a horrifying thought. For some reason, she had thought they were too far away from St Helier, living in the north-west of the island, to have to do the same. How naïve of her to think that they could avoid becoming involved with these men.

The horror must have been evident on her face because he continued: 'I am aware that this is not going to be favourable to you both, but we must arrange billets for many soldiers now across the island.'

Estelle recalled his almost perfect English and hoped that when the time came for him to discover they had two bedrooms lying unused since her father's death that another soldier would not then also come to live with them. She wondered how long she and Gran had to prepare for this uninvited guest to move in. Didn't they have enough to deal with? Had they not been punished enough? When he didn't elaborate further, she decided to ask him.

'When do you plan to move in, then?' She was irritated that they had no choice.

Her grandmother stiffened but didn't want him to get the idea that just because they were two women living alone they were able to be pushed around.

'I will be moving in this evening and will require dinner tonight.'

'Oh, will you?' her grandmother snapped. 'Then I'll expect you here no later than six-thirty. We don't like to be up too late in this house.'

Estelle knew her grandmother was being contrary. She might like an early night but she was perfectly aware that Estelle never retired to her room earlier than ten-thirty most nights.

'Of course,' he replied. 'That will suit me well. You will be paid for my room and meals of course and I will expect my laundry to be taken care of. I hope that is acceptable to you?'

It made little difference if it wasn't, Estelle thought angrily.

When the two women just stared back at him, he placed his cap on his head, gave a final curt nod, turned and left the house. Neither Estelle nor her grandmother spoke, waiting until they had heard the car engine start and disappear down the driveway. Estelle then moved over to the window to look out, just to be certain one of them hadn't stayed behind, and then went to close the front door.

Returning to the living room where her grandmother was now sitting in her favourite armchair, one hand covering her mouth, Estelle crouched down in front of her.

'Are you all right?' Gran. 'Would you like me to make you a cup of tea?'

She shook her head. 'No, I think we need to decide which room to put him in, don't you?'

Estelle was confused. 'But I thought he'd have Rosie's room.'

'No, he should have your father's room.'

Estelle hated the thought of the officer taking over her father's room. He had been murdered by German bullets and now one of them was going to be staying in his room. 'Daddy would turn in his grave,' she said, without thinking.

Her grandmother glared at her. 'What would you suggest, then? Rosie will be back, Estelle, and, like it or not, your father will not. I can't bear to think of that little girl going through all she is now in London and having to return and sleep in the same room that a German officer has occupied for however long he's here. Can you?'

Estelle shook her head and got to her feet. 'No, but, then again, the thought of one of them sleeping in Dad's room is horrible, too.'

'I agree,' Gran said, rising up from the chair slowly. 'But we're not in a position to do much about it. Now, unless you'd like to move your things into your father's room before this evening, I suggest we go and clear out all your father's things and make it ready for Captain Bauer.'

They made an immediate start deciding that for the time being they would store her father's belongings in Rosie's bedroom, until they could sort through them and pack away whatever they decided to keep in the attic. Estelle stifled a sob as she caught a faint waft of her father's scent from one of his old pullovers she was folding before placing it into a case to put away. Had he really only been dead for less than three months? It felt like a lifetime ago since she had last been able to give him a hug. She had barely had enough time with all that had happened since then to be able to sit and grieve properly for him.

'Right, I'm going to leave you to finish off this room while I visit Mrs de la Haye. Her boy was one of those who were sent away with Gerard and she's finding it hard to cope. I said I'd take her some of my rock cakes today. You'll find the rest in the cake tin after you've finished in here.'

Estelle finished making the bed. She would rather not have been left to make the room nice for the captain but didn't dare argue with her grandmother. For someone who was only four foot seven, Marnie Le Maistre could be fierce.

Estelle picked up the clock from on top of the chest of drawers and stared at it, an idea coming to her. She moved the dials, turning back the clock one hour to Jersey time. It was a small retaliation, but a satisfying one to think their uninvited guest might be late.

Her thoughts returned to her grandmother and her visit to Mrs dele Haye. So that was why she was dressed to go out when Estelle had arrived home to find her grandmother with Captain Bauer.

It was only when she had placed the clock back on to the chest of drawers that it occurred to her that her grandmother had taken rock cakes to Mrs de la Haye just three days before. And her grandmother never made rock cakes twice in one week, not since rationing had come into force and their flour and butter supplies had been reduced so much.

'Where have you really gone?' Estelle murmured to herself. Her grandmother was hiding something, she was certain of it. But what could someone her age, someone who had spent the past twenty years living peacefully on a farm in St Ouen, have to hide? She didn't know, but she had every intention of discovering what it was.

TWELVE

Estelle

E stelle hoped her grandmother would be back at the farm by the time the officer returned with his belongings. She kept herself busy by cleaning out the chicken coop. 'Get away, Dotty. And you two, Clover and Cilla,' she hissed, waving her wet brush at them to keep them from going back inside before she was finished.

The house had felt strange and too empty without her father and sister around, though she much preferred that option to now having to share their space with a Nazi. 'Well, I'll be damned if I'm going to let this German be too comfortable in our home.'. Turning her thoughts to what to prepare for their meal tonight, Estelle took a colander out to the storeroom at the side of the house, grateful to be in a position to make their measly rations more substantial by growing her own potatoes and vegetables. What would their enemy eat? She had to remind herself he was just a man. A man who would need to eat and drink just like they did. She wondered what he would be like to live with. He hadn't seemed too bad from what she had seen but she could never forget that despite his smile he was still a Nazi, and she hated Nazis. They would soon find out what it was like to live in close proximity to one and she wasn't looking forward to it.

Estelle left the vegetables on the worktop and hurried upstairs to wash and change. She was brushing her hair when it dawned on her that with only one bathroom in the house she would have to share it with the captain, and she didn't want to be in the bathroom when he returned. Estelle also didn't want him to think that she had made an effort just for him, but knew her grandmother would expect her to show that however difficult life was for them right now they still had pride in themselves.

She returned to the kitchen and grabbed her grandmother's pinny, tying it around her waist to protect her clean skirt. She had just finished peeling a small pan of potatoes when a knock on the front door disturbed her. Rinsing her hands, she dried them on the hand towel hanging over the bar in front of the range cooker, wishing Gran was with her. She noticed her hands trembled as she reached behind her in an attempt to untie the pinny.

'For pity's sake,' she moaned through gritted teeth when all she managed to do was to knot the ties even tighter.

Her hands struggled with the cloth as she twisted the pinny round to better get at the knot. Then there was another knock on the front door and Estelle could feel herself getting hotter by the second. Unable to free herself of the pinny, she rushed to answer it.

Opening the door, Estelle found Captain Bauer standing

there, his expression serious and a bag at his feet. He looked younger than she had realised earlier and appeared surprised to see her. She realised it was probably because of her flustered state. She glanced down at the pinny twisted around her. Mortified, her face reddened further and she couldn't think what to say.

He looked down at the tangled knot of ties. 'Allow me.'

Estelle stared at him in surprise as he turned her around and proceeded to work on the knot.

In silence, he undid the cords and handed the released apron to her. Taking it from him, she wasn't sure what to say.

'Good evening, Miss Le Maistre. Are you ready for me to bring my belongings into your home?'

She wanted to say that there would never be a point in her life when a Nazi would be welcome in this house but, remembering his authority, she nodded and stepped back. She realised she couldn't recall his name. 'You did introduce yourself but…'

He didn't seem surprised. 'I am Captain Hans Bauer of the Wehrmacht.'

'That's a bit of a mouthful,' she said, shocked when his eyes widened and she realised she had spoken the words out loud. 'Sorry, I mean, do I address you as that, or is there a shorter version?' She knew she was pushing her luck by being cheeky and that her grandmother would not approve, regardless of who she was addressing, but Estelle was too irritated by having this tall, broad-shouldered man – who, at a guess was probably only a couple of years older than her – about to move his things into her dear father's bedroom.

He seemed a bit disconcerted. 'Please, you may call me Hans while I am in this house, if you like. Captain Bauer, when we are in public.'

Estelle had no intention of ever being too familiar with this man. She studied him in silence, staring into his navy eyes, his blond hair combed back from his face. He was immaculate, like all the other Jerries she had seen before him, and maybe back in Germany the girls thought him handsome, which she, secretly, had to admit he was. However, he was still a Jerry and stood for everything that had torn her life apart in the past few months.

'No, I think Captain Bauer will be fine.' It was best to set the boundaries straight away, she decided. This captain couldn't get too comfortable. 'Shall I show you up to the room?'

She wasn't sure but he seemed a bit deflated. He gave her a nod and motioned for her to lead the way. Estelle walked up the stairs. It was a weird sensation having a stranger – a male stranger, at that – following her up to the first landing. She stopped outside her father's bedroom door. She still found it hard to believe this was happening and a fist of rage clenched in the pit of her stomach.

She pushed the door open a little too forcefully so that it slammed against the bedroom wall and light flooded out of the large room into the hallway. 'This will be your room while you're billeted with us.'

He strode right in and placed his bag on the floor, standing with his hands on his hips as he studied the room.

He walked over to the window and stared outside for a few seconds before turning to her.

'Thank you, this looks very comfortable.'

'It should do,' she said, 'it's the best room in the house.'

'You have given me the best room?' He seemed surprised.

'It's my father's bedroom. That is, it was. Until he was killed at the harbour in June.'

They stood in silence. Estelle dared the young officer to say something.

'By a German pilot,' he finally admitted, not tearing his gaze away from her, but so quietly she almost thought she had imagined it.

Estelle needed him to know what his people had done to her family. Now he did, she turned to leave. 'I trust you have everything you need.' Without waiting for him to reply, she added, 'Your towels are over there.' She pointed to a wooden towel rail in front of him. 'And the bathroom is the next room along after this one. There is only one bathroom, so we'll all have to share.'

She didn't know why she needed to elaborate this point in particular but maybe it was because she wanted to get across how inconvenient it was to her and her grandmother that he was staying with them.

'I wasn't certain whether there would be a bathroom inside the house.'

Estelle was aware that a lot of the farms still didn't have the luxury they had of a pleasant bathroom. 'My father had one put in when my grandmother came to live with us. He thought it only right as a man living with all women.'

'A man of sense.'

'My father is none of your concern.'

He studied the room and his gaze settled on a picture. Estelle blushed and walked towards it. 'I'm sorry, I forgot to remove this.'

He waved for her to stop. 'Please do not feel you must take it down. Did your mother draw this?'

She could understand why he would think such a thing, especially as she had told him this was her father's bedroom. She reached out and lifted the framed drawing of an evening dress she had done in memory of her mother's birthday one year. Her father had loved it and said it made him happy to think of Estelle designing dresses for her mother who, he knew, had she lived, would have been delighted to wear one of her daughter's designs. 'No, this is my design for my mother. She died when I was seven.'

'I'm sorry to hear that.'

Estelle held the picture to her chest. 'It was a long time ago now.' She looked at the empty nail poking out of the wall. 'I'll replace the picture with something else, unless you have something you wish to hang there.'

He smiled. 'There is no need to replace the picture.'

'Fine. I'll leave you to settle in.'

'Thank you, Miss Le Maistre,' he said, looking over at her. 'That is very kind of you.'

She stared at him, trying to gauge if he knew that being kind was the last thing she was trying to achieve. 'My grandmother insists on good manners.'

His expression was not of amusement, but something else. Something that seemed to say that he appreciated her spirit. Well, he could go to hell. She had no intention of impressing this man in any way at all.

It was then that she heard the back door close announcing her grandmother's arrival. 'We eat supper at six-thirty.' Leaving the room, Estelle closed the door quietly behind her, her heart pounding.

As she walked along the landing, Estelle could hear her grandmother humming, though she had no idea what she could find to be cheerful about. She took the framed drawing to her room and slid it into one of her clothes drawers before going downstairs to join her.

Closing the door behind her to allow them to speak without being overheard, she whispered, 'He's here.'

Her grandmother spun round as if surprised to see her there. 'Oh, it's you?'

Estelle frowned. 'Yes. Did you hear me? He's here.'

Her grandmother's mood seemed to slip. 'Already?'

'Yes. He arrived a short while ago. I showed him up to… his room. He liked it.'

'As he should do.' She picked up the pinny Estelle had left lying on the back of the chair and tied it around her own waist.

'I didn't lay the table in the dining room,' Estelle said, unsure where her grandmother wanted them to eat their meal. Whenever they had a guest to dinner, they always ate in the dining room. Estelle found it rather oppressive with its old-fashioned heavy dark wood furniture and red walls, so never minded when they ate in the kitchen. It was much brighter and cosier in there with the heat emanating from the old iron range her father had refused to replace. This man, though, wasn't an invited guest. His presence had been forced on them.

'I don't see why we should heat another room,' Gran said. 'We can have our meals in here. Unless he dictates otherwise, of course. I've seen these Jerry officers in town. Buying up all the stocks of champagne. They seem to like the finer things.' She moved the pan on to the heat for the potatoes to cook. 'I see you've peeled the spuds. Well done, my love.'

'I didn't have time to buy in more meat for him so we'll have to divide the pork I had already between the three of us.'

Pork was a real treat since the war began. Her grandmother took a knife and cut down an onion hanging from the wall in a platted row. No doubt the German was expecting to be well fed. A farmhouse like theirs, unlike many on the island who didn't grow their own produce, would have been sought after as a billet, Estelle was sure. She thought back to her brief meeting with the captain that day in the meadow. Had he known she lived here, or was it just a coincidence that he ended up being billeted with them?

Captain Bauer joined them in the kitchen five minutes before supper was due to be eaten. As she had expected, he was punctual and wore his uniform. He automatically assumed he was sitting at the head of the table, which Estelle found infuriating, but a quick sideways glance from her grandmother stopped her from reacting in any way.

The three of them ate their meal in awkward silence. For once, the creamy Jersey potatoes didn't seem as pleasurable to eat as they usually did. She sneaked a peak at the captain to watch this stranger sitting so stiffly at their table. He caught Estelle's eye and she instantly looked away, mortified to have been caught looking at him.

'This meal is delicious, Frau Woods. Thank you.' He cleared his throat and focused on eating another mouthful of food. 'You live on a beautiful island. You are very lucky to have been born here.'

Estelle opened her mouth to speak but she caught her grandmother giving her a warning glare and decided against telling him how much they did love their island, especially before he and his cohorts arrived to take it over like cuckoos in a very beautiful nest.

'I was born in England, Captain, but I've lived here for many years now.' Her grandmother replied, formally.

The small talk turned to safer topics like the weather and he asked what produce they grew and which animals they kept. Estelle didn't volunteer any information. She decided to let her grandmother do the talking.

Apart from them exchanging a couple of sentences, the only sound in the kitchen as they ate was the movement of cutlery against the plates as they cut through their food and the occasional sound of one of them swallowing their water.

Supper over, Estelle was relieved when the officer thanked them, asked for a glass of water to take up to his room, and bid them good night.

She and her grandmother washed the dishes in silence before sitting sat back at the table.

'I don't know about you but I found that exhausting,' her grandmother whispered. 'Isn't it bad enough that they've come here, without forcing us to have one of them sleeping under our roof, too? Two women alone with a strange man; it isn't right.'

Estelle couldn't have agreed more. How were they going to be able to spend every morning and evening with this man?

Her grandmother frowned and stared at her wrinkled hands. 'I don't imagine I'll ever feel at home with him in this house.'

THIRTEEN

Rosie

LONDON, 16 SEPTEMBER 1940

I t's been really hot here in London, Essie. Aunt Muriel says it's stifling and that's the right word for it. I miss the sea breezes that we are used to but barely notice and being able to walk down to the beach at Grevede Lecq with our swimsuits and towels on hot days and swim in the sea. I must stop going on about how much I miss everything about home. Aunt Muriel said it will try and help me settle in better if I focus on what I do like about living here rather than what I don't. Right now, though, I can't think of much.

I'm getting used to seeing the silver barrage balloons floating high above us now. They're almost fish-shaped and are at the end of a long metal rope. They're there to stop German planes flying low over London and they wind them closer to the ground during dog fights so our pilots don't get their planes caught in them. I saw a dog fight yesterday when two German bombers crashed after they were shot down by the RAF. Lots of people were cheering and I was, too. One man said he thought there must be *fifty Spitfires flying around in the sky above us. I saw a German bomber fall to bits as it came down. I even watched as a German pilot bailed out. I wanted to stay to see more but Aunt Muriel made me go with her to the shelter, so I missed the rest.*

I have to not show how scared I am whenever I hear bombers flying overhead. They've bombed London every night for the past week, apart from one. It's the most frightening thing I've ever experienced, Estelle. I wanted to go to Trafalgar Square and see Nelson's Column and the huge lions, but on our way there the sirens started screaming and we had to run to the nearest shelter. Glass from broken windows and bricks and stone were crashing to the road all around us. I clung to Aunt Muriel's jacket so tightly that she had to prize my fingers off her to take my hand and drag me into a nearby doorway for shelter. My entire body was shaking. I was sure we were going to die horribly.

The first day it happened, Aunt Muriel treated me to tea at a Lyons Corner House. The waitresses there are called Nippies, because they nip here and there very quickly. Don't you think that's funny?

I was frightened when a fire engine raced passed us during another raid on our way home, it was swerving to miss the bombs that had exploded in the road. I saw something I wish I could forget but doubt I will ever be able to. It was a man, he was running past where we were standing when a flame from one of those bombs, incendiaries, I think Aunt Muriel called them. It set his clothes on fire... the screams. I can still hear them and I still feel sick every time I think of him and what happened. People ran past him screaming and crying. We didn't know what to do. I'll never forget his screams, Estelle. It was like being in a nightmare that I couldn't wake up from.

Aunt Muriel pulled me from the doorway shouting at me to run as fast as I could. We darted between falling bits of building and hot shrapnel. I stumbled once, but thankfully Aunt Muriel was holding very tightly to my hand and pulled me forward.

In the end, although we're not supposed to go down to the Underground, we bought penny tickets like lots of other people and went down anyway. We had nowhere else to go but people said it's the safest place to be during a bombing raid. We stayed down there all night. It was hot and smelled disgusting because we were all crammed together on the platform and we were forced to go to the lavatory in corners. The whole place shook when a bomb landed somewhere nearby. I shook the whole time and couldn't sleep a wink.

The next day, we made our way home passing people some who had blood and dust covering parts of their clothes and bodies. We walked most of the way and caught a bus for the last part of our journey to Hammersmith. I don't think I'll ever forget the sight of those smouldering buildings. Some houses and flats had their entire front walls missing. It was like the family had only stepped into another room. In one the table still laid and pictures hanging on the wall. It was so sad to think that those had been people's homes hours earlier.

There was so much glass crunching under foot I was scared a shard would pierce my shoe, but it didn't. The air was very smokey. Aunt Muriel kept saying, 'Look at poor, dear London, Rosie.' She pointed out where the worst of the fires and smoke was and said it was the direction of the docks and then she cried but tried to hide it. The poor docks had such a hammering, Estelle. It's heart-breaking to see the devastation and it made me think how frightened Daddy must have been to be caught by that plane when they bombed our docks.

Aunt Muriel and I were frightened in case we had lost the flat, but it was untouched. We were the lucky ones that day.

FOURTEEN

Estelle

E stelle's chance of taking back some control from her oppressors came sooner than she had expected when, the following day, a patrol car arrived at the farm.

'What do they want with us?' Gran grumbled, peering over the sink where she was washing the breakfast dishes and out of the open kitchen window.

Estelle wished for the first time that Captain Bauer was still at the farmhouse and not out. She ran over to stand next to her grandmother to see who was outside.

Estelle groaned as a German in his immaculate uniform strode purposely up their garden path. She took a deep breath to calm herself as much as she could manage.

They stood still and stared at the front door, waiting for him to knock. Finally, there was a loud rapping on the wooden door.

'I'll go and see why he's here,' Estelle said, determined to show her grandmother that she was capable of dealing with their uninvited guest.

Her grandmother didn't look very happy with the idea, but Estelle rushed out of the kitchen across the hall to the front door before she could argue. She took a deep breath and, pulling her cardigan sleeves down from her elbows to her wrists, cleared her throat and opened the door.

'Do you want something?' she asked, glowering at him, happy to show her distaste.

'I am told that we may buy eggs from this farm. Yes?'

She wasn't sure who by but didn't dare argue. 'Is that so?' Would they be collaborating if they sold eggs to Nazis? Then it occurred to her that they didn't really have much choice.

'I'll ask my grandmother,' she said, her tone more pleasant than before. 'Wait here for a moment.'

Estelle hurried back to the kitchen and explained what he wanted from them. 'What should I do?' she asked, aware that Gran would have to approve the sale of the eggs, especially to one of the soldiers.

'They've requisitioned a lot of our produce, but I haven't heard about selling to individual soldiers. I don't suppose we have much choice,' she said, a look of resignation on her face. 'Just to be sure. We don't want them to single us out. You never know where that might lead. I'd rather they barely knew we existed than cause them to find reasons to give us a hard time,' she said, half to herself.

Estelle moved her weight from one foot to the other, anxiously waiting for Gran to give her permission.

She puffed out her lined cheeks. 'Go on, then. Ask him to bring some sort of container with him next time.'

Estelle returned to the front door. The young soldier

listened as she explained what her grandmother had said. His face lit up. He reminded Estelle of a small boy who'd been given permission to have a treat.

'I'll pop some in an old basket, but if you could bring your own container next time that would be better.' She went into the kitchen and a thought crossed her mind. She smiled to herself as she deliberately ignored the freshest, largest eggs they had and instead chose the smallest, least appealing ones from the basket in their pantry. The ones that had been there a good long while. She handed them to him. 'There you go.'

'Thank you, *sehrgut*. How much do I owe you?' he asked.

Estelle told him, he paid, gave a quick nod and left. She watched him walk away. All right, so he wasn't going to know that she had given him the smallest eggs but maybe from now on she could keep some back to go rotten. Slip a couple of bad ones in for any other Germans who might find their way to their farm. They had to start somewhere, she reasoned, and, although small and perhaps inconsequential, this felt like her first act of resistance. She quite liked the feeling of power it gave her.

Estelle then went down to the greenhouse and began picking tomatoes to take to the parish grocer to sell, as she usually did twice a week.

As she worked picking the juicy ripe bright red tomatoes and carefully packing them into a wooden tub, she thought back to Captain Bauer. His manners were impeccable and he had kept pretty much to himself since he had moved in. She wondered if in any other world they might have been friends. He was handsome with his tanned skin, navy eyes and blond hair and it made her sad to think that two people who, through no fault of their own, were on opposing sides of a war and never able to be relaxed with each other. Then she thought of Gerard and her father and shook her head, irritated with herself for acting so foolishly. He was the enemy, never mind how polite he might be. She was being utterly ridiculous and letting herself and, she thought horrified, Gerard, down by allowing such unwarranted thoughts to enter her mind.

She felt something drip on to her foot and, looking down, saw a splash of bright red on her shoe. It made her think of the blood her father would have spilt when he had been shot. She noticed the tomato in her hand and realised she was holding it a little too tightly.

FIFTEEN

Rosie

SEPTEMBER 1940

I think of how you and Gran are every day, Estelle. It must feel like you're imprisoned on the island right now. I long for this war to end, so we can all see each other again. I can't believe I've never noticed before now how bright the colours are at home. Even the grey clouds in Jersey seem to make the green of the fields brighter in contrast. I didn't think I could but I'm slowly settling in and getting used to living in London now.

I was out buying fish and chips for our supper the other night ready for when Aunt Muriel arrived home from work and the bombing began. Everyone was running in different directions trying to get to a shelter, or home. A lady grabbed hold of me and told me to go with her. She dragged me into a house and before I had a chance to be scared she took me down a cellar where several other people were that I recognised as stallholders from the market in Shepherd's Bush.

There was a lady with a little baby that screamed until it fell asleep. Poor little tot looked exhausted. There was a boy a few years younger than me with his terrified dog. He said the dog was a Jack Russell and his name was Geoffrey. Don't you think that's an odd name to give a dog? It made me think of Rebel and how frightened he would have been to have all that bombing going on around him. We were so scared we were all quiet at first but we then managed to talk a bit and I found out that the woman who took me down to the cellar was the boy's mum.

The whole house shook several times and bits of plaster rained down from the ceiling, getting in our hair. I was worried about Aunt Muriel, but I prayed quietly that she was safe somewhere, probably in the shop basement where she works.

There was an older lady. She's got a loud voice and I could tell that everyone in the cellar loved her. She introduced herself to me and said her name was Queenie. I really liked her. Even though we could have died at any minute, she told some of us stories and laughed a lot. I couldn't help smiling. I really liked her and when the all-clear sounded and we were leaving the building to return home she asked me where I lived. I told her I was staying in my Aunt's flat in Coulter Road and she said that if I was ever in trouble to come and find her either on her stall in the market or in her flat, which was on the ground floor of the building where we were sheltering. It made me feel a bit better to know that I knew another adult to turn to in London if I ever needed one. She reminded me a little of Mrs Le Marrec, not because she looked like her, but because she was kind and wore a similar cat brooch on her dress.

It was such a shock to see all the black plumes of smoke rising from the burning buildings and the debris on the streets. I know I should be getting used to this sort of thing by now, but I can't seem to be able to. I noticed smoke coming from the same direction as Aunt Muriel's flat, so I ran back as quickly as I could hoping the house was still there. Only the other day, a house round the corner lost the entire front. You could see the pictures hanging crocked on the walls and the bedspread from one of the upstairs rooms hanging down where the floor had been torn apart. It was really sad. Thankfully, the building where our flat is was untouched and soon after I got there Aunt Muriel arrived.

Aunt Muriel helped me send you a telegram. We could only do a few words, so I hope it makes sense. I was trying to be cunning and send you a coded message, but I got a little confused. I'll make sure that I spend time planning my next one, just in case I have to do that one with little notice, too. More than anything, if I can't send you any further messages before then, I'll be hoping you all have a safe and happy Christmas. It doesn't feel like Christmas will ever happen. And Christmas, when I'm not on the farm, just won't be the same. Will Father Christmas even know how to find me? What will happen to him with the bombing, I'd hate to think he'd get shot down.

SIXTEEN

Estelle

OCTOBER 1940

Estelle was wrapped up warmly in her father's old jacket against the drizzly morning weather. It had been four months now since she had last seen her father or sister and she desperately needed to find a way to make contact with Rosie. Having a German living in their home was inconvenient and she hated not being able to speak freely with her grandmother as she had always felt able to do. Her grandmother was also outside this morning, sweeping the yard. They had been discussing ways of getting a telegram to Rosie and Muriel in London.

The front door opened and the captain stepped outside and raised his hand in a welcome. 'Good morning. Not a very pleasant one, today.'

'Good morning, Captain,' her grandmother replied, nodding.

Estelle turned to her grandmother and said, 'I had better get on back up to the top field. If you go and work out what twenty-five words you want to include in our telegram to

Aunt Muriel and Rosie, I'll cycle into town later to the post office to see if I can send it.' She looked directly at the captain before going on. 'I'm just glad the authorities saw sense and now allow us more words. The twelve that we were originally restricted to were far too few to say anything worthwhile.'

He stood in silence, unwilling to rise to Estelle's pointed remarks, which only frustrated her further. 'Of course the last time we tried to send a telegram, we were turned away. The post mistress told me that they are only allowed to accept and send two hundred and twenty telegrams every so often and I had just missed out.' She swallowed to clear her throat and stop herself from tears forming with the frustration she had been feeling since then.

'I am very sorry to hear this.'

She stared at him, desperate to say that she blamed him. Blamed him and his stupid leader for taking her sister away from her. From stopping them from even being in touch. 'All the islanders are in the same position. It's not just us.'

Gran patted her hand. 'Leave it now, lovey, there's nothing we can do.'

Estelle caught the captain watching her. 'Is something wrong?' she asked barely able to hide the sarcasm in her voice.

'I…' He hesitated briefly. 'I would like to help you.'

She looked at her gran unsure what he meant or how she should answer. Her grandmother gave her hand a gentle squeeze to let her know she would reply for them. 'How can you help us?'

'I could take your message and arrange for it to be sent for you.'

'No.' Estelle didn't want his help.

He widened his eyes in surprise. 'Why not?'

'Estelle, love,' her grandmother said quietly, and Estelle knew she was trying to warn her to hold her temper.

'I only wish to be of some help to you both. I know how it is to be parted from family for many months.' He looked questioningly at Estelle.

'Estelle? What harm could it really do?'

She could tell by her grandmother's expression that she wanted to accept his offer of help. Who was she to refuse something that would make her loved ones so happy? She turned to the captain. 'All right then. We will accept your help.'

The following afternoon, Estelle walked into the kitchen after feeding the animals and was pulling her boots off when Captain Bauer arrived home.

'Did you have a good day today?' he asked, looking, she thought, rather pleased with himself.

'The same as it is most days,' she said, standing with one socked foot on the wooden boot jack and resting the other heel in the 'V' of the wood her father had carved years before for the purpose. 'You?'

'I did, as a matter of fact. I am happy to tell you that I was successful in arranging for your telegram to be sent.'

Estelle pulled her foot back out of the boot and sat on the nearest chair. '*You did?*'

Gran entered the kitchen, then, holding a laundry basket of clean, freshly dried sheets. 'Did I just hear you say that you sent our telegram, Captain Bauer?'

Estelle couldn't mistake the excitement shining in her grandmother's eyes.

'Yes, Frau Wood. I do not know how long it will take to reach them but, hopefully, it will not be *too* long.'

Estelle watched the captain speaking to her gran – it was clear that he took pleasure in her grandmother's delight. Perhaps he wasn't so bad, she thought, despite her feelings towards him. Then, again, maybe he was just telling them he had sent their message so that they would trust him? Only time would tell.

SEVENTEEN

Estelle

CHRISTMAS EVE 1940

The captain was turning out to be a pleasant house guest, Estelle had decided, feeling conflicted by the thought. He had always been polite but his help with sending their telegram had led to her attitude towards him softening slightly and he had taken to spending an hour or so in the living room with them after supper before he respectfully retired to leave them to their evenings. He was always up early and out of the bathroom before Estelle got up and, on the whole, kept out of their way.

The long winter nights had set in and the biting cold and continuous rain dampened an already dwindling mood both on the farm and the island. It was to be the first Christmas of the Occupation and Estelle's first Christmas without Rosie, Gerard and, of course, her father. His seat at Christmas lunch would remain empty now for ever. But would Rosie's and Gerard's? It was a prospect Estelle tried her hardest to push to the back of her mind.

Determined to try to keep positive, she had gone up the

ladder into the attic space on Christmas Eve and was grumbling to herself as she rummaged around looking for the right boxes she needed.

'Where are those ruddy decorations,' she moaned, opening what must have been the tenth or eleventh box only to discover she still hadn't found the family Christmas box.

'May I be of some help?' Captain Bauer asked from the ladder, giving Estelle a shock.

She stood upright and smacked her head hard against one of the beams. '*Bloody hell!*' she cried out, wincing, placing her palm against her head.

'Miss Le Maistre,' he said, horrified. Then, climbing the last few rungs of the ladder to join her, he asked, 'Are you hurt?'

'No, no,' she said, leaning away from him, too embarrassed to admit that her head felt like she had just split it. 'I'll be fine. It was just a bit of a knock, that's all.'

He crawled towards her, not looking at all convinced by her protestations. She wished he would leave her and her pounding head alone so that she could gather herself.

The captain studied her face and reached up, then taking her hand gently by the wrist he pulled it slowly away from her head and frowned. Estelle looked down shocked to see blood on her fingers.

'Oh, I've cut myself.' She wasn't sure why she said something so unnecessary, but before she knew it dizziness overcame her, and everything went black.

The next thing she knew, she was lying on her bed, her head resting on a folded towel and her grandmother sitting on the edge of her eiderdown next to her. It took a moment for Estelle to recall the last few minutes before she had passed out.

'How long was I out?' she asked, wincing at the pain caused by the sound of her own voice in her head.

'You are awake.' Captain Bauer came into the room, another damp towel in his hand. 'I'm sorry, I don't wish to intrude.' Seeing the stricken look on his ashen face reminded Estelle what a fool she must have made of herself in the loft

She didn't know what to say, so closed her eyes, hoping it would help dispel the throbbing in her head.

'Please accept my sincerest apologies,' the captain continued.

'What for?' her grandmother asked. 'You were the one to carry her down.'

He blamed himself, Estelle realised. 'Don't apologise,' she murmured. 'I should have been more careful.' Her head pounded painfully, she closed her eyes again. 'Please don't feel badly,' she continued quietly, hoping the pain wouldn't increase if she kept her voice low. 'It really was my own stupidity.'

'You are too kind, Estelle. I am at fault and it is unforgivable.'

She opened her eyes, squinting at him. 'Captain, that's enough. I'm fully aware how low those beams are, I've been up there hundreds of times and should know better.' She reached out for her grandmother's hand. 'Gran, I think the captain has probably had a bigger shock than me. Maybe you should offer him a drink of some sort.' She gave him a sideways glance and smiled weakly to show she was teasing him. He smiled back shyly and looked down.

'Please, will you not call me Hans now?'

She felt her grandmother's weight lift off the side of the mattress and suspected she was giving his request some thought. 'All right, then. Hans, why don't we leave Estelle to lie here quietly for a while and I can make us both some tea.'

By the sound of their footsteps on the wooden floor, they had left the room and were now in the hallway.

Estelle thought back to her grandmother saying that the captain had carried her down the ladder. It was a thin flimsy one and she found it difficult to imagine anyone being able to do such a thing. Despite the pain thudding in her head, Estelle needed to know how he had done it. She winced as she opened her eyes again and saw that he was still hovering outside her bedroom. His air of authority, that of a German officer, their occupier, had completely disappeared.

'May I ask how you managed to carry me down the ladder without breaking both of our necks?'

He stepped back into the room and smiled. 'It was not a problem, you are not very heavy.'

That didn't answer her question. 'But it still can't have been easy to do.'

He shrugged. 'Before I joined the military, I was a...' he thought for a moment for the English word. 'I worked as a fireman.'

Estelle wondered if it was the bang to her head that had confused her as he remembered the captain had briefly mentioned before that he himself grew up on a farm. 'But I thought you were a farmer?'

'No. My father is a farmer. I must correct myself. He was a farmer. I grew up on the farm. But the farm will...' he hesitated. 'Was going to be passed to my older brother. My younger brother is helping my mother with the farm now.'

Estelle noticed the change of tenses and suddenly felt a pang of pity for him. But also something else. Recognition. His presence in their home might have been forced on them but hearing him talk about his life before the war with his own family loss helped her see him as a man rather than simply the enemy. They were in similar situations. Dealing with grief and the loss of loved ones. Living in a new world unrecognisable from their lives before the war.

Her grandmother called him to follow her downstairs and Estelle couldn't help thinking of Gerard. He was an only child and if anything happened to him his father would have no one to leave his farm to. What would happen to their family? She prayed every night that he was safe in the camp in Europe where he had now been interred for almost five months. Although she looked out for the post, there had been no word of him.

Early the next morning, Estelle woke to find that although her head still ached, it wasn't nearly as bad as she had expected it to be. It was just after four thirty am. Christmas morning. It was dark outside and cold in her bedroom but she was very thirsty and desperately wanted a drink of water. Pulling on her dressing gown and slippers and not expecting either the captain or her grandmother to be awake yet, she crept downstairs. The house was quiet, so unlike the previous year when Rosie's delighted shouts, calling for her, Gran, and her father to get out of bed and go see what Father Christmas had bought, woke them all. Her whole body seemed to ache with sadness at the memory. Today was just going to be a day to endure and get through.

Estelle quietly turned the door handle to the kitchen and pushed it open, looking forward to being in the warmest room in the house. She stepped in and gasped to find a man reaching down scruffling Rebel's head. He stood up abruptly and spun round to grab her with both hands. 'Estelle, hush. It is me, Hans.'

Estelle was mortified for him to catch her in her old dressing gown. 'I thought I would be the only one awake. Why don't you sit down and I can put the kettle on?'

He looked down at his hands on her arms before letting go and lowering them to his sides. 'My apologies.' He clasped his hands together. 'Please sit.'

He pulled a chair out carefully for her and motioned for her to sit down. 'I will make *you* a drink. Would you like a tea?'

Surprised, Estelle couldn't think of what to say apart from, 'Yes, that would be nice. Thank you.'

Estelle watched as he lifted the kettle from the range and shook it gently to see how much water was left in it. Then taking it over to the tap under the window, he took off the lid and partly filled the kettle, before replacing the lid and putting it on to the range for the water to boil.

He took two cups and saucers down from the rack and leant against the work top. 'You are up very early? Couldn't you sleep?'

'I'm not the only one,' she pointed out. He was probably missing his family at a time like this. 'It's a strange time of year,' she explained when he didn't say anything further. 'I'm missing my little sister Rosie and my father more than ever today. To be honest, I was probably thinking about them when I should have been concentrating on what I was doing in the loft.'

He looked confused. 'Loft?'

'Attic.'

'Ah, your head.' He raised his hand to touch the back of his own head. 'How is it this morning? I checked on you last night, with your grandmother, of course. We wanted to be certain you were well.'

'Thank you.' It still surprised her how thoughtful he was. 'It's sore, but I'm sure it'll be fine after a couple of days.'

'I hope so.'

He picked up the kettle and poured a small amount of the hot water into the blue teapot her grandmother liked to use and swilled it around to heat the pot. Then pouring it out, spooned a couple of teaspoons of tea leaves in and poured on the boiled water.

'You didn't say why you were down here so early. Is it because it's Christmas?' she asked. 'It is a difficult time when you're separated from those you love.'

His face showed a flicker of emotion. 'That is true. Christmas is not a time to be away from family.'

His voice sounded so gentle that if she had known him better, or maybe if he wasn't German, she would have felt compelled to offer comfort to him for his pain. But he was. And she couldn't lose sight of who he was and what he represented. Rebel stepped out of his bed in front of the range and stretched languidly before making his way to sit next to the captain. Even the dog liked him!

Hans poured their tea and carried their cups over to the table, placing hers in front of her and then sitting at the other. They sat in companionable silence and Estelle wished she had at least brushed her hair before coming downstairs. What a mess she must look.

Eventually, Hans finished his drink and pushed away his cup. 'You wish to know what I have been doing down here so early?'

He was smiling, so Estelle didn't imagine it was something untoward, or he wouldn't be sharing it with her. 'Yes, I do?'

'Follow me,' he said, standing and walking to the kitchen door.

He crossed the hall and nodded to the living-room door. 'Please, go on.'

Was he teasing her? She wasn't sure. He stepped back to let her pass and once she was in the room, he closed the door quietly. They were in almost complete darkness, but before she managed to say anything, Hans switched on the light.

Estelle gasped. It was magical. There was holly on the top of the pictures and all their Christmas decorations from the box in the attic had been strung across from one side of the room to the other. The mantelpiece had been decorated with their small Christmas ornaments and instead of a tree, delicate glass baubles were hanging from what looked like the small branch of a little tree in one of her grandmother's stoneware pots.

'You did this? For us?' She looked behind her to smile at him questioningly.

'It is Christmas. And I wanted to show my gratitude to you and your grandmother. I know what you must think of me but you have both been very kind.' Estelle opened her mouth to argue, but realising he was right, closed it again.

Estelle turned to face him. She hated to think that all his hard work for this surprise might be ruined by something she said. 'I can see you're a decent man and I really am touched with your thoughtfulness. It's the best present you could have given us. Thank you.' Without thinking, she took his hands in hers and stood on her tiptoes to kiss his cheek.

Realising what she'd done, she dropped his hands and stepped back. Horrified. What was wrong with her? And what was she doing kissing a German, and in her nightclothes, too? 'I... I shouldn't have done that. I only meant to say thank you.'

'Please do not concern yourself,' he said, his face reddening with embarrassment. 'I am happy that you like what I've done.'

'I know my grandmother will be delighted, too. Rosie and I usually put up the decorations. It's one of our traditions, but this year, without Rosie...'

'I understand.' He seemed thoughtful. 'In Germany, we

open gifts on Christmas Eve.'

'You must miss your family very much right now?'

'I do. It helped to decorate this room for you and made me feel closer to my mother.' He smiled. 'I always take her to the local market for a glass of Glühwein. I am hoping that I will be able to do so again next year.'

'I miss my family, too.' Their eyes met and they stood in silence. Both thinking of lives that felt a million years ago and far away from the horrors they were living now.

This was not the Christmas Estelle had ever imagined while laughing and joking with her sister, grandmother and father as they took down the decorations the previous year. The captain had done a fine job decorating their home for them and she appreciated his efforts but there was one particular decoration he hadn't included and it wouldn't feel like Christmas to her or her gran if it wasn't on display.

Later that morning, she quietly made her way into the living room and closed the door behind her.

She crouched down next to a box of baubles and delved into the tissue paper until her hand found what she was looking for. Estelle smiled as she held up the tatty papier-mâché star that Rosie had painted in her first term at Kindergarten soon after starting at St Ouen's Parish School. Each year, Estelle would lift it from the tissue paper she had wrapped it in the previous year and hold the yellow ribbon threaded through the hole at the top in front of Rosie. 'Look, Rosie,' she'd say. 'I've found your masterpiece.'

Rosie always pulled a face and complained when Estelle hung the tatty-looking object on the Christmas tree, but Estelle knew that her sister was only hiding her enjoyment that something she had made was loved so much by the rest of the family and brought out each year. Estelle's heart ached. She missed her sister every day but taking out this treasured bauble made the pain even more acute. This would be the first year in over a decade without Rosie's excitement echoing through the farmhouse and, she thought as tears constricted her throat, the first year ever without her father to hug her on Christmas morning and tell her how proud of Estelle her mother would be.

She cleared her throat and took a deep breath. She needed to keep strong for Gran. As if thoughts of her grandmother had materialised her, a second later, the living-room door opened and in she walked, holding a small sheet of paper. She looked, Estelle noticed, as if she were in some sort of trance. Estelle's stomach did a flip and she braced herself for yet more bad news.

'What's the matter?' she asked quietly, going to stand in front of her grandmother, whose hands were trembling terribly. It was then that Estelle realised Gran was holding a telegram! *Rosie?* 'Gran, please, your frightening me.'

Her grandmother blinked a couple of times as if bringing herself back to the present and Estelle suddenly relaxed as her thin lips drew back in a wide grin. She handed the sheet to Estelle. 'Read it. It's from Rosie and Muriel.'

Estelle took the telegram from her grandmother and read all twenty-five words several times before allowing the tears that she'd been holding back to run freely. 'They're well.' The relief was almost too much for her and Estelle had to sit down. 'They've wished us Happy Christmas. Oh, Gran.'

Her grandmother grinned, giving Estelle's cheek a gentle pinch between her right thumb and forefinger. 'Read it out loud to me, dear.'

Received Oct Message. Missing you all. Keeping well. Thinking of you always. Wishing you Merry Christmas and Happy Birthdays. Keep safe. Love, Rosie and Muriel.

The telegram Hans had sent for them had got through!

'This is the very best present either of us could have hoped for, isn't it?' she said, her voice barely above a whisper.

Her grandmother sat on the arm of Estelle's chair and put her arm around her. 'It is, sweet girl, it truly is.'

Estelle rested her head against her grandmother's chest and closed her eyes. Her grandmother's arms tightened around her in a hug and she kissed the top of her granddaughter's head.

'You know, Estelle,' Gran said, thoughtfully, 'our captain, Hans, he's just a young lad who was called up, like Gerard and the rest. He can't help who he is, no more than we can.'

They both stared in silence at the telegram in Estelle's hands as if it was a precious treasure.

'I know. I can see that now.'

EIGHTEEN

Rosie

26 DECEMBER 1940

Well, Essie, I've just experienced my first Christmas without you, Daddy and Gran. Aunt Muriel did her best to make it fun and we even went to Queenie's flat for a sing-song on Christmas Eve. You'd love Queenie, she's always the loudest at any gathering, but I have to admit that she is a lovely person and I pretend sometimes that she's my gran. She gives perfect hugs and even gave me a present, which I thought was unnecessary but very kind of her. It's a knitted scarf, in bright red, and I love it.

It was strange not waking up and coming downstairs to find you in front of the Christmas tree waiting for Gran to finish her breakfast and Daddy to feed the animals so that we could all open our presents together in front of the fire. Did you put up my ugly papier-mâché star on the tree again this year? I bet you did! I hope you did, despite me moaning each year.

I hope you received our telegram. Aunt Muriel and I wanted to send you Christmas cards but she thought that there was more chance of you receiving a telegram.

She wanted to take me to Midnight Mass on Christmas Eve but a bomb had exploded near there a few days before and she was worried the church might not be safe enough for us to be there. You wouldn't believe how many damaged buildings there are, Essie. It frightens Aunt Muriel when I'm gone for too long in case an air raid begins and we might be separated and not find each other in time to go to the shelter together, so she likes me to stay nearby the flat.

I was worried about her, Essie. We have a lot less food here than I'm used to back home, less bacon and butter, tea, that sort of thing. Aunt Muriel says she's fine but she's ever so thin. But, Pierre seems to have cheered her up. I can hear you thinking, 'Who is Pierre?' He's a Canadian soldier, Estelle! Strangely enough, he's one of those rescued from St Malo when Daddy went over with Gerard and his father last year! I asked him to describe the men who rescued him or the name of the boat but it wasn't Daddy. Still, it made me proud to think that Daddy and your Gerard helped save these brave men, and now they're stationed here. He's in the 1st Canadian Division and he's got the funniest accent. He can speak French, don't you think that's funny? He's very nice and I know Aunt Muriel goes pink every time she sees him. I've pointed this out to her but she scolds me and tells me to shush. I hope he isn't sent away anywhere, I'd hate for her to be unhappy again. I know she likes to pretend she's tough, and I think she is, mostly, but London has been so badly battered, and it doesn't look like there'll be any end to this horrible war right now.

I hope you and Gran are coping with those horrid Nazis marching all over the island. They say here that you're being treated all right, but I can't imagine what it must be like to be so close to... to... them. We've seen a few dog fights in the skies and it's so scary, Estelle, but when one of our boys gets one of theirs the streets are filled with cheers.

I suppose you have rationing, too. I'm longing for a bar of Cadbury's Dairy Milk, but Aunt Muriel said that by having to wait for one will make it taste all the better when we do get to enjoy one again.

I'd better go, I can hear Aunt Muriel in the kitchen preparing our breakfast and I need to go and help her. I hope we never have another Christmas apart as long as I live.

NINETEEN

Estelle

17 MARCH 1941

C hristmas was more pleasant than Estelle had expected it to be. Even her grandmother and the captain commented that they had enjoyed it, too. They toasted absent friends over cocoa before retiring to their bedrooms at the end of the day and Estelle couldn't help wondering how different Gerard's Christmas must have been to hers.

Gerard... there were times when she lay awake all night turning over everything in her mind. How she was here, living with Hans, the enemy, sharing meals with him and even laughing with him now, occasionally. All the while, Gerard, her sweetheart, was locked up in a camp in Europe – a prisoner of war! Was she being disloyal? Or was she just trying to get by in the best way she could?

Christmas had also brought a relaxation in the rules of listening to the wireless. The BBC reports were still forbidden, so Estelle and her grandmother secretly listened on the evenings when Hans was out of the house. It seemed that, although London was still being bombed by the Luftwaffe, their focus since November had diverted to other cities, with Coventry, Liverpool and Clydebank being the most recent targets. Estelle was relieved for her sister and aunt but she couldn't help thinking about how many other families were still losing loved ones and their homes. What was worse – live side by side with the Nazis or face the sheer terror of daily air raids and the thought that you or your family might be next?

Everyone's mood locally seemed to shift up or down depending on what was discovered through the news. British and Australian forces had captured somewhere called Tobruk in North Africa in January but it had come with heavy fighting in the Western Desert. Then they'd heard that Plymouth had been blitzed by the Luftwaffe, killing hundreds of innocent souls, and Estelle hadn't been able to stop herself from running into her room and burying her head in her pillow to stop herself from crying aloud. Tears wouldn't help anyone and they certainly didn't bring back the dead.

Despite listening to reports from all over the globe, Estelle's world seemed very small. She had given up trying to find some of the items she had always thought of as essentials, even the soap they used to use had now been replaced by a nasty cheap one that made her skin sore. It was frustrating and degrading that they couldn't find shampoo, or soap to keep themselves clean, and she wondered how long she could make her meagre wardrobe last now that it was impossible to purchase new clothes or shoes. She reminded herself that everyone was in the same boat when it came to these things, however. The whole island was suffering.

The weather had been very cold at the beginning of the year and fuel was scarcer than ever. They had even taken to wearing several layers of clothes and their outdoor coats in the house just to keep warm. With the fuel shortages, they had given up using Estelle's father's tractor and stored it safely under a tarpaulin at the back of the barn behind boxes, pallet boards and old milk churns and anything else she could find to make it as inconspicuous as possible so that it wasn't stolen by any light-fingered Germans.

The captain had even taken to helping out on the farm when he wasn't on duty. She had tried before to tell him she didn't need his help but he had insisted that it was in lieu of their hospitality towards him. If he was to live under their roof, he wanted to help keep that roof secure.

Estelle couldn't help noticing the transformation in Hans when he worked on the land. Out of the harsh, imposing grey uniform and away from the strict rules that went with it, he was cheerful and relaxed. She enjoyed listening to his stories about his childhood on his own family farm and working beside his father and brothers.

———————

It was now March and early one morning a car called for the captain just before six o'clock. As she watched him from where she was working in the barn, Estelle could feel the tension as he greeted his driver and got into the car. Something serious was clearly going on. The whispers in town were full of how a group of young Frenchmen escaped from Brittany and were on their way to England to join the Free French.

Yesterday, Madame de la Roche had called in for a cup of tea and informed them that the recent bad weather had meant the young lads had ended up on what they thought was the Isle of Wight, which, of course, it wasn't. They had been washed up on Vazon Bay in Guernsey and had since been arrested and brought back to Jersey for trial.

'What do you think will happen to them?' Estelle had whispered to her grandmother after Hans had gone up to his room for the night. 'Do you think he might know?'

Her grandmother frowned. 'You can't possibly ask him about something we're not supposed to know anything about. Now promise me, you'll keep quiet.' When Estelle didn't reply immediately, she snapped at her. 'Promise me, now.'

She had no choice but to do as she was told.

'Anyway,' Gran continued, 'he's definitely been quieter the last few days but that could because of any number of things. Maybe it's his mother's birthday, or his wife's?'

'Hans has a wife?' Estelle asked, for some reason shocked to discover he was married. She didn't know why the thought of this news seemed to matter and she was irritated with herself for reacting. Why wouldn't he have someone waiting for him back in Germany? He was a handsome, hard-working young man. But she couldn't help thinking how strange it was that he hadn't thought to mention his wife at all to her, especially when he had been living with them for so many months now.

'I'm not saying he has,' her grandmother replied, 'only that he *might* have someone.'

Estelle couldn't hide her irritation. She hoped her grandmother hadn't picked up on her confusion. 'But why wouldn't he mention, if he was married?' Estelle said, mostly to herself.

She heard her grandmother sigh in irritation. 'It's not our business whether he does, or he doesn't.'

She was right. It wasn't.

Later on that day, Estelle was walking along the edge of the top field with Rebel, inspecting the potato crop, when she heard the unmistakeable echo of gunshots, all within a split second of each other. Rebel immediately sprung up and barked and Estelle whirled round, ducking slightly, trying to listen to which direction the shots had come from. Rebel's hackles rose as they both stared in the direction of St Ouen's Manor, where the sound seemed to come from. Estelle loved the ancient and beautiful manor house which had stood on the island for over a thousand years. Charles II had even been a visitor there during his exile and, whenever Estelle cycled into St Helier, she rode along the road that ran along one side of the property under an archway of branches formed by Dutch elms that grew on either side. Since the invasion however it had been taken over by the Germans and Estelle did her best to avoid it as much as possible.

'It's okay, Rebel,' she soothed, a shiver running through her as she frantically tried to work out what might have happened and whether she was in danger herself. Rebel looked up at her and tilted his head, seemingly confused.

She crouched next to him and gave him a hug. It was soothing to press her face against his warm fur and breathe in the familiar earthy smell. One further shot was fired after about half a minute and then there was nothing further.

When she returned to the farm, Estelle removed her jacket and hat before pulling off her boots and placing them next to her father's work boots that neither woman had the heart to give away. Estelle looked up at his old tweed jacket, its elbows having been patched with pieces of leather by her grandmother had several times. Her father's folded cloth cap was still in his right-hand jacket pocket where he'd pushed it that day in June when he'd left the farmhouse for the last time. Estelle kept her back to her grandmother, who was by the range, as she brushed away her tears and walked over to the sink to wash her hands. Her head was full of the day her father died and the sound of gunshots ringing out across the valley.

'I've made a fresh batch of bread,' Gran said. 'It's only small as we barely have any flour, but it's better than nothing. We've some tomato soup still left over from yesterday, I thought we could eat that.'

'That sounds perfect, Gran,' Estelle fibbed. She decided that once the war was over, if it ever was, that she would never eat tomato soup again! She also knew, though, that she was luckier than most to have something as nourishing as tomatoes to eat. Many were surviving on far less and both she and her grandmother were doing all they could to help supplement their neighbours' meals with produce that was left over from the German quotas. They all had to pull together and help out each other.

The captain arrived back at the farmhouse some time later. Estelle spotted him as she came out of the barn and gave him a cheery hello, surprised when he appeared not to hear her the first time.

'Hans? Is everything all right?' she asked, catching up with him just outside the kitchen. His expression was serious and his face pinched.

Estelle placed the bucket of water she'd been carrying on to the cobbled yard and it splashed around her feet. He looked across at her as if he'd only just noticed she was there. 'I will retire early to my room. I am not hungry this evening. I would be grateful if you could please let your grandmother know.'

He didn't seem himself at all. Had he had bad news from home? 'Would you like me to bring you up a hot drink?'

He shook his head. 'No. Thank you.'

He barely looked at her as he walked past her. Something terrible must have happened and she wished she knew what it was. She didn't have to wait long to find out.

The following morning, Estelle walked to Mr Gibault's shop and joined the queue.

'You know my daughter took her eleven-plus in January?' the woman in front of her was saying as she clutched her wicker basket to her stomach. 'Well, she passed.'

'You must be pleased?'

'Very, especially when you think how strange it is for the kiddies right now,' she replied proudly.

Estelle let the conversations carry on around her. It was amazing the things she picked up in queues while waiting to be served. She heard someone else enter the shop and then Hans's voice asking the two boys behind her whether either of them would like to earn a little pocket money carrying out a few chores for him. Estelle smiled to herself at his attempt to be friendly with the locals. The boys began speaking in Jèrriais and acting as if they didn't understand him. She had heard from her gran that some parents insisted their children spoke the Jersey patois when in the presence of the soldiers. Many families only spoke it at home. Estelle would have liked to practice the language with her grandmother, especially now that Hans lived with them but, as with her mother, both women had grown up on the British mainland and neither had been interested to learn the language. Unlike her and Rosie, who were brought up speaking it with their father.

She heard Hans try once more to make conversation before she stepped in and translated. Once she had their reply, she changed it to make it more acceptable before relating it back to Hans as they giggled behind her. Hans thanked her and looking a little frustrated, left the store.

Her father had enjoyed chatting to her in Jèrriais when they were alone together, or even sometimes when he didn't want her mother to know something, like what he'd bought for her for her birthday, or other surprises he might have had in store for her. She smiled at the memory of how he'd told her he had bought some sweeties for her and hidden the small paper bag in the barn and that as soon as she'd finished feeding the chickens she could have one or two.

'You're the Le Maistre girl, aren't you?'

Estelle heard her name being called out and the harsh accusatory tone in which the question was asked. Before she had time to react, she received a sharp tap on her shoulder and turned round to face the person addressing her. It dawned on her then that everyone else in the queue was staring at her.

'Well, aren't you?'

'I am. What of it?'

'People like you make me sick.' The woman sneered at her.

Estelle winced in shock. 'Excuse me, do I know you?'

'Never mind me, it's you we want an explanation from.' A thin pinch-faced woman with her hair tied up in a scarf wound round her head like a turban glared at her.

Estelle recognised her as someone who lived on the other side of the village, but she doubted she'd ever said more than the briefest greeting to her over the years. The woman had no reason to be giving her such a hard time. She jutted out her chin and placed her hands on her skinny hips, looking confident that she would have the backing of the others.

Estelle could see that a couple of the others in the shop now looked uncomfortable, not wishing to get involved in the unnecessary nastiness, probably, Estelle thought, or because they were relieved the spiteful woman's attention wasn't on them. These weren't times where you wanted to fall out with people. She recalled hearing rumours that the

Kommandant was receiving daily letters from islanders snitching on friends they had fallen out with or neighbours they had long held a grudge against.

Estelle glanced around at the other women in the shop. It dawned on her that they all knew something that she did not. No one was going to corner her in this way, she decided. How dare they all gang up on her? She had always worked hard, been polite and kept out of any trouble.

'If one of you would be so kind as to enlighten me, I'd be very grateful,' she said, doing her best to sound tough as sarcasm dripped from her words.

The skinny woman shook her head in disgust. 'We'd like to know just how you and your grandmother sleep at night? Living all cosy with the enemy up there at your big farmhouse?'

Estelle felt as if she'd been slapped. 'If you mean Captain Bauer then he was billeted at our home, we had nothing to do with deciding who moved in with us. You know we have no power against the Germans.'

'No, but I'll bet you were all for it when you met him and saw how handsome he was, weren't you?'

'Chantal, I don't think that's very fair.' One of the other women at least seemed shocked by her accusation. Estelle noticed that it was Sylvie, a girl who'd been in the class above her at the parish school.

'He is a Nazi officer!' Estelle snapped, but, disconcertingly, felt slightly disloyal to Hans, who had been nothing but a gentleman since moving into the farmhouse.

Chantal sniggered. 'Them being Nazis hasn't deterred other young women though, has it?'

Estelle could feel her cheeks becoming hot and knew her face was red. Rather than embarrassment, which she assumed these people probably supposed her reaction to be, it was her rising temper and she was rapidly losing control of it. She desperately wanted to storm out of the shop but had no intention of doing so until she had defended herself. How dare this woman question her reputation, especially in such a public way? She took a breath to reply, when Sylvie, stepped forward.

'Chantal,' she said again. 'You can't say something like that to Estelle, she's a good girl.'

'Hah, they were all good girls at one point, weren't they? And we don't want a Jerry bag living in our parish.'

Estelle gasped at the mention of the dreaded name: *Jerry bag*. It was a name a few of the local girls had been called due to their intimate relationships with some of the soldiers. She couldn't understand how those girls justified having relationships with the enemy, no matter how handsome he might be. Estelle wondered, though, how many of them had been accused out of spite yet had done nothing wrong. And now this Chantal woman was accusing her.

'Now, you listen to me, you young–' Chantal pushed Sylvie aside and stepped forward, her nose almost touching Estelle's.

Estelle winced at the woman's sour breath and desperately wanted to move back but she stood taller and refused to give in to her intimidation, especially when she had no idea what she had done to cause this woman to accuse her in such a way.

'That's enough!' Mr Gibault's booming voice silenced

the muttering in the shop. 'I'll not have that sort of behaviour here. Estelle Le Maistre and her grandmother are good people and I won't have you insinuate otherwise.'

Estelle looked across the counter at him as he marched back in from the storeroom. She hadn't noticed him leaving, but was relieved that he was back to help her.

'Don't you listen to them, Estelle.' He glared from one woman to the other, resting his attention on the skinny mealy-mouthed woman who had taken it upon herself to accuse her. 'And you, madam, should be ashamed of yourself. You've only lived in this parish for three years. Miss Le Maistre's family have lived here for well over a century.'

The woman clamped her mouth shut. Estelle suspected it was because she didn't fancy having to register for her rations at a shop further away. Knowing Mr Gibault, Estelle believed he was capable of sending Chantal on her way and telling her never to come back if she didn't behave. But why was she at the centre of such malicious attention? They weren't the only people in the parish to have officers billeted with them. Once Mr Gibault had spoken, everyone turned back to face the counter and carried on waiting for their turn, trying to pretend nothing had happened.

Following the confrontation, the atmosphere in the shop was now palpable and Estelle willed him to hurry up and serve everyone. He did seem to be chatting less than usual, she noted, gratefully, which was a relief, but the queue still took ages to move. She could still feel eyes on her. Watching her. Judging her…

Finally, when she reached the front of the queue, Estelle

quietly asked him why Chantal had singled her out. The silence in the shop was almost deafening.

'I wish you hadn't asked me that, young Estelle,' he said, his voice barely a whisper as he measured out some bacon for her and her grandmother. 'But I know you well enough that you'll not leave until I tell you.' He stopped what he was doing and gave her a questioning look.

'Please, tell me. I'm not a – I'm not a Jerry bag.' She said firmly. 'And I feel like everyone here knows something I don't.' Part of her wished she didn't have to know, because, by the look of regret on his kindly round face, she sensed that whatever he was about to tell her was going to be upsetting.

Sighing, he finished wrapping the bacon and handed it to her. Estelle placed it into her basket and waited for him to find the words.

'It's that Nazi fellow that lives in your house. The one in here earlier.'

She knew that much. 'What about him?'

'Oh, for pity's sake,' Chantal snarled nastily. 'What he's trying to spit out is that your Nazi officer is the one who gave the order for that poor young French boy to be shot.'

French boy? Shot? Estelle took a moment for her brain to process the woman's words. 'What? No, he can't have done.' Estelle looked in disbelief from the woman to Mr Gibault and she could see by the look on the shopkeeper's face that it was the truth.

'She's right, I'm afraid. I've got it on good authority that he's the one who gave the order for the boy to be executed by the firing squad. That poor lad was only twenty-one. All he'd done wrong was try to escape from France and join the Free French in Britain and for that those bastards tied him to a tree and executed him.'

Estelle's mind whirred as she thought of Hans and struggled to reconcile the young man who had decorated her family home for Christmas – with a cold-blooded killer.

'Yes,' snarled Chantal, giving a satisfied knowing nod to those around her. Estelle was relieved to note that the other women were now looking rather more shame-faced than they had done earlier. Sylvie looked as if she, too, wanted to cry.

'You must have heard the shots yesterday?' Chantal asked, an unpleasant grin on her face. 'You live close enough to the manor. Did you give him a nice dinner when he came home, too? Bet he wasn't even put off his food by that young lad's brains blown all over the ground. Barbaric the lot of them.'

Mr Gibault slammed his hands down hard on his wooden counter. 'I said that's enough, Chantal. Now, if you can't hold your tongue, you can get out and shop elsewhere.'

'Well, I was only saying what you were all thinking,' she argued, giving Estelle a sideways stare as if she had been the one to start the drama.

'Are you going to stop this nastiness or are you leaving?' he growled. 'The choice is yours.'

Estelle cleared her throat and straightened her shoulders. She wanted to cry.

Mr Gibault chatted quietly, no doubt, she thought, because he was trying to keep her calm until she was finished with her shopping. She was grateful for the slight distraction but could sense all eyes were still on her as she paid for her goods. She didn't know what was worse the pitying glances or the accusatory ones.

'Thank you, Mr Gibault,' Estelle said, leaving the shop with as much dignity as she could muster. She walked slowly and steadily along the main road until she could turn into her lane. As soon as she was sure that no one could still see her, she ran as fast as she could back to the farm. Once inside, she dropped her basket and purse, leant against the sink and burst into tears.

TWENTY

Estelle

How could she have been so wrong about someone? For the first time, Estelle realised just how much she had grown used to Hans in the house, his presence so calming. And, yes, how much she liked him. She had thought him to be a man of principal, despite his uniform. She had been wrong. Completely and utterly wrong. Hans was not the man she thought she knew, after all. Chantal was right. He was the enemy. She had been so stupid to forget that.

Estelle heard the heavy sound of Hans's jackboots coming down the stairs. Desperate to conceal any evidence of her upset, she hurriedly blew her nose on a hanky and wiped her wet cheeks with the back of her hand. She turned to see him standing in full uniform, his cap under one arm in the kitchen doorway. His face was pale and drawn.

'You know, don't you?' he asked, his voice quiet and emotionless.

She stared at him, unable to speak for a moment. 'How could you? How could you murder a young man – *a boy*?'

Hans flinched as if she'd hit him. 'He was not a boy and not innocent. He was a man who had been found guilty of a crime.'

She rounded on him. 'He was barely more than a boy and all he did was try and escape to fight for his country.'

'His country is at war with mine.' Hans's voice was monotone as if he was repeating a line he'd been practising.

Estelle marched the few steps up to him and, raising her hand, slapped him hard across his left cheek. 'You are a monster, just like all Nazis. I hate you for it and I'll never forgive you for what you've done.'

His bright blue eyes narrowed and the softness she was used to seeing disappeared, replaced by icy glints as he grabbed hold of her wrists.

'I did my job. I do not like it any more than you do. But I made sure that he had a quick and painless death. It was the only thing I could do for the prisoner.' When Estelle groaned, he added. 'Yes, I gave the order to shoot. I admit that. But I ordered my best soldier in the firing squad to shoot him directly in his heart and not miss so he would not suffer.'

She gasped at his honesty.

'I am aware that is no solace to you but we are at war, Estelle.'

'Not suffer? Are you mad? The poor man must have been terrified out of his wits. 'How does it feel to cross a line from which you can never return?' Estelle questioned in frustration. She turned to walk out of the back door, desperate to get away from him.

He followed her, his arm reaching over her shoulder and slamming the door closed as soon as she began to open it. Estelle spun round.

His face was only inches from hers. He was breathing heavily and stared into her eyes for a few seconds. Then he lowered his focus to her mouth and for a split-second Estelle thought he was going to kiss her, but the moment passed and his eyes rose a few inches to look deeply into hers once more.

'Whatever you may think of me,' he said, his voice low and fracturing with emotion, 'this is not something I've ever done before nor wish to repeat.'

She had no idea what to do next.

He looked distraught. 'I had no choice. I have to follow orders.' He waited for her to reply but when she didn't, he added, 'As a fireman, before this war began, I'm trained to save lives not take them. But now, I must follow orders and, in doing so, find a way to live with my actions. When you say you will never forgive me, know with certainty that I will never forgive myself.'

A tiny part of her brain willed her to try to understand what he was saying. This was a new version of Hans. A different man to the one who had helped her and her grandmother on so many occasions. He had stopped her leaving the farmhouse and by doing so had shown her once again that he was in charge here. She had already assaulted him. She knew now how far he would go for his country and she daren't give him the opportunity of turning on her and reporting her for defiance to a Nazi officer.

He took a deep breath and before she could reply, placed his hand on the doorknob. 'If you will move aside now?'

She did as he asked and he immediately opened the door and marched out of the farmhouse. She took the few steps over to the kitchen window and watched him reach his waiting car. His driver got out and opened the door for him and, after giving one last look at the farmhouse, Hans stepped into the car and was driven away.

Estelle stared at the retreating vehicle, wondering if she would ever see him again, or if she even wanted to. Then, as the car turned to leave, she noticed there was another officer in the car. He reminded her only too well of that horrible officer who had stopped her on The Parade the previous year. Before she had time to look away, she saw a hand raise up and wave at her and as the car drove down the drive, a face moved closer to the back window of the car. Estelle gasped to see it *was* the officer from The Parade. He smiled at her. Now he knew where she lived.

TWENTY-ONE

Estelle

She was still in shock after the events of the day when her grandmother returned from visiting her friend Violet half an hour later, explaining that she had decided to learn Jèrriais as a surprise for Estelle, having now thought that it might be useful at some point. 'So, you see,' she said excitedly as she took off her coat and draped it on the back of one of the kitchen chairs, 'I'm not too old to learn something new, after all.' Estelle didn't like to interrupt her chatter and murmured reactions in what she hoped was all the right places. 'Violet said I had to speak it at every opportunity,' Gran added. 'Which is why I've been popping to her place so often.'

Estelle found it difficult to remain still and not pace back and forth. She was unsure how much to tell her grandmother about what had happened between her and Hans before his hasty departure. Not that she was completely sure what *had* actually happened between them. The look he had given her when his face was so close to hers had made her wonder if he was about to kiss her. But that was mad, surely? She had just accused him of murder and he was devastated, that much was certain. How could a man so hurt by her words have to resist from kissing her, it made no sense at all.

She became partly aware of her grandmother taking off her scarf and chatting about Violet's leg trouble, but was too troubled by her own feelings to take in much of what was actually being said. Estelle needed time to clear her head, or at least work out what was going on inside it. She made an excuse to go and check on animal feed in the barn and, when out there, sat on one of the large old milk churns and rubbed her face. Hans was handsome, he was also helpful around the farm and had seemed very decent... till today. That much she knew.

However, it was the other side of Hans she found difficult to separate from the man who lived in her house. Whichever way she tried to look at it, he was a German soldier. Plain and simple. And now she knew for certain that he had killed a man – not in battle, but a young man who had done nothing more than try to escape from his captors. A sob escaped and she began to cry. He had given the order to fire, for pity's sake. Hans. How could she now then be thinking of the way he had looked at her? How could she even give space in her brain to try to work out he had wanted to kiss her? What the hell was wrong with her? She should be thinking of Gerard – her sweetheart – the man she loved and missed, not this Nazi enemy officer. Guilt flooded through her and she began to sob.

Rebel nudged her with his face. 'Hello, boy,' she said,

stroking the top of his warm head, the softness of his fur soothing her. Estelle crouched down and hugged him. 'I'm beginning to think that you're the only one I can share my deepest thoughts with. I know you won't judge me.' She kissed the top of his head. 'You are such a loyal boy.'

She noticed it was getting dark. How long had she been out here, she wondered. Her grandmother would be preparing supper now and it would be selfish of her to let her make some for Hans if he might not be coming back to the farm. It was time to go inside and tell her grandmother what had happened.

Estelle had finished relaying to her grandmother the incident that had occurred at Mr Gibault's.

'I've been hearing things about that Chantal,' Gran said, grimacing. 'Some folk around here suspect her as being the one who sent a letter to the Jerries accusing her next-door neighbour of hiding a pig.'

Estelle gasped at the spite of the woman. 'And had he got one?'

'Yes, poor devil. It's been confiscated and he's locked up in prison, waiting for sentencing right now.'

Estelle took a moment to mull over this shocking news. 'That's not all, though,' she said miserably. She went on to explain about Hans's reaction at the farmhouse, leaving out the bit about how close they got.

Gran's mouth dropped open. 'No, he didn't do it,' she said, sitting down heavily on to one of the kitchen chairs.

'Oh, that's such a terrible shame. And here was me thinking he was one of the good ones. I'd said as much to you, hadn't I?'

Estelle nodded. She had wanted her grandmother to be right about him, too, very much. She didn't know who she felt most let down by, Hans for giving the order to shoot the young prisoner or herself for believing that a Nazi could be capable of decency.

She looked over at her grandmother and saw how worn out she seemed. Estelle supposed it was one of those days when this horrible situation got the better of her.

'You're a good girl, Estelle. Never let anyone tell you otherwise,' she said raising her right hand and resting it against Estelle's cheek. 'I think I'll have an early night tonight. For some reason, I'm feeling exhausted.'

'I'll bring up your knitting, if you're quite ready to sleep, and also a mug of warm milk. You'll probably feel back to your old self tomorrow after getting a good night's rest.'

Her grandmother didn't argue, which troubled Estelle. Usually, she didn't like her granddaughter fussing.

Estelle set to warming the milk then took it up to her grandmother's bedroom, only to find that she was already asleep. Bringing it back down to the kitchen, she sat at the table to drink it herself. She yawned. Gran wasn't the only one who had been exhausted by the day's events. Estelle washed up and wiped the sides to keep busy, keeping an eye on the clock and listening out for sounds of a car engine. She didn't know if she was wanting Hans to return that evening, or if it would be a relief for him to stay away.

Eventually, though, she decided that he wasn't coming back and went to bed.

However, it was impossible to sleep with her mind so full. So much had happened to them all in the past ten months. This time last year, she thought, she and Gerard were looking forward to the summer and going swimming down at Greve de Lecq beach. Rosie would have been humming up in her bedroom, grumbling about homework and making plans for her summer, or troubling Estelle to take her to the pictures. Estelle lay in bed and looked up at her ceiling. She missed hearing Rosie's footsteps from her bedroom above. Thankfully, the house was so old that the floorboards always creaked, especially at night, as the cooler air contracted the wood, so she could still pretend that someone was up there when she missed her sister most.

She must have eventually dropped off because the next thing she knew her grandmother was in her bedroom opening the curtains and blinding her with the sunlight as it streamed across her pillow.

'Ooh, that's bright,' Estelle groaned, shielding her eyes with the back of her right hand. 'Has something happened?'

'No, you've just overslept,' Gran replied, coming to stand by her bed. 'He came back at some point …' she whispered, 'Hans … But he's already left again. Do you think he's avoiding us?'

'Possibly.' Estelle wasn't surprised. 'Although it's probably more likely that he's just busy. If these French guys were caught trying to escape then others will be trying to do the same from Jersey, won't they?'

Her grandmother sighed. 'Let's hope they're more successful than that poor lad.'

Estelle didn't have to face Hans for three days. He managed to arrive home very late and leave before she or her grandmother rose in the mornings. She was relieved. She still didn't know what to say to him and preferred not having to confront him again or make excuses to avoid him.

A part of her knew that she was being unfair. She hated the Nazis for bombing London and the other cities and ports on the mainland but she also knew that the RAF were doing the same thing across Germany, and she thought of those pilots as heroes. Her thoughts were a mess. If nothing else, what had happened was a stark reminder to not get too close to Hans. He wasn't her friend, not really. He never could be. He was an uninvited guest in their home, and on their island, and she would have to put up with him for as long as was necessary.

Now Estelle had recovered from the shock of Chantal's verbal attack, she had no intention of letting her, or anyone else, for that matter, give her a hard time, and she purposefully walked to the parish shop at exactly the same time as she had done on the day of the incident. She slipped her list into her pocket, pulled on her coat and grabbed her basket and purse.

Estelle arrived at the store and joined the back of the queue.

She exchanged a few words with those shoppers she

knew well but could tell by the surreptitious glances and whispers from some of the women that it was common knowledge what had happened the other day. Estelle was almost at the front of the queue when the brass bell rang and the atmosphere in the shop changed noticeably. Estelle turned to see that Chantal had arrived.

Estelle decided to let Chantal and her audience stew for a while. She would have her moment, but she wanted to be served first. Finally, Estelle reached the front of the queue and was welcomed by Mr Gibault. She gave him her list and waited for him to weigh and wrap her groceries.

'We don't have too much at the moment,' he said, 'but I do have a nice mackerel for you and your gran's tea,' he said, keeping his voice low and being careful not to let too many of the others see what he was wrapping for her.

'Thank you, we're very grateful. I don't think I've had mackerel for months, not since they put a stop to the fishing in September.'

She paid for her purchases and turned to leave. As she reached Chantal in the queue, she could see the smirk on her face, obviously thinking that Estelle was going to leave without saying anything and might – thinking her too nervous, perhaps? Even if she was nervous, Estelle was damned if she was going to show it.

'Ah, Chantal,' she said, forcing a smile. 'I didn't see you come in. Any more accusations to fire at me today before I leave? Or have you quite finished?'

Chantal's eyes narrowed, as if she'd love nothing better than to slap her, but Estelle didn't care. It gave her satisfaction to take charge of the situation. 'Well?'

Chantal looked at the others in the room. All of them were staring and not bothering to hide their interest. 'You want to watch yourself.'

Estelle had had enough of this woman's threats. 'I don't think you're in a position to threaten me, or anyone else. Not when you're sending letters to the Kommandant snitching on your neighbours.' She leant in slightly closer, lowering her voice but keeping it loud enough so everyone could hear her. 'The pig was it? How could you do something so despicable?'

Before the woman could reply, Estelle turned away and walked out the shop with her head held high.

TWENTY-TWO

Rosie

11 MAY 1941

W e were beginning to hope that Hitler might have had enough of trying to bomb London, but we were wrong. Last night at eleven o'clock, the bombs began falling all over the city. Oh, Estelle, it was terrifying. I truly thought we were for it. Hundreds and hundreds of bombers were flying over us. It's said they came up the Thames and poor Westminster got the biggest hammering. I don't know, all I do know is that even Aunt Muriel couldn't hide how frightened she was, nor Queenie.

We were in Queenie's basement because I didn't want to go to the Underground again, I hate it down there. But we were only at Queenie's half an hour when I realised I'd been selfish to poor Aunt Muriel and wished I'd done as she asked. The entire building shook and at one point I expected it to crumble on top of us. The bombs were so loud my ears hurt. It's as if the entire world is trembling when those things come down nearby. The ack-ack guns blasted continuously. I do admire those brave men who remain outside doing their best to defend the rest of us.

Aunt Muriel said they probably chose last night as it was a

full moon and 'the damn Luftwaffe would have a clear view of London to be able to aim better'. I'm quoting Aunt Muriel, so you can't tell me off for swearing. The raid lasted seven hours and by the time the all-clear went just before six o'clock this morning, I don't think any of us got a wink of sleep.

The thing is, Estelle, that I don't know how much longer I can take all this. I need one of Daddy's bear hugs and for him to tell me it's all going to be fine. More than anything, I need to know this awful bombing will stop and I'll be back on the farm again with you all.

If we are lucky enough to be together again, I promise to behave and not be so annoying. I wish I had realised how lucky I was before all this happened. Now I don't know if I'll ever see you and Granny again. I love you both and miss you so very, very much.

TWENTY-THREE

Estelle

1 JUNE 1941

O ne of the unexpected bonuses of Hans keeping out of their way was that Estelle and her grandmother had more opportunity to illegally listen to the BBC on the wireless. Not that the news had cheered them at all. They had just listened to the reports of the devastation London had suffered the previous nights before. The Luftwaffe had been out in force.

'They said that it's one of the worst bombing raids over London yet,' Estelle murmured, terrified for her sister and aunt. 'I do hope they're all right.'

'As do I. But there's no point in harping on about it. Muriel is sensible and knows London better than anyone, she's lived there her entire life, after all. She'll look out for Rosie and do her level best to keep them both safe, you mark my words.'

Estelle knew her grandmother was right and that it was pointless worrying about them, but that didn't stop her from doing so. She noticed her grandmother's hands trembling as she read the *Evening Post*. 'What's the latest in the paper tonight, Gran?'

'Nothing good.' She finished reading and then handed it over to Estelle.

Once again, she saw on the front page that another Order had been given, this time it was concerning Jewish residents on the island. '*Any person having at least three grandparents of pure Jewish blood shall be deemed to be a Jew,*' she read out loud, getting more affronted by each sentence. Estelle shook her head. 'It says here, "A grandparent having belonged to the Jewish religious community shall be deemed to be of pure Jewish blood. Any person having two grandparents of pure Jewish blood…", and it goes on and on. Gran, these poor people.' Estelle felt sick at the thought of locals being singled out in such a way. 'This is disgusting.'

Her gran leant over and took the newspaper from her hands. 'It is appalling. I don't think I can even stand to have this in my sight.' She folded the paper, shaking her head, and stuffed it out of sight. 'I've been worried about you.'

Estelle could tell she was trying to change the subject. The article they had just read was clearly affecting her more than she let on but Estelle didn't want to push her grandmother when she was looking so tired. 'You have?'

'Yes. You've been working hard over the past few weeks and I haven't noticed you going out anywhere apart from to the shop,' her grandmother said, clucking disapprovingly. 'It won't do you any good to dwell on things. It's time you popped into town and paid your friend Antoinette a visit. I've knitted her little boy a sweater, although I've done it a little large because I'd rather it too big for him to grow into than too small and impossible for him to wear.' She pointed to the sideboard.

Estelle looked in the direction of her grandmother's finger and saw a blue sweater that looked the perfect size for a small child. 'Thank you, Gran. I know she'll be very grateful for you thinking of her.'

'Yes and I'm sure she'd welcome a few veggies from you, too. Take enough so she can give some to her mother and grandmother.'

Estelle gave her grandmother's idea some thought. Despite her assurances to her grandmother and Mr Gibault that she was fine, the incident in the shop had shaken her and made her feel anxious.

Estelle put together a basket of a few potatoes and tomatoes, and some carrots that she'd been growing secretly in the hedgerows surrounding their land. The authorities were extremely strict about what farmers grew and commandeered the majority of it to feed their soldiers. She suspected Hans might have worked out what she was doing but he never mentioned it.

'I'm off now,' she called from the front door, before going to the barn to collect her bike. It was a warm, sunny day and Estelle set off.

When she reached town and neared The Parade, she heard the distinct sound of jackboots stamping their way in unison before she saw the rows of proud Nazis marching along the wide road. Estelle dismounted from her bike and pushed it along. She wondered what they could be showing off about now. Probably displaying their strength after the horrific bombings in London a few days earlier. How she hated them and their grey uniforms and tin helmets as they goose-stepped over streets that her ancestors had proudly walked along.

She heard a woman shout out but quickly the local bobby took her arm and said something quietly to her as he pulled her away from the crowd. Poor lady, Estelle thought, knowing how much she also wanted to scream in the soldiers' faces and tell them all what she thought of them. For the first time in her life, Estelle felt claustrophobic living on the island, feeling that there was nowhere to go. No way to escape.

She pushed her bike in the opposite direction and looked forward to seeing her friend again. Antoinette knew what it was like to miss someone. The thought of Antoinette missing her husband, Paul, made Estelle feel guilty, though. If she was truly honest with herself, she hadn't wanted to give Gerard much thought recently. Her head had been so full of what had happened with the French men, the cruelty of François Scornet's execution and the thought that Gerard could end up facing something similar was always in the back of her mind.

She neared her friend's home on Hue Street, unable to shake off a sense of being watched, but, each time she stopped and turned round, no one was there– or, if they were, they weren't looking at her. She was being ridiculous, she thought, as she spotted Antoinette standing at the front door to the tiny terraced house she lived in with her mother. Estelle waved at her friend, smiling. It was good to see her again and she wished she had made the effort to come a few weeks before.

'You're here, finally. It's been too long,' Antoinette said, her smiling face belying that she was teasing.

'Yes, I know. Sorry,' Estelle said, kissing her friend on both cheeks. 'Now, where can I put my bike? I don't want it pinched. I've heard that many are going missing.'

Antoinette pushed her front door open. 'I think it'll be safest in the hallway. It's only narrow in there, but we can just about pass by.'

Estelle pushed her bike inside with a little difficulty. The basket kept getting in her way, so she took it off and handed it to Antoinette. 'Here, take this, will you? What's in there is for you, anyway. I've bought a few bits and some extra for your gran, too. There's also a jumper in there for little Louis that Gran knitted for him.'

'That's so thoughtful of her. Please thank her for me. I'm desperate for clothes for him, he grows so quickly and there's so little around to buy.'

Estelle could hear happy garbled chatter going on in the next room and assumed it must be Louis. 'It's getting worse, isn't it? But I heard that Summerland takes in old cast-off clothes and remodels them to make smaller outfits to sell on to people. Have you tried there?'

'They do,' Antoinette replied, smiling, as she led her friend into the room where little Louis was playing in his pen. 'In fact, I've got a job there. Now that Paul is away, I need to bring in some money and Mum was only too happy to look after little Louis for me when I'm at work.'

Antoinette bent to kiss her little boy on the top of his head as he played in the small wooden playpen. He raised his arms wanting to be picked up, but Antoinette picked up a battered looking wooden car from next to his foot and handed it to him instead. It looked homemade and with love, causing Estelle to speculate that it was something his father had carved for him before leaving the island. How many children must there be who had been made fatherless by this war? Would Louis's father ever return? She hoped so. The thought reminded her of her dear Papa and how different life would be to have his comforting presence during these dark days.

Antoinette walked back to the door they'd just come through, before turning to face Estelle. 'Would you like a cup of tea? It is rather weak, I'm afraid, but it's just about drinkable.'

Estelle shook her head. She didn't want to offend nor did she want to take any of her friend's valuable ration of tea. 'A glass of water will be perfect, thank you.'

Antoinette nodded and left the room to go to the kitchen. Seconds later, there was a whoop and she came back into the room holding up a rock cake that Estelle recognised as one of her grandmother's.

'Is this from your Gran?'

Estelle smiled. 'She must have slipped it into the basket when I wasn't looking. She knows how you always loved sampling her rock cakes whenever you came to the farm to see me.'

Antoinette smiled. Estelle was pleased to see her friend's cheerfulness return and made a mental note to thank her grandmother for her thoughtfulness when she returned home.

'This is such a treat,' Antoinette called back from the kitchen, before re-entering the small living room with a tray – which she placed on to the small coffee table in front of them – containing two glasses of water and two plates with the half a rock cake on each. 'I love your gran for doing this,' she said, handing Estelle her plate.

Estelle took a bite, aware that there would be less sugar in it. She didn't mind, though. This rock cake was much smaller than before the war but was a welcome reminder of normal times, pre-Occupation times, when life seemed so carefree. With the increasing rationing they were all experiencing, she knew that Gran's stocks of things like the few raisins she could taste wouldn't last and that the time was coming when treats like these would be a thing of the past.

The two sat, eating in silence until the thunder of marching started up again. It was so forceful that the house seemed to tremble in their wake.

'They like to make themselves known, don't they?' Estelle remarked, relieved that she didn't have to put up with hearing them marching past her front door like this.

'There are so many of them now,' Antoinette said, thoughtfully. 'And I think that although most of them were fairly pleasant when they first arrived, it was because they only thought they were stopping here for a brief summer break before heading across the Channel. Now they know that's not happening any time soon, they seem less impressed to be in Jersey and letting their resentment of us known. Don't you think?'

Estelle agreed. 'They don't seem to be nearly as determined to try and fit in with the locals as they did last year. Either they're tiring of us, or it's dawned on them that none of us want any part of what they're doing.'

Antionette finished her water. 'I wouldn't say none of us. There are some girls who are enjoying having strapping young Adonises prancing around, exercising on the beaches and being charming.'

An image of herself walking through town on Hans's arm suddenly popped into Estelle's head unwanted and she felt a surge of disloyalty towards Gerard for having such a thought. What was wrong with her?

'I don't know if they don't understand the seriousness of what they're doing or if they're just making the most of today without thought to the consequences later on,' Estelle pondered.

'By later on, I presume you mean when this is all over?' Antionette replied.

Estelle nodded.

'We don't know if that will happen next year – which I very much doubt, the way the war seems to be going – when we're sixty, or ever? Who's to say those girls aren't the clever ones?'

Estelle gasped. 'You can't honestly mean that?'

Antoinette sighed heavily. 'No, I don't. I'm grateful I have a husband to love, even if he's been taken away. But I won't judge those girls as harshly as some are doing. I don't think any of us should.' She gave Estelle a pointed stare. 'Do you?'

Estelle became lost in thought: Who was she to judge? She could never be intimate with a German but was that because she had Gerard. She thought of Gerard's sweet face. She had loved him for as long as she could remember and had always assumed they would spend the rest of their lives together, but the Occupation and heavy burden of grief had taken their toll. She wasn't the same girl any more. No matter how hard she tried, she couldn't forget Hans's face so close to hers that dreadful night when he had stormed off. The memory still stirred strange emotions in her that she couldn't quite place. Was it because he was the enemy? He had looked hurt by her criticism of him. Hurt one minute and seemingly wanting to kiss her the next. And if he had kissed her...? Would she have dared kiss him back?

'Estelle?'

She realised Antoinette was waiting for an answer. 'No, I think it's very easy to judge someone without knowing all the facts,' she said, finally, aware how much of a hypocrite she was being. Hadn't she done exactly that?

TWENTY-FOUR

Estelle

AUGUST 1941

E stelle walked into the kitchen one evening in early August. As soon as she opened the door, her grandmother spun round, her mouth open in shock, the plate she was drying slipping from her hands and crashing on to the tiled floor.

Estelle rushed forward. 'Whatever's the matter?'

Her grandmother's breathing was shallow and her whole body was shaking. She looked as if she was about to pass out.

'Come and sit down,' Estelle said, taking her by the shoulders and leading her to a chair, which she pulled back from the table, before pouring her a glass of water. 'Here, drink this.'

Her gran blinked then, as if noticing Estelle for the first time. 'I'm fine, my love.'

She didn't look it, Estelle thought as she crouched down to carefully pick up the pieces of the broken plate. Taking the dustpan and brush she swept up and disposed of the smaller fragments of porcelain. As she washed her hands, it occurred to her that the broken plate was one of the last few plates that her mother and father had been given as a wedding present. Estelle realised that her gran must be in a bad state not to have commented on breaking it because she was the one who had always made a fuss when Estelle or Rosie used any of the four remaining plates, saying how precious they were to their parents.

'Are you going to tell me why you had such a shock when I walked in? I know something's frightened you, I can tell by your reaction, so please don't bother trying to deny it.'

Her gran shook her head and attempted to smile, but failed pitifully.

'Gran, I told you, I'm not going to let you get away with not telling me. Wouldn't you be hurt if I kept something important from you?'

Her gran stared at her and after a few moments nodded. 'Yes, I would.'

'Right. We've only got each other now, here on the island, for as long as this damn war lasts, so we need to be able to confide in one another. Tell me what's upset you. Please.'

Her grandmother seemed to be struggling to explain. 'Take your time. There's no rush. It's just the two of us here.'

Her grandmother clasped her hands together. 'You saw that new order in the paper a couple of months' ago. The one about people having to declare if they are Jewish?'

Estelle nodded.

Her grandmother gave a slight shrug and seemed to

make a concerted effort to straighten up. 'It's upset me, that's all. Haven't you read about those poor people having to wear yellow stars on their coats, losing their businesses and being treated like pariahs these past few years. All over Europe. And not just those who are Jewish, either.'

'Yes, and I agree it's horrific. The Jewish community haven't been made to wear yellow stars on their coats here now, have they?'

'Not yet.'

Her grandmother stared at her momentarily and then rested her right hand on Estelle's left. 'I have a friend who's Jewish, Mrs Green. She lives in Roseville Street in town and she had to register two months ago. I'm concerned for her, that's all. I was deep in thought when you came in and hadn't been expecting you then. Just a silly old lady lost in thought. Nothing more.'

Estelle had never heard her grandmother mention a friend by this name, but she was obviously in too much of a state for her to question the point now. 'You're certain it wasn't anything else?'

'Yes.'

Estelle wasn't sure if she believed her. 'You'd tell me if it was, wouldn't you?'

Her grandmother rested her hands on her slim hips and tilted her head slightly. 'You know I would.'

Comforted by her reassurance, Estelle smiled. 'This is Jersey. If they haven't made those who've registered over here wear the Star of David yet, then maybe they won't? They'll be treated better here, surely.'

Her grandmother sighed heavily, as if the weight of the

world were on her shoulders. 'I don't know, my love. I hope you're right.'

They sat in silence for a few minutes, each lost in their own thoughts.

Her grandmother smiled sadly. 'Never in my years did I imagine we'd end up like this. Thinking too of Rosie and Muriel and how long it's been. The separation is hard to bear.'

'Hopefully, this will be the last time this happens to the Channel Islanders.'

'Yes, let's hope so.' Her grandmother finished her water and studied Estelle's face. 'I've been concerned about something.'

Estelle wasn't sure she would like what her grandmother was about to say. She had that determined look on her face she used when she was about to broach a difficult subject.

'You need to be sensible and find a way to overcome your differences with the captain.'

Estelle was shocked by the change of subject. 'What? How could you say that? Why think of that now?'

'I've noticed how he seems to be avoiding you. When you enter the room, he makes an excuse to leave, saying he's got reports to write, that sort of thing.'

'He does?'

'And he's not the only one. You're barely in the same room as him before you find a reason to go and do something in your room, or out in the yard.' Her grandmother stood. 'Because no matter how pleasant and well-mannered he is to us, Estelle, we have to remember he is a Nazi Officer.' Estelle went to argue, but her grandmother raised her hand to stop her speaking. 'As much as I agree with you and I can't believe these words are even coming out of my mouth, we don't know when we might need him. I think you need to repair your –' she struggled to come up with the word – 'friendship with him. And soon. This is about survival now, my love.'

Estelle stood and, with a laugh, pushed her chair back under to the table. 'I can't see us needing him for anything. And, anyway, as you said, he is a Nazi Officer. If he can shoot a young man on an order, he can turn us in for something. Not that either of us have done anything to warrant him reporting us.'

'Apart from listening to the BBC on the wireless, hiding the tractor in the barn and the secret supplies of food we are hiding for neighbours. But it's all beside the point. Please. Do as I ask, just in case.'

In case of what? But Estelle didn't like to ask. She was more convinced than ever that her grandmother was hiding something from her but, in the end, it wasn't Estelle who instigated a conversation with Hans, but the other way around. And just at a time when Estelle, though she was too proud to admit it, needed him the most.

A few days later and Estelle was irritated that wood had now been rationed on the island and that anyone wanting to cut firewood, even on their own land, needed a permit. The restrictions were getting tighter and she was beginning to feel like they had been at the mercy of the Wehrmacht for far longer than a year.

She turned on the radio that evening as she sat down in the sitting room where her grandmother was knitting.

'Listen, Gran,' she said, leaning closer to the wireless, excited. 'The BBC is appealing for people to put 'V' signs – V for Victory – in as many places as possible. As an act of resistance and to boost morale. Isn't it brilliant?' The thought of taking part, being a part of something that would connect her to a larger campaign of resistance beyond the beaches of the island inspired her. She just wasn't sure where, or how she would do it and get away with it.

'Lovey, I don't want you doing anything silly now,' Gran said, her knitting forgotten for a few seconds. 'We must be especially careful having the captain living here and we both now know for certain that he will carry out his orders, don't we?' Estelle nodded. 'I couldn't bear it if you were arrested and thrown in prison. You don't want to be deported to France, do you?'

She didn't, but she also couldn't sit back and not get involved in this movement.

Over the proceeding days, she heard more and more whispers from friends and neighbours about V signs having been left around the island in various different ways.

She wanted to do the same thing. Here she was, growing food on her farm, which, for the most part, kept the Germans fed, being polite to them, even, obeying their commands, and for what? She wanted to be doing something more like others who were out there facing the enemy and trying to stop them. She felt useless and frustrated. But could she, in some small way, make her own mark? Show the Nazis she wasn't a pushover. That she wouldn't make life easy for them.

It was a damp evening. She had worked hard all day, yet again, on the farm and was completely exhausted. She didn't know how she was going to keep up with all the jobs she needed to do and was relieved that David Bisson and two of his schoolfriends were helping her out. She was in a daze, transfixed by her grandmother's knitting needles clicking away so effortlessly when her eyes focused and she suddenly noticed something strange in the pattern on the pullover she was knitting.

'Are you're trying something new with those different colours?'

Her grandmother didn't answer for a while and then stopped when she reached the end of her next row of stitches. She held up the knitted panel and gave Estelle a secretive grin.

'Can you spot them?'

'What?' Estelle looked at the russets and browns in the stripe across the panel. She wasn't sure what her grandmother meant. Then she saw it. Estelle bit her lower lip and giggled. 'Gran. Those are Vs, aren't they?' she asked, keeping her voice low. You never knew who was listening these days.

Her grandmother's lips slowly drew back into a wide smile. 'You can see them? Are they too obvious?' She frowned slightly and studied the work hanging from her needles. 'It's difficult for me to tell because I already know they're there.'

Estelle shook her head slowly. She was in awe of her grandmother's actions. 'No. In fact, I wasn't sure why you were using two colours that were so alike, but now I know they're there, I can see them.'

Her grandmother began knitting again, the *click click click* of the needles amusing Estelle until she laughed in delight, in awe of her grandmother's quiet act of rebellion. 'I'm very proud of you, Gran.'

Then she asked, 'Who is that pullover for?'

Her grandmother stopped what she was doing and tilted her head to one side. 'It's not a pullover, it's the back of a cardigan. I thought the colours might suit you this autumn?' She smiled at Estelle and the younger woman's mouth dropped open. 'Really? Oh, I'd love to wear it. Thank you.' She would be proud to do so. 'Now what can *I* do? I have to find something that I can do.'

Estelle decided to take a piece of chalk with her whenever she went out. She would need to keep the chalk hidden, in case she was stopped. There were reports in the paper of serious repercussions for locals leaving V signs in all sorts of places and warnings that the Jerries were becoming more determined to track them down and punish those caught with fines and prison sentences.

It wasn't long, though, before Estelle had the opportunity. She was on her way to visit one of her grandmother's friends in Trinity, with a basket of vegetables and some milk, when she realised how quiet the area was. Not a single soul was out and there were no houses nearby except for a fine house that Estelle knew had been taken over by one of the more senior Wehrmacht officers. It was the perfect place. This was the home of an islander – and now invaded and tainted by the enemy. There were granite pillars either side of the large entrance. Glancing around and thankful to see that she was alone on the road, she stepped off her bike, her breath coming in light pants, as if she had been running.

She quickly kicked off her left shoe and took the small piece of white chalk from the place where her little toe had been pressing against it for a week. If she saw someone she would drop a small stone she had kept in her pocket for this purpose. At least then, if she was caught, she could pretend to have stopped to remove the stone from her shoe and no one could argue with that.

Before she could change her mind, she pushed the chalk deep into the granite and scrawled a large 'V' on the right-hand pillar. It must have been ten inches in height and Estelle was terrified but thrilled to have finally done something in retaliation. She stepped back, unsure whether to chance repeating what she had done on the other pillar, when she heard the sound of a car approaching. Trying not to panic, she threw the chalk into a nearby bush and slipped her foot into her shoe, hurriedly mounting her bicycle and pedalling off at a wobble. Estelle pedalled as fast as she could, desperate to get away from the property, just in case anyone caught up with her. Her heart was pounding as her mind raced with the consequences of her actions. What would happen if she was caught?

Estelle rode home, the rush of adrenaline making her

feel heady and more alive than she could recall feeling since the Occupation began – or, if she was honest with herself, since she and Hans had argued. Pedalling along the road, she relished the warmth of the sun on her skin and the cool sea breeze blowing through her hair. For a few minutes, it felt good to be alive.

'You're looking pleased with yourself,' Mr Gibault shouted as she cycled passed and waved to him. His comment took away some of the euphoria she felt. She couldn't let on what she had done. No matter how triumphant she felt.

Arriving home, she ran upstairs, to change out of her summer dress and sandals and into her father's old work overalls with a small sleeveless vest underneath. Tying her hair back with an old ribbon, she then went downstairs, pulled on her boots and went back out into the yard.

Since the Occupation had begun, many islanders had complained that their animals had been stolen and Estelle, not wishing to give anyone the chance to do the same to them decided that now was the time to move their chicken coop down from the area behind the barn closer to the house, where she or her grandmother could keep an eye on it. First though, it needed to be cleaned.

She let the chickens out, smiling as they ruffled their brown feathers and noisily ran to the bank at the side of the yard. Then, taking a bucket to the tap in the yard, Estelle turned it on and waited for the water to fill up. As she watched the bucket fill, she smiled to herself as she thought of the V she had left behind on the pillar. V for victory. This was her own small victory – a clear message to the enemy that her spirit hadn't been – and couldn't be – broken. Just as she reached out to turn the tap off, someone grabbed her right arm and pulled her around.

'What on earth do you think—' she shouted, coming face to face with Hans. It was the first time she had seen him this close up for months. He stared down at her, his mouth tight and eyes narrowed. She didn't know what could have annoyed him and frankly didn't care. All she knew was that his grip was hurting her.

'Let go of my arm.' She shrugged him off. 'What's the matter with you?' She rubbed her muscle lightly, certain there would be a bruise where his fingertips had held so tightly on to her.

He seemed unable to speak for a moment. 'What is the matter with *me*?' he asked, sarcasm dripping from his question. 'You ask me this?'

She wasn't sure if she was supposed to answer, so kept quiet. They were so close to each other. She could see the lines of his face – new ones, that hadn't been there before, and he'd lost weight.

'Look, I don't have time for this,' she snapped. 'If I've done something to offend you, then tell me. Otherwise, please leave me to get on with my work, Captain.' She felt cornered and that was something she wouldn't stand for, not even from a Nazi – not even from Hans.

His eyes widened and his mouth opened, as if he was going to say something further. Then he closed it again and, turning on his heels, marched off to the farmhouse. Estelle stared after him. The Hans she thought she had known would never have acted in such a manner. He rarely showed such emotion, always so polite and controlled... apart from the last time she had spoken to him, her conscience reminded her.

Focusing her mind on the task in hand, she returned to her work and was halfway through cleaning out the first part of the chicken coop when the back door to the farmhouse flew open and Hans marched out again. This time, he was wearing an old pair of trousers and a shirt with the sleeves rolled up. Estelle was still smarting from him grabbing her arm so roughly, so decided to ignore him and see what he did next. She continued scrubbing the floors and walls of the coop while several of the nosier chickens clucked around her.

She heard his footsteps coming up behind her and sensed by the slowing of them that his anger was diminishing, which was a relief. Finally, he stopped next to her. She could hear his breathing but waited for him to speak before acknowledging him.

'Miss Le Maistre,' he said, then, 'Estelle.' When she didn't react, he added. 'I must speak with you. Immediately.'

Now he had her attention. Trying not to show her irritation, Estelle sat back on her heels and, with the back of her hand, wiped away a tendril of hair from her face. 'Yes, what is it?' She looked up at him and, as much as she was still annoyed with him, she didn't like to see him in such a state. What on earth could be the matter?

He glanced back at the kitchen. 'Would you walk with me, so I may speak with you in private?'

Estelle followed his gaze to the house and spotted her

grandmother standing at the kitchen window, surreptitiously watching them as she washed something in the sink.

'Fine.' She stood up and brushed the dust and muck from her legs. 'I'll just need to wash my hands, but we can walk that way.' They went into the barn and Estelle used the tap to wash her hands as well as she could. Then, wiping them on her top she gave him a nod.

She led him up the pathway at the furthest gable end of the barn to the house and then around the back.

'Here is good,' he said, stopping.

She crossed her arms in front of her chest. 'Well, go on, then. Tell me what's bothering you.'

His eyebrows lowered into a frown and once again he seemed angry. 'I saw you,' he said through clenched teeth.

Her stomach dropped – the car engine – but she feigned ignorance. 'Where?'

'It's not so much where, as *what* you were doing that concerns me.'

Not wishing to admit to anything in case she was wrong, she asked, 'Oh, really. And what *was* I doing?'

'You have put me in an impossible position, Estelle.'

'Why?'

He closed his eyes and she could see he was battling his inner conflict. Then opening them, he looked directly into hers, and said. 'I know it was you.'

His hands clenched into fists and she noticed the muscle working in his jaw as he struggled to contain his temper. 'I saw you, cycling away from that sign you left. That V sign.'

'Ah ...'

'That is all you have to say?' He lowered his head close to hers and, in a quieter voice, said, 'Do you not know how much trouble you could be in for carrying out such an act, Estelle? If you're not thinking of yourself then what about the people who lived nearby.'

'But I made sure there were no neighbours and I know no one was watching me because I checked, first.' As soon as the words were out of her mouth, she realised what she had done and closed her eyes. Thank heavens others weren't relying on her to keep secrets, she was too honest by half. And more than a little stupid, she thought, irritated with herself for not keeping her mouth shut.

He shook his head slowly. She wasn't sure why he seemed so disappointed in her admission, especially as he'd already said that he knew what she had done.

'Please, you must not do this again. If I saw you, then my driver could have done. Thankfully, he was looking in his rear mirror at me and speaking as I watched you cycle around the bend in the road. By the time he looked to the front, you were out of sight. Why would you do such a reckless act?'

'Why do you think?' She stood up straighter and stepped closer to him. 'Because I feel completely trapped and helpless in this situation that is none of my doing. I want to – I want to *feel* that I'm doing *something*, however small. Something more than just meekly bowing and scraping to my enemy.' Hans winced as if she'd just slapped his face again. She groaned. 'Look, I know it was a silly, reckless thing to do, but it felt so good at the time.'

'Would it feel good to be arrested, too? I do not think it

would. What you have done is considered sabotage. There will be severe consequences for you if you are caught, and for others if you are not.'

If she was caught? But no one had seen her except him. Was he saying he was going to turn her in? Estelle couldn't bear the thought of others suffering for her actions. All she had thought was that she needed to do something in retaliation. They had murdered her father. Imprisoned her sweetheart. She needed to show she wasn't weak and powerless. She had been foolish, and for what? To be able to hold her head up when others boasted about their own acts of resistance.

'The island is too small for you to be able to escape justice,' Hans continued. 'Your actions left me with the impossible choice of handing you into the local police myself, or sparing you, which would, inevitably, lead to repercussions for other people.'

Not quite understanding, Estelle asked, 'What will you do?'

He raised his hands, palms upward in a hopeless gesture. 'If they do not catch the culprit – *you* –then all neighbours in the area will have their radios confiscated.' He watched her silently for a few seconds while she processed his words. 'You know as well as anyone how difficult that is for people. How all of you here on the island feel disconnected from everywhere else. At least with their radios, they can hear voices from far away and may not feel quite so detached. What would *you* have me do?'

He was right, she realised with horror. She had put him in an impossible position. Accuse her and take her in, knowing that to do so would devastate her grandmother, a woman he respected, not to mention what might happen to her, or turn a blind eye and allow others to suffer and lose their only lifeline to the outside world.

'Estelle? If you are unable to answer my question, I shall put it another way. What would you do if you were me?'

It was impossible. She hung her head miserably. 'There is no right answer,' she said quietly, close to tears for inadvertently causing so much trouble. 'I must do what's right and turn myself in.'

'No, you won't.' He stared at her without speaking for a moment. 'Thankfully, for you, I respect your grandmother too much to put her through the ordeal of losing you.'

'But what about the neighbours?' she asked close to tears.

'The V sign has gone. It was never there and no one is going to be punished.' It had gone? But that would mean Hans had... Estelle was still struggling with her feelings of relief and guilt when he added, 'You must not do anything like this ever again. I am very serious. The mood in the Wehrmacht is not as positive as when we first invaded the islands. Acts of sabotage like yours will not be tolerated. I hope you understand how close you came to being arrested.' His face clouded over with something that she thought could be shame. 'Estelle, I do not know how long I will remain here, or if, like others, I will be sent to the Eastern Front. If I leave, I will not be able to help you should you do anything else.' He shook his head, frustrated. 'I am going against my country by warning you. Covering for you. My loyalty to my people. I hope that if the situation was reversed, you would do the same for me.'

Estelle didn't think she had ever felt so ashamed. She knew him well enough to be aware of how important his loyalties were. Now he was turning his back on everything he felt honour-bound to follow and he was doing it to keep her safe. Whatever she may have thought of him these past months, he was a loyal man. Only this time, his loyalties were towards her.

TWENTY-FIVE

Rosie

SEPTEMBER 1941

W e've just returned from sending you all another telegram. Aunt Muriel and I are very grateful to the Red Cross for setting up the message system and allowing us to be able to contact you. We couldn't say much, as usual, because you can't with only twenty-five words, but it's enough to know that we are able to let you know we're fine and send our love to you. I'll wait anxiously for your reply, but don't expect to receive it for a few months. But at least I'll know one is coming.

You'll never guess what? Even though Aunt Muriel insists that Canadian soldier is just a friend, I caught them kissing a few days ago! It wasn't anything like the kisses in the pictures, I have to say. I can't help thinking it's funny and rather nice that he's called a French name like Pierre and one we might hear in Jersey yet he comes from so far away. It made me feel a little homesick at first, but now it makes me feel a little closer to home. I know that probably seems odd, but it is how I feel.

I love his funny accent and he's very kind and brings us little gifts each time he comes to call or invites us out for tea. She says *that he's here to help defend Britain. I wish the Canadians Daddy and his friends helped rescue were able to stay in Jersey and help defend you all, too. Maybe Daddy wouldn't have died?*

I worry about you and Gran so much now that you are by yourselves at the farm. I hope you're both safe and, although I can't imagine you would ever use Daddy's gun to defend yourself, if you weren't, I feel better knowing you have it. I hope you never have to defend yourself. I wish I could bring Pierre and his soldier friends and Aunt Muriel and sail over to rescue you and Gran. I wish more than anything that we could be together again.

TWENTY-SIX

Estelle

OCTOBER 1941

E stelle finished her ersatz tea, which this time she and Gran had made out of bramble leaves, dried carrots and peapods. They didn't dare waste anything now that supplies coming into the island from France were so unreliable. They made a pact not to moan about their lack of comforts and knew through the news that they were luckier than a lot of people on the mainland to still have their home.

'We can enjoy proper tea again when this is all over,' Gran reassured her at least once a week. Estelle suspected she was trying to reassure herself more than anything.

She noticed how thin her grandmother was becoming. Like everyone else, worry was never far away from her mind. She washed out her cup as she watched Hans being driven away. There had been a bit of a stalemate between the two of them since their confrontation behind the barn. Estelle still felt guilty for his kindness towards her and her grandmother and that his cleaning away the V sign meant that others hadn't suffered. And it was a relief not to have to read anything about repercussions in the *Evening Post*.

She was grateful to him for his consideration, for risking his own safety by removing her act of resistance and not turning her in, but a little embarrassed that her attempt had been such a failure. She dried her cup and hung it up on the hook on the wall. The wind was still howling outside from the previous night's storm. She had been waiting for this moment to be able to go outside and check on any damage to the barn and their fields, as well as to collect in as much wood from debris that she could in case their farm was checked by Germans for any fallen trees. The soldiers needed fuel as much as the islanders and knew to look for it after storms, no doubt suspecting that locals would make the most of unexpected supplies.

She wrapped her scarf around her neck and buttoned her coat as high as it would go before pushing her feet into her boots and going outside. She hoped to find a decent amount of wood to hide in the barn so it could dry out. They needed all they could lay their hands on to heat the house for the coming winter. She believed her father would be proud of her efforts in looking after the farm and her grandmother, especially now that fuel was rationed as well as the fish, milk and potatoes of the previous few months.

Mr Gibault was warning the villagers that he'd heard talk from older farmers who were able to read weather signs through observation to crops, soil or even the birds of this being an exceptionally cold winter, and she had a horrible feeling he was right. As she walked passed the barn and up the slope to the field behind it, Estelle recalled the conversation in the village store earlier that morning when she had gone to buy their rations.

'And how could old Mr Le Blond know what the weather's going to be like weeks from now?' Chantal asked, scowling as she placed her meagre rations in her basket.

Estelle had heard some of the older farmers repeat their sayings in the past and although she would never disrespect any of them by questioning their comments, she was also interested to know more.

'For a start,' Mr Gibault said, handing her back her ration book, 'haven't you noticed the extra pinecones on the trees recently?'

Estelle hadn't but waited patiently in the queue to hear more.

'I can't say I've had much time to notice those sorts of things, Mr Gibault,' Chantal sneered. 'Not with little ones to clean up after. Is that it, or was there more?'

Mr Gibault glanced at Estelle and pulled a face. 'Chantal, all I know is what I was told and as I'm a shopkeeper and not a farmer, I choose to listen to the reason of those who know the land and nature better than I. I think you should take the advice you're given and do your best to prepare for a cold winter.'

'It's always cold during the winter, Mr Gibault.' She pushed her ration book into her bag and rested her hand on her right hip. 'And was there any more to back up this weather forecast, then?'

He waved Estelle forward to the counter. 'Only that there are far more berries on the bushes. Now that's something even I've noticed.'

Estelle wasn't sure if she had noticed anything about an increase in the number of berries but watched Chantal's reaction with hidden amusement.

'And the berries are ones we can eat, are they?' Chantal asked in a sarcasm-filled tone.

'You can, if you wish,' he said with a grin, 'but I think Mr Le Blond was meaning the berries as being extra food for the birds rather than us humans.'

'*Really?*' Chantal said, sarcastically, as she turned and walked towards the door, stopping and addressing him again before leaving: 'Well, as I'm not a bird, I think that information is completely useless. Good day, Mr Gibault.'

The brass bell jangled furiously as Chantal opened the door before walking out and slamming it closed behind her.

'Now,' Mr Gibault said, wiping his hands on a tea towel he had hanging from his belt, 'what can I do for you, young Estelle?'

Fishing had been banned in September the previous year and fish was now rationed, each household only being allowed a pound of fish per week from May. Milk was rationed to half a pint from October and, worst of all, the use of radios had been outlawed and everyone ordered to hand theirs in. Everyone suspected it was to keep islanders from knowing what was going in the outside world and who was winning the war.

Estelle knew that her grandmother was finding it upsetting not to be able to hear the news from the BBC and she felt the isolation from the rest of the world so much harder now that there wasn't even the most tentative connection with it. She had even quietly paid her friend Antoinette money to give to a young boy she knew who was secretly making up crystal sets for the locals.

Today was the day they could collect theirs and Estelle couldn't wait to try it out. Estelle wasn't sure if her grandmother would approve but was happy to take the chance and had already decided to hide it in Rosie's room.

Estelle was lucky to live in such an old house, which had been extended this way and that over the last two centuries, with small outhouses like the washhouse where they did their laundry and the old pig sties that had never been used in her lifetime but where they now stored old bits of machinery and tools.

One of the things her grandmother had insisted they had done when the island had first been occupied was to search every room in the house and their outbuildings, looking for ideal places to hide items. They might need to store away food, or precious jewellery – not that she had much of that – and it had made them feel more secure to know that they had made a few plans, just in case.

Cycling home with the crystal set hidden in the basket of her bicycle, Estelle had to hide her panic every time a soldier passed her by, or even when she saw a car coming in the opposite direction. She still had a feeling that she was being watched some of the time when she left the farm and it wasn't helped by soldiers constantly stopping and searching the locals now, just for the hell of it. She seemed to be stopped more often than not and wasn't sure if it was because she had a guilty look on her face or simply because she was a young woman. The latter, her grandmother said.

She cycled up the lane and, not bothering to put her bike away in the barn, for once, she stepped off it, resting it against the granite façade of the farmhouse. She collected her purse and the crystal set from the basket and quickly went inside, running upstairs without bothering to take off her scarf, coat or outdoor shoes. Estelle ran up to the attic and into Rosie's room, where she pulled back the small bookcase and revealed the secret compartment where she had planned to store it.

'There,' she murmured satisfied with where it was hidden, for the time being at least. She decided she would come up here to listen to the set when Hans was out and her grandmother was in the kitchen, or knitting in the living room. That way, no one would be near enough to hear her footsteps on the squeaky wooden floorboards in the bedroom.

She thought she heard a sound outside. In fact, she was sure of it. She doubted it was her grandmother because she had gone to spend a few hours with Violet Le Marrec, to keep her company. If it was Hans returning, he'd be suspicious to find her up here and still wearing her coat.

She quietly closed the bedroom door, her heart thumping, and ran downstairs to the kitchen. Estelle peered out of the window but didn't see a car so relaxed slightly. Then, something caught her eye. She saw the hint of a shadow moving across a small part of the yard. There *was* someone there, after all, but who?

'My bike!' Why had she not thought to put it away

before now? Estelle wanted more than anything to stay inside and lock the doors, but she had no way of replacing her bike if it was stolen. She had heard many tales of locals losing theirs when the Germans had decided to requisition or simply 'borrow' them, and knew that they could be sold for much more than they had been worth before the war. It was her only mode of transport and if she wanted to keep her bike safe then she needed to be bold, force herself to go outside and lock it away in the barn. Or, she could bring it inside until her grandmother or Hans returned home and then, when she had someone else with her, she could take the bike and store it away properly. Yes, she decided, that's what she would do.

Estelle pushed her feet into her boots and told herself not to be such a baby. She pulled open the back door and stepped outside, slamming straight into a hard body. She shrieked and closed her eyes. It was what she feared – that the officer from The Parade had finally come back for her. She was desperate to run back into the house, but her legs refused to obey her brain and she just stood there, shaking.

Two hands gripped the top of her arms and held her. 'Estelle, it's me.'

She hoped she wasn't conjuring up Hans simply because she was so frightened, but when he said her name a second time, she peeked up at him, relieved to see it *was* actually him.

'Oh, it *is* you,' she said, breathless with relief. 'You gave me such a fright.' Now she knew she was safe, her irritation with him bubbled over. 'Why were you creeping around the farm like that. You almost frightened me half to death.'

He frowned down at her and then pointed to where she'd left her bike.

'Blast. My bike's been stolen,' she shouted, furious with herself for being so careless. 'I'm such an idiot. I knew I shouldn't leave it there, but I—' She remembered at the last moment that the crystal set was a secret from Hans, instantly breaking off her sentence.

He narrowed his eyes. 'Did something happen, Estelle?'

She could feel her cheeks reddening and hoped he couldn't tell in the darkness. For once, she was grateful it was winter and that the light faded earlier. 'I, er, don't remember.'

He didn't look convinced. 'Your bike is safe. It is why I was here, 'creeping around', as you put it. He mimicked her local accent and Estelle laughed.

'Well, that's a huge relief. Thank you.'

'It is my pleasure.' He gave one of his brief nods. 'You should know that it is dangerous to leave your bicycle outside. Someone could borrow it from you without asking and might not return it.'

'I *do* know. Mainly one of your lot. I'll try to remember not to do it again.'

'Good, because I won't be here to put it away next time.'

Estelle's smile disappeared. Had she heard right? 'Why not? You're leaving us?'

He nodded. 'I am going home, Estelle. To see my family. We are usually given leave twice each year but I didn't have any last year because it was too difficult for me to make the journey home and return in time. This year, my mother is unwell and I am being allowed to go for longer.'

Once again, she was reminded that he wasn't so different from her and the islanders. What must it be like to be so far from home when you knew your mother was sick? 'I'm sorry to hear about your mother. Will she be all right?'

'We think so. She has had to endure a long operation and I will be able to help on the farm while I am there. I am lucky they are allowing me to do this.'

'They must value you.'

'I do not know about that, but I am grateful.'

Estelle knew she should be happy for him to be able to visit his family, only someone entirely selfish wouldn't be. So, why, then, was she so upset? 'I'm happy for you,' she said, meaning it. 'How soon do you leave?'

'In two days. But there will be another officer billeted here while I am away. He is... Well, he is awaiting somewhere to become available elsewhere but asked if he could take my place here while I am away. I had no reason to refuse. I will need to bring him here tomorrow, so we will both be here for one night. Is that too difficult?'

'No, that's fine,' she said, relieved to know that Hans would be with them for any first awkward encounters. 'We can put him up in Rosie's room for the night.' She made a mental note to remove her crystal set and anything of great importance that belonged to Rosie into her own room. She was glad that Rosie wouldn't know that a Nazi officer would be sleeping in her bed for the time being. Even Hans being with them was still a little strange. Occasionally, she was able to forget his allegiance to the Wehrmacht and think of him just as a pleasant houseguest, but would it be the same for this officer.

'What is he like, this new officer? Can you tell me anything about him?'

Hans thought for a moment. She could see he was struggling to decide what to say but, in the end, he shrugged. 'He is very different to me. A little older and harsher in his manner, perhaps. Hopefully, I won't be away too long and then he will be moved to another place.'

What an odd thing for Hans to say, she thought. She knew he was excited to be returning home, so must not like the new officer very much. 'He isn't very friendly, then, this man?'

Hans shook his head. 'No, not very.' He stared at her thoughtfully before turning away.

An icy shiver ran the length of Estelle's spine and she suddenly knew without asking exactly who the officer would be.

TWENTY-SEVEN

Rosie

OCTOBER 1941

I can't believe it's almost sixteen months since we last saw each other Estelle, but it feels much, much longer. Last night, I dreamt I was back at the farm. I was lying in the grass in the top meadow and laughing as you and Gerard pretended to waltz in front of me. There was a breeze and I could smell the saltiness in the air. The grass was dotted with daisies and buttercups and you and I were wearing matching daisy crowns that Gerard had made for us both. It was a lovely dream, Estelle. I was woken by a seagull making a dreadful din and when I came round I realised it was someone outside the flat hooting their car horn. It was horrible waking to discover I wasn't with you in the field and it's made me grumpy all day.

I really miss the Jersey autumns. It gets very airless here for some reason and I miss the salt in the air coming off the sea during the high winds that we sometimes get this time of year. Oh, Estelle, there's so much I miss from home. You, Gran, Daddy, of course, but we'll both be missing him but I also miss my friends, Rebel and the other animals. I miss my bedroom and my things. They might not be valuable to anyone else, but my shell collection in the basket on my dressing table and the opaque glass that I've collected over the years from the beach and that driftwood Gran hates me keeping in my room. I just wish this would just hurry up and end and then we can be together again and I can nuzzle the back of Rebel's furry head.

Aunt Muriel is missing Lieutenant Wilson because he's been sent away for some sort of training exercise. I'm longing for some of the chocolate and fruit he brings us. He brought two oranges the other day and a tin of strawberry jam, at least I think it was strawberry. He does spoil us but says it's because we're his British gals. He brings Aunt Muriel lipstick and stockings, which makes her very happy.

I hope he survives the war because he's a really kind man and very funny. I know that Aunt Muriel likes him very much and I tease her that she loves him. She says I'm not to say such things but her face goes red when I do and I can tell she loves him very much. I think she's scared he'll be sent back to Canada, or worse, somewhere in Europe, where the fighting is, and she won't ever see him again. I hope that doesn't happen. Imagine if she married? I could go and stay with them in Canada, once I've been home to see you and Gran first of course.

I asked Aunt Muriel if she would like to go and live there but she said we're not to make plans because there's a lot that can happen during war time, isn't there?

TWENTY-EIGHT

Estelle

OCTOBER 1941

Estelle paced in the kitchen. Hans had told her he would be popping in with Oberleutnant Kurt Fischer to introduce him to her and her grandmother. She prayed silently that her instincts were wrong and that this would be an entirely different officer to the one she dreaded seeing again. The thought of him knowing where she lived had terrified her since that day he had been in the car collecting Hans. She had been waiting for him to turn up again but never imagined it would be to share the same house and bathroom with her. She hoped that she was wrong.

Estelle turned to leave the kitchen to go to the bathroom when she heard the sound of a car engine drawing up outside in the yard. No time now, she thought nervously.

'Gran, they're here. We'd better go outside to greet them.' Get it over with, she thought, miserably.

She heard her grandmother's bedroom door close and then her footsteps coming slowly down the stairs. 'Right, my love, let's go and see what this new officer is like, then.'

She widened her eyes at Estelle and grimaced. 'I hope he's as pleasant to live with as Hans, but I doubt we can be so lucky twice.'

Estelle refrained from answering and opened the back door for her grandmother before following her outside. They arrived in time to see Hans step out of the car. He gave them a brief smile before Estelle turned her attention to the driver as he walked around to the other side and opened the door for the other officer who obviously expected to be waited on. This didn't bode well. She could barely breathe as she waited to see if her worst fears were right.

The person inside stepped out and straightened up. He looked around the yard with his back to them and then turned slowly. His eyes rested on her and Estelle felt as if the air had been sucked out of her lungs. He walked over to them, a grin on his face, and, standing in front of her grandmother, clicked his heels together and gave a curt nod.

'Frau Wood, Fräulein Le Maistre.'

Hans walked up to his side. 'This is Herr Fischer. He is the officer being billeted with you until my return.'

Another nod from the man who had occupied many of Estelle's thoughts since they had first met. She knew instinctively that he had arranged his stay with them. She felt sick but, hearing her grandmother welcoming him, forced herself to put on a dignified act of welcome.

'We meet again, Fräulein Le Maistre.'

He said it in such a friendly way that for a second Estelle wondered if she had been over-sensitive about his attentiveness to her and her efforts to attempt to avoid him.

'You know each other?' Hans gave Estelle a questioning look, which she ignored.

'Estelle will show you up to your room,' her grandmother said, oblivious to any atmosphere. 'We decided to give you my youngest granddaughter's room for now, Herr Fischer.'

The driver removing cases from the trunk of the car brought them over, standing silently behind the two officers.

'Please, do not trouble yourself, Miss Le Maistre,' Hans said. 'I need to fetch something from my room and will show Herr Fischer where he is to sleep.' Without waiting for a reply, Hans turned to the driver and motioned for him to follow them up the stairs.

Estelle and her grandmother stepped back to allow them to pass and watched silently as the three uniformed men walked through their kitchen, into the hall and disappeared up the stairs.

'Your father will be turning in his grave to know those three are inside his beloved farmhouse.'

Estelle agreed. If nothing else, she was relieved her father wasn't around to witness this situation. Now that revolting Oberleutnant was moving in, she was also relieved her little sister wasn't having to share the house with him. There was something about him that made Estelle's skin crawl and she hoped he would find another billet to move into. Preferably sooner, rather than later.

Unable to bear being under the same roof as him, Estelle said, 'I'd better go and check the chickens' water.'

Her grandmother gave her a knowing look. 'How did

you meet the Oberleutnant, Estelle?' she asked. Estelle told her about running into him on the Parade and how she'd tried to avoid him since then but had felt his eyes on her at other occasions in town. Her grandmother stared at her thoughtfully. 'He doesn't look like the sort of man who would take kindly to being rebuffed.'

Was her grandmother giving her a warning? Estelle wondered, reminded of Hans' words. She opened her mouth to reply.

'Hush, hush.' Her grandmother reached up and stroked Estelle's hair. 'I only mean that I think he's someone you need to watch out for, nothing more.'

'I agree and I can reassure you, I'll do my best to keep out of his way.'

'You're a good, sensible girl. I know you'll do your best. Now, run along then,' her grandmother said, interrupting her thoughts.

As she made her way across to the barn, Estelle couldn't shift the horror she felt having the devil moving into their home. 'We should feel safe here,' she mumbled to herself. 'It's our home. Maybe he's not all that bad. It's not as if I've even given the poor man a chance yet.'

'Make sure that you don't.'

Estelle gasped hearing Hans's deep voice behind her. 'I didn't know you were here,' she admitted. 'I apologise. I shouldn't speak badly of the Oberleutnant.'

Hans glanced over his shoulder and then taking her hand, pulled her deeper into the barn, checking once again that they hadn't been followed. 'Estelle,' he said, his voice low, 'you are right not to trust him.' He shook his head and she could see he was battling with his conscience. 'I should not speak ill of one of my own, but I do not wish to lie to you.' He hesitated. 'To me, we are all equal.'

She believed he meant what he said, but couldn't hold back from replying, 'Yes, but some of us are more equal than others. Isn't that the case?'

He frowned. 'It is, I suppose, true.' They stared at each other. 'Please listen to me when I say that you must take care not to upset him.' He seemed to struggle to find the right words. 'Or you have to be careful not to give him the wrong idea.'

She was incensed. 'What? How could you even think that I would do such a thing. I am engaged. Have I ever given you the wrong idea?'

He clamped his hand over her mouth. 'Shush. He must not hear me speaking to you.' He removed his hand and put his finger up to his mouth. 'We must be very careful. I would not usually take it upon myself to interfere, I have no right to do such a thing. However, in this case, I worry for you and I wish to warn you to be careful.' Estelle thought about what he was trying to say and appreciated him taking the time to do so. 'Estelle, I am making a clumsy attempt to do this, but I hope you understand what I am trying to say.'

She did but his words unsettled her even more than before. She nodded, hoping to reassure him. 'Thank you. I believe I know what you mean and will do my best to stay clear of him whenever possible.'

'That is good. I will instruct him and remind him to act as a gentleman at all times. However, you do not have any close neighbours and I will be away for several weeks and will be unable to watch out for you.'

She smiled at his concern. 'I'm sure Gran and I will be fine. You should forget about everyone here and enjoy seeing your family again. You must be looking forward to it.'

He nodded. 'I am. Although I am worried about what I will find. I haven't been back home for nearly two years now and much will have changed.'

'Not too much, I hope.'

'We shall see.' He glanced at the barn door. 'I must go before he misses me and comes looking. It would not do for him to find me in here with you. He would imagine all the wrong things.' He took her hand in his and gave it a gentle squeeze. 'Please be careful.' He let go of her hand and gave her one last smile and left.

Estelle watched his retreating back. He tried his hardest to be good and kind to them and she was grateful that up until now their experience of the enemy close up, in their home at least, had been one of politeness. She closed her eyes to squeeze the tears away and finally let herself admit that she would miss him.

———

The following day Hans's departure seemed to come by only too quickly. It helped when he gave her and her grandmother a smile as he and Herr Fischer got into the vehicle to be driven away.

'At least he's taken that other one with him,' Gran said as the car turned out of the drive and on to the lane.

Estelle sighed. 'Yes, it is a bit of a relief to see the back of him, even if he will be back later.' She hugged her gran. 'I'll go and strip Hans's bed and clean his room.'

Estelle took a duster from the cupboard underneath the sink and went upstairs to his recently vacated bedroom, opening the door slowly. She hadn't been in here since the day he moved in as he had always insisted on stripping his own bed and recalled how she resented him for coming to stay in her father's bedroom. It had upset her to show him up to her father's room on that first day but now she felt his absence acutely and wished Hans was back with them again. What would her father think of how she felt now? She pushed the thought away, not wishing to dwell on it. Estelle stood in the doorway and breathed in. It still smelt of Hans somehow. The smell was a mixture of the pomade he used in his hair, the polish on his boots and the leather holster and belt but also the smell of the books he always seemed to be reading.

The window was open and the bed made although he must have known she would come up and strip it and take his bed linen and towels downstairs to be washed.

A breeze from the open window brushed against her face and Estelle's eyes were drawn to the table underneath the bedroom window which Hans used as a desk and she noticed a tall glass he must have taken from the kitchen for the water he brought up to bed with him. In it was a pink Jersey Lily and underneath she spotted a folded piece of paper.

Was it for her? Estelle stared in amazement at the solitary flower in front of her before reaching down and carefully sliding the folded paper from underneath the glass. She unfolded it slowly, nervous in case anyone caught her.

Estelle, I recently came across a flower like this one and was told it was a Jersey Lily. You are like the Jersey Lily, strong and beautiful. Please accept this as a small token of thanks for all your kindness and especially your friendship. I will be thinking of you while I am away. Please know that I will return.

Until then, take care, Hans

Estelle re-read the note several times. She closed the bedroom door and sat on the bed, staring at the flower. It was such a lovely gesture and although it made her want to cry, it also reassured her that Hans would return. But why did she even want him to return?

She spotted her grandmother going outside to cut a few herbs. She glanced up at the window.

'Do you need any help up there, Estelle?'

She shook her head and smiled. 'No thanks, I'm almost done.' She picked up the glass with the flower inside it and took it to her bedroom, placing it on her windowsill. She could always say she had found the flower if her grandmother spotted it. As for the note, that would need to be hidden or destroyed. Estelle couldn't bear to burn it, though, so she went to the framed photo of her father, Rosie and herself and unclipped the back. Removing the photo, she carefully placed the unfolded note between the picture and the cardboard backing before replacing the back on to the frame once more. There. It was hidden and only she would ever know it was there.

'Can you come down yet?' her grandmother called up to her. 'I need you to help peel some of these spuds when you're done stripping that bed?'

She tiptoed across the landing and back to his room. Stripping the bedclothes off the bed, she folded them roughly, then, grabbing the bath sheet, hand towel and flannel carried them back downstairs to the kitchen.

'You took your time, my girl.' Her grandmother shook her head. 'Put them in the laundry basket in the washhouse, then come back in here and help me.'

'Yes, Gran,' Estelle said, grinning widely as she did as she was asked.

TWENTY-NINE

Estelle

DECEMBER 1941

I t was looking like they were in for a miserable winter, Estelle decided, and not simply because it was already freezing cold and they were struggling to find a decent amount of food despite their rations being increased for Christmas and everyone receiving a small amount of real tea. If she had hoped that Herr Fischer might not be as bad as she dreaded, then she had been very wrong. He seemed to find fault in everything she did. It was as if his interest in her had changed from a leering fascination to one of irritation, or, Estelle wondered, feeling unnerved, was it one of frustration?

She had heard of one or two of the soldiers trying to force their attentions on to local girls, although for the most part they kept their distance and remained quite well-mannered. As some of them left the island for the Eastern Front, other less-professional soldiers seemed to be being brought in to replace them. Or at least that's how it seemed. Maybe they had simply given up trying. Whatever it was, the atmosphere on the island seemed even darker and more frightening than it had been the previous summer. It didn't help that the officer living upstairs in the bedroom above hers was one of the least pleasant men she had ever met.

Estelle felt sure that if she and her gran could cope with the situation they now found themselves living in then they could cope with anything. She had received a letter from Gerard and he seemed well but she knew he would want her not to worry about him so it was difficult to tell how he was exactly. The thought frustrated her. She would rather know more than the vague niceties he gave her, at least then she would get a better sense of what he was facing.

She hadn't heard from Hans, but then she hadn't expected to. It was inappropriate for him to write to her and the last thing she wanted was to draw any unsavoury gossip or even stoke the embers of whatever it was she was already feeling. Life on the island was hard enough.

Estelle was washing some of the tools at the water pump near the shed when the hairs on her arms stood up on end and she realised someone was watching her. She tried to focus on what she was doing and not give in to the temptation to look behind her to check. Unable to stand it a second longer, she snapped her head round but no one was there. For a second, she thought she must have imagined it and then she looked up to Rosie's bedroom window and saw him staring at her, a grotesque smile on his thin face.

An hour later she watched, Oberleutnant Fischer be driven away. He was immaculate, as ever. She presumed he was going out for dinner but unlike she had used to do with Hans, she didn't bother to ask. That night, while Herr

Fischer was out, Estelle took the opportunity of setting up her crystal set in her bedroom. It was the first time in several weeks she had dared to do so and she was itching to hear news from outside the island. She always felt comforted by the broadcaster's clipped British voice saying, 'This is London calling' but then had to pay attention to the news, which was mostly upsetting at the moment.

She listened intently as he reported on the Red Army's counteroffensive in Russia and ended with the announcement that Pearl Harbor in Hawaii had been bombed. She had no idea where that was and felt for the families as well as the men in their thousands who had been killed or badly injured. The war was spreading around the world, destroying everything and everyone in its path. When would it end?

The following morning, Estelle woke and yawned, her breath frozen as she breathed out. She hadn't heard Herr Fischer return the previous night and realised he must still be out. He had probably spent the night in one of the brothels that had been established, she thought, with revulsion. The Germans had brought women over from the Continent to keep their soldiers *occupied*. How much of a choice had it been for the poor women to be brought here to service these men? Though when Antoinette had pointed a couple out in town, Estelle couldn't help but think how impossibly glamorous they looked. She shuddered at thought of what they had to do.

It was a relief to get out of bed and know she wouldn't have to find ways to avoid him that morning. Mornings were the worst when she suspected him on occasion of waiting for her to leave her room to use the bathroom. He would then come out of his room and act surprised to find her there, his amusement obvious at her discomfort in speaking to him while wearing her dressing gown. Sometimes she was even sure she could hear him breathing on the other side of the bathroom door when she was washing before he continued on his way downstairs.

She hated this cold weather, especially now that they had little heat in the house. Estelle grabbed the clothes she intended wearing for the day and pulling on her dressing gown crossed the hall and locked herself in the bathroom. She couldn't be too careful. She had no idea when Herr Fischer would return and the last thing she needed was for him to walk in on her.

She cleaned her teeth as best she could. Then, after running a small amount of cold water, she took off her father's old woollen socks, which she had begun sleeping in to keep her feet warm, and washed before hurriedly drying herself and dressing. She had just returned to her room when she heard Herr Fischer arrive, so stayed where she was and did her best to not make any noise. His footsteps came to a halt outside her door and she held her breath, not daring to move a muscle. Minutes later, she heard him go back down the stairs and out of the door. She stayed to the side of her window so she couldn't be seen from the yard and peered out to make sure he had actually left.

After sharing an egg with her grandmother, she decided now was the best time to pay Mr Gibault a visit. She wanted to see if he had anything at all to sell them that they could possibly eat for their supper that evening. How different it was now to last year when the old man's shelves had been full to the brim. It was bitterly cold, yet again. Estelle wrapped up well buttoning up her coat as high as it would go. Gran had knitted her new mittens and Estelle was relieved they hadn't ever got round to throwing out old clothes before the war. The material and wool were proving to be very useful now that everything was so scarce. Her shoes were worn and the boots she wore when she wasn't working could do with new soles, but there wasn't the money or the material to replace them. She pulled the hat her grandmother had made to go with her mittens knitted for her from an old jumper of Rosie's and picked up her purse and basket.

'I'm off to Mr Gibault's now, Gran,' she shouted, waiting for a reply.

'If he doesn't have what you need and you've got time, why not walk up to Mrs Gould's shop and see if she can help you?'

Estelle assured her she would and then left the house out of the back door, crossed the yard and went up to the chicken coop.

'Have you got a treat for me this morning, Clara?' she asked of their one remaining hen. She bent to stroke the brown feathers hating that they had been forced to give the others away to the Germans for their table. They had been lucky enough to be able to share an egg for breakfast this morning, but Estelle was hoping to find the second one she'd noticed earlier before Herr Fischer returned and saw what she was doing.

There was one egg, so she carefully picked it up and

placed it on to a clean pair of socks she'd put into her basket for that reason. She didn't chance doing anything so daring while Herr Fischer was in the house because she knew he would be watching her, like he usually did.

Not that she was expecting there to be anything much to buy at Mr Gibault's, but the villagers had begun bartering when they had something they didn't need in exchange for something they wanted, or could use. Mr Gibault always did his best to help feed his customers, but it was becoming more difficult. He did though occasionally allow Estelle to swap one or two eggs for something that might take her fancy. She suspected he was giving one of the eggs to his aged mother, who, Estelle couldn't help noticing seemed to be deteriorating more each time she saw her.

She walked quickly to try to keep warm and had just entered the shop when she noticed Herr Fischer's car passing through the village, presumably returning to the farm. He could only have been gone about ten minutes. Why would he need to return to the farm so soon after leaving? Either he had forgotten something, which she doubted – he seemed to be meticulous with his preparations before leaving each day – or maybe, he was hoping to catch her out. Or catch her alone. Had he expected her grandmother to be the one to do the shopping today? She had been doing it for the past few days, so it was likely.

'You all right there, Estelle love?'

She turned away from the window and nodded. She was glad to be alone in the shop with the kindly shopkeeper for once. 'Yes, thank you, Mr Gibault.'

He indicated to her basket. 'You seem to have a pair of

socks in your basket, Estelle. Does that mean you've forgotten to put away some of your laundry, or maybe you have an egg for me today?'

She laughed and placed her basket down on to the wooden counter. 'I have an egg. Only one, I'm afraid. Gran and I shared the other for our breakfast this morning. It was delicious.'

'Hmm,' he said carefully, lifting the precious egg from its sock nest. 'You'll need something just as tasty in return for this. Did you have anything in mind?'

Estelle shrugged. 'Maybe if you have any slices of bacon, or ham?'

He tapped the side of his nose. 'I have bacon. I can let you have a couple of rashers. How does that sound?'

'Perfect. Thank you.' She giggled. 'One of these days, we'll have bacon and eggs to eat at the same time.'

'Won't that be nice.' He took the egg to his storeroom at the back of the shop and brought back two thin slices of bacon. 'I dream of eating a big roast lunch with all the trimmings. You know, thick gravy and as many roast potatoes and Yorkshire puddings as I can cope with, together with perfectly cooked beef.'

Estelle's mouth began watering at the thought. 'I dream of a cream tea, with scones, jam and thick Jersey cream. Oh, and chocolate. I'm desperate for some chocolate, and a vat of tea.'

They laughed together and Estelle relished the moment.

'Right, let me see. I can give you one candle and a pound of fish for your weekly household ration.' She nodded and handed him her ration book. 'There's not too much else here at the moment, I'm afraid,' he said, apologetically, as if it was his fault he couldn't supply his customers with the food he had been able to before the war.

'Please don't apologise. We're luckier than most on the farm. The Jerries take a huge chunk of our food and we've only got one hen left, so she's more precious to us than any jewellery ever has been.' Estelle patted her hat, relieved to wear it and that it covered her greasy hair. 'I'm longing to have some shampoo, or even soap. I think I miss those things most of all,' she admitted.

'You'll have them again one day,' he said, giving her a reassuring smile.

'Do you really think so though?' When her hair wasn't clean and she couldn't find soap anywhere in the shops it made her feel less like a woman. She'd almost forgotten what it felt like to have a long luxurious soak in a bath.

'I do, young Estelle. Just do your best to hang in there.'

She hoped he was right and not just giving her false hope. It had been almost eighteen months now since the soldiers had invaded the island. Nothing seemed to be getting better, only worse and according to the news she picked up from the BBC on her crystal set, things were also getting worse for the allies all over the world. She said as much to the kindly shopkeeper.

'Ah, but I think that's where you're wrong,' he said, tapping the side of his nose with a finger.

Estelle was confused. 'What do you mean? Have I missed any good news then?'

'The latest gossip is that the Americans will now have to enter the war. After the bombing of that harbour in Hawaii.'

He folded his arms across his chest. 'What's more, I have a feeling it will happen.'

Estelle felt a sense of hope, something she could barely recall feeling seeping into her. 'Do you really think so?'

He nodded. 'I do.'

She bit her lower lip thoughtfully. 'Then maybe we might be able to fight back and send these greenfly packing.'

He laughed. 'Greenfly. That's the nicest thing you've called them yet.' He took a piece of paper and wrapped her fish before placing it in her basket. 'I think that the tables might have turned. Or, at the very least, have cause to start turning. We'll have to pray that it's the case.'

The bell jangled and the shop door opened. Two women walked in, chatting to one another.

'Right. Enough chat,' he said. 'Here's your candle. I suggest you keep a couple of tins because it seems that we're going to need them to make lamps in the not too distant future. Cut one in half and try to buy some paraffin from the chemist when you're next in town,' he whispered.

'Thank you,' she said, gratefully, as she paid for what she'd bought. She dropped her change into her purse and placed her ration book in afterwards before closing it. 'You've been ever so kind, Mr Gibault. I appreciate you taking the time.'

'Your dad and I were friends since we were toddlers and it's what he would want me to do. You take care now.'

'I will, Mr Gibault. Thank you.'

THIRTY

Estelle

APRIL 1942

C hristmas came and went and Estelle was relieved when it was over. She had expected the previous Christmas to be bad but thanks to Hans and his thoughtful decorations and sending their telegram for them, it hadn't been nearly as bad as it could have been. This year though they had the Oberleutnant and neither she nor Gran felt inclined to do more than hang up Rosie's star. The only saving grace was that he had left them mid-afternoon to attend celebrations with other German officers. She couldn't help wondering how many more Christmases they would face under occupation.

Christmas had morphed into a freezing January and February, which was followed by a bitterly cold March. One season blurred into the next with food becoming ever scarcer if that was possible. But April had brought something far worse... Her grandmother's friend, Mrs Green, had been deported with a group of other women from the Jewish community earlier in the month and hadn't been heard of since. No one would tell them where the ladies had been taken or how to contact them. Her grandmother's mood took a downward turn.

Hans had been away for months now and she wasn't sure if he would ever be returning. The only news to boost their morale was the knowledge that the Americans had now joined the war.

Mr Gibault had been right when he had said this would happen after the terrible bombing at Pearl Harbour. As always, when there was a massive boost to the local morale, it was down to something dreadful happening against the enemy. But the consequences would be felt by the islanders, as some of the Germans would turn their frustrations on them. Only now, when things were worse, could the locals see it was much easier to live alongside cheerful officers and they might even have said they missed the days of the early months of the Occupation when excited young German soldiers smiled and waved at them as they shopped in town. At least then, the islanders hadn't known that almost two years later they would still be controlled by the Germans or that things could become so much bleaker than they had been.

Everyone on the island now knew that the Germans were working hard to fortify Jersey, building concrete bunkers across the headlands and above the beaches and installing massive guns like canons to defend the island from any attempts to rescue to take them back by the Allies. Estelle discovered for herself how large scale the operation was when she rode on her bike down to St Ouen's Bay and saw that Chateau Plaisir, the holiday camp on the edge of the shore overlooking the wide bay, had been requisitioned and demolished.

Her grandmother hadn't left the farm in months now and Estelle was determined to raise her spirits. Back at the farm, she found her in their small washroom at the back of the house. It was a small brick extension that had probably been something else years ago, but since Estelle's childhood had been where they kept the copper to heat the water and wash their laundry.

'Gran,' she said running over to take the heavy sodden bed sheet from her grandmother's hands. 'That's far too heavy for you.'

Her grandmother glared at her and snatched the sheet from her grasp. 'I'll thank you not to presume I'm in my dotage yet, young lady.'

'Maybe not, but that water must be freezing and your hands are bright red.'

'I'm almost done, then I can hang this outside on the line.' She gave Estelle a half-smile. 'You can hang it up for me, if you like, you're taller than I am.'

Estelle stood and watched as her grandmother tried her best to clean the once-white sheet. It was strange to think how the only time she had thought of soap flakes before the war was when she had to carry them back from the shops and the box was heavy. Would they ever have the luxury of being able to wash their sheets in soap flakes or detergent again?

Her grandmother looked up at her questioningly. 'Is

there a reason you're hovering over me while I see to the laundry?'

Estelle feigned innocence and grinned. 'Sort of. I thought it would be a nice idea if we went for a bit of a walk together.'

'Where?' She handed Estelle one end of the sheet and began twisting her end in the opposite direction to remove as much of the excess water as possible.

'Anywhere. The village would be a good start.'

Her grandmother stopped what she was doing and stared at her. 'Why?'

Estelle didn't bother to fib as Gran always saw through her whenever she tried to hide something. 'You haven't been out for a while and I thought it'd do you good.'

'I've been out into the garden. But I've not been further because it's so cold and miserable.'

Estelle didn't believe her. 'That's never stopped you before. Admit it, you haven't ventured out anywhere for far too long and I don't think it's good for you. For anyone. Come with me to the village and maybe we can have a walk along the lanes. I know there's nothing much to see by the way of flowers, but it's a sunny enough day and I'm sure we'll both feel better for doing it.'

Her grandmother watched her for a few moments. Estelle didn't like to point out that the sheet was dripping on to the floor and on to her grandmother's boots. 'Fine. You hang this up then and I'll go and fetch my coat.'

Estelle nodded, happy with her grandmother's reaction.

Half an hour later, they set off out of the back door. The weather had brightened up a little, which was a relief, at least. Estelle didn't mind the cold, especially when it wasn't windy or raining.

'I'm glad you've come out with me,' Estelle said as they turned left out of the driveway and on to the lane.

'I am too now that we've got going,' her grandmother said, smiling as she linked arms with Estelle. 'I sometimes feel a little claustrophobic at home, or even out of the house knowing that we have to watch everything we do and say now.'

Estelle heard a car and turned to see Herr Fischer's driver pull into the yard. He slowed down briefly before continuing to the farmhouse. 'That was close. A couple of minutes later and we'd have to pass our house guest before leaving.'

'Horrible man,' her grandmother murmured almost under her breath.

Estelle knew her grandmother liked to keep her feelings mostly under wraps. When she had asked her about it a few years before, she said that she believed everyone was entitled to their own opinion and that she didn't like to foist hers on anyone else. Estelle was sure that her reason for doing it now was so that she could give Estelle a chance to speak up about the Oberleutnant, especially knowing how Estelle found it increasingly difficult to live with Herr Fischer.

'At least with Hans, I never felt he was constantly watching me. And waiting for us to make a wrong move.' Estelle replied.

She spotted three ducks flying past and pointed to them, smiling. 'Look Gran. Aren't they lovely?'

Her grandmother put her right hand up to shield her eyes against the watery sunshine and grinned. 'How wonderful it must be to have wings and the freedom to go where you want whenever you choose.'

Estelle wished she could be like those ducks, spread her wings and fly off to visit Rosie right now, or Gerard. Or better still, bring them back to her. But, then again, would she want to put those she loved through this ordeal? Living with the enemy. Powerless to fight back.

She felt her grandmother's arm stiffen. 'What's the matter?'

'Can you hear footsteps?' her grandmother whispered, her voice shaky and her eyes scanning the surrounding land.

Estelle listened and could hear them quite clearly by the sound their heavy boots made as each step made contact with the road. She turned her head nervously, horrified to see Herr Fischer walking quickly up the lane behind them. 'It's Herr Fischer,' she murmured, keeping her voice low. 'He's trying to catch up with us.'

Without saying anything further, they stopped and turned to face him. 'Herr Fischer,' Gran said, sounding more polite than Estelle knew she felt. 'Are you wanting to speak to us about something?'

He looked rather red in the face while they waited for him to reach them. 'Ladies,' he said, bowing his head slightly. 'You are out for a stroll, it seems?'

The women exchanged glances before nodding. 'Yes,' Gran said. 'We thought we'd make the most of the better weather. You?'

'Me?' He looked a little dumbfounded. 'I wish to join you. You do not mind, I hope?'

Neither dared look at the other. Estelle knew without seeing her grandmother's expression that she would be trying to appear relaxed about the prospect of his company.

'We don't mind, do we, Estelle?'

'No, of course not,' Estelle lied. 'Good afternoon, Herr Fischer.'

'Gut afternoon.' He went to walk on. 'Shall we?'

They did as he asked and Estelle wished now that they had left early enough not to have been spotted by him.

'I do not know Jersey as well as I would like,' he said, hands clasped behind his back as he walked. Estelle wondered if he was this stiff in stature when he was with his family in Germany.

'Have you been for many walks on the island, Herr Fischer?' Gran asked.

'No, but I believe I should take more when I have the time. It is a small island, but beautiful.' They walked on for a few strides when he asked, 'You have always lived here, Frau Woods?'

'Yes,' Estelle heard her grandmother say. She tried to hide her shock. It was a lie. Why would her grandmother give him false information?

There was an awkward silence until he then asked, 'You were born here, too, Fräulein Le Maistre?'

'Yes, I was.' She couldn't understand why he was asking such questions. Then again, she wasn't sure why she should be surprised by him acting in such a way, she decided. He

always seemed to be nosing around and trying to find
information about them.

A military car drove along the lane and the three of them
went in single file. It slowed and the driver wound down
the window. He spoke rapidly at Herr Fischer in German,
before giving a knowing snigger and driving off. Estelle
managed to catch her grandmother's eye. She seemed to be
sending her a warning to be careful, but it wasn't necessary.
Estelle was more than aware that she needed to be alert
around this man.

As they walked on, he manoeuvred himself between
them. After a few more minutes, as he casually pointed out
birds, asking the English names of them, he slipped his arm
seamlessly around Estelle's waist. She stiffened and he
smiled down at her, unconcerned and without missing a
step. His grip on her tightened so she couldn't pull away or
stop walking.

'I will be leaving you in the next few weeks and I
thought that maybe you would accompany me to a dance
one evening, Fräulein Le Maistre.'

The blood drained from her face. 'Thank you, Herr
Fischer,' she said, desperately trying to find a way out of his
invitation without appearing rude or insulting him. 'I, er,
well, that is, I don't socialise. I never have liked to venture
out in the evenings, to be honest.'

'Then you must make an exception for me.'

Her stomach clenched in fear, as his hand rested heavily
on her side just above her hip. 'I would in normal
circumstances,' she said, remembering too clearly the
advice Hans had given her – she had to be careful of

rebuffing his advances. 'But I am engaged,' she lied. 'I don't think it appropriate that I accept another man's offer of an evening out.'

'She's right,' her grandmother said. Estelle looked across at her and could see she was forcing her mouth into a smile that didn't reach her eyes. 'It wouldn't really be appropriate.'

'I am not asking *you*, though, am I, Frau Woods?' he snapped. He stopped walking. 'I am asking Fräulein Le Maistre. If she is old enough to be engaged, then surely she is old enough to answer for herself? No?'

Estelle could see he was furious with her attempted refusal. Her head pounded with the pressure of finding a way out of this difficult scenario that seemed to be escalating only too quickly. She desperately didn't want it to get out of hand. Whatever they said next could determine the rest of the time he lived at the farmhouse. He had the power to make their lives hard, if not, in fact, impossible.

'I would accept your kind offer,' Estelle said, keeping her voice as light as she could manage. 'But I didn't think your authorities liked soldiers to fraternise with the local women?'

He blinked rapidly as he considered her words. Estelle heard the sound of a car engine approaching and the next thing she knew it slowed to a stop next to them.

'Oberleutnant Fischer,' said a voice that sounded very like one she had longed to hear for the last few months now. 'May I offer you a lift.'

Herr Fischer's hand dropped from her side. His eyes

lingered on Estelle for a moment longer and she could sense his annoyance at being interrupted.

The voice from behind her spoke again. 'Herr Fischer. Now.'

Estelle's heart pounded with relief. She hadn't imagined she had heard Hans's voice – it *was* him. She turned to look at him.

'It's good to see you again, Captain.'

THIRTY-ONE

Estelle

JUNE 1942

H ans had been back at the farm for two months but despite their excitement that his return would mean the departure of Herr Fischer, it seemed that the other officer would be staying with them for a few months longer. Estelle noticed that even Hans was less relaxed around the Oberleutnant and she longed for the vile man to finally leave the farm and move on. At least now, both she and her grandmother felt safer with Hans back at the farm. His seniority to Herr Fischer helped keep the dreadful man in his place, but he still tended to appear when Estelle least expected him to, and questioned her grandmother relentlessly.

It was a warm, humid day and by the time Estelle reached town, to visit Antoinette, she was feeling sticky and uncomfortable. The two friends decided to take a stroll.

'It's far too hot to stay in this house,' Antoinette grumbled settling Louis in his pushchair.

Estelle asked for a glass of water to quench her thirst

before leaving. 'I've bought us some apples. We can take those and eat them sitting down in the shade somewhere, if you like?'

There seemed to be more soldiers on the streets than the last time she had visited St Helier, but maybe, Estelle thought, she was imagining things. Antoinette slowed her walking and Estelle did the same, unsure why.

She looked at her friend, concerned. 'Is something the matter?'

'I'm not sure.' She indicated the thickening of the pedestrians further up the road. 'I think something might be happening and I'm worried about taking Louis there, if it could be dangerous.'

Estelle understood. There was a definite atmosphere that was impossible to miss. 'Don't worry. I'll go ahead to have a look while you wait here for me.'

She walked on, her hearing alert to anything she should be aware of. As she drew closer, she heard the shout of a German order and a dog snarling. Estelle hesitated. No one was speaking. Usually, when something was happening, whispers would pass through the crowd and she would be able to pick up some information, but not this time. Everyone appeared to be transfixed by some horror she had yet to witness.

Estelle walked on nervously. Something was very wrong, but she couldn't fathom out what it might be. She reached the back of a row of locals and manoeuvred her way forward so that there were only a couple of people standing in front of her. She didn't want to be conspicuous, just in case something happened.

Another order was barked out in German and Estelle looked to her left. Her breath caught in her throat when she saw what was causing such horrified attention from the other locals. Coming down the street were men and women and others that seemed no more than children. Most appeared to be wearing nothing more than sacking, their dirt-ingrained feet shoeless. Some were barely able to walk, hobbling on the tarmac and all of them were near starvation. This was like nothing she – or anyone on the island – had ever seen before. Estelle could barely comprehend what was going on.

For the first time, she spotted a soldier, then a second one, both holding tightly to dogs on thick leads. The dogs' teeth were bared, pulling at their leads to reach the poor people making their way along the road. A whip cracked. Estelle gasped. What was this? Where had these people come from? She didn't recognise any of them as locals. Had they been brought over from the Continent? But why?

The islanders stared in horror. Then, suddenly, as if someone had given a silent signal, a few women broke away from the watching crowds and ran forwards. Each held out a piece of bread or whatever food they could retrieve from their shopping bags to the starving people in front of them. Estelle pushed forward too holding her bag with one hand and pulling out the three apples she had been saving with the other. She managed to hand two apples to two prisoners and then went to pass the third apple to a young girl. Their eyes locked and Estelle's heart broke to see such haunted sadness mixed with gratitude. She wished she could whisk the girl away somewhere safe.

She gasped when the girl dropped the apple and both bent to retrieve it. Estelle's hand had almost reached it when a whip snapped down on to the girl's back causing her to cry out in pain. The next thing Estelle knew, a large hand slammed into her chest and pushed her roughly with such force that she tripped backwards. She braced herself for the inevitable pain when she hit the ground, but someone grabbed hold of her at the last moment and helped her to her feet.

She was too stunned to mutter more than a brief thank-you but watched the wretched souls wending their way painfully down the street.

'You won't be able to help them,' the man who had caught her said. 'Not unless you want to be punished for doing so.'

Estelle watched the last of them limping away. 'Who are they?' she asked to anyone who would listen.

It was a few moments before a women replied. She was wiping her eyes with her sleeve. 'Prisoners, someone said. To build the fortifications.'

Strangers in the shocked crowd were comforting each other and parents holding more tightly on to children.

'But they look so badly cared for,' Estelle replied horrified that those she had just seen were mostly barefoot, some only wearing sacks instead of clothes. 'How will they ever have the strength to do anything at all, let alone be used for such hard labour?'

Estelle returned to where Antoinette was waiting.

'You're crying,' her friend said, resting her right hand on Estelle's left arm and stroking it lightly. 'What happened up there? I heard shouting but didn't dare move any closer to look.'

Estelle explained what she had witnessed. 'I thought we were luckier here than in France or the rest of Europe not to have the nastier Jerries, but these men were brutes. They're not at all like the first ones who came over, they're much, much worse. I saw one whip a young girl and her only crime had been to try and take an apple from me.' A sob rose in her throat and before Estelle was able to suppress it, she cried out. 'I'm so sorry. I can't seem to help myself.'

Antoinette pulled her into a hug. 'Let's go back to my house. I don't really feel like taking a stroll now, anyway, do you?'

Estelle shook her head, unable to speak.

That afternoon, back at the farm, she recounted what she had seen to her grandmother, stopping several times to catch her breath or wipe the tears from her eyes. 'It was the worst thing I've ever seen, Gran. The state of those poor people and the way they were being forced to walk with dogs and whips, it was barbaric. They were starving and in so much pain.' Estelle closed her eyes unable to push away the vision of the grey faces of despair that she had watched earlier.

Her grandmother hadn't spoken since her arrival back at the farm. 'We need to find a way to help them, but how are we supposed to do that?' she said now.

Estelle shook her head in despair. 'I've no idea. I was

trying to think how while I cycled home.' She stared at her father's old coat hanging from the hook on the back of the kitchen door and then to his boots, the dried earth still stuck to them. 'What would Dad have done, do you think?'

Gran shrugged. 'I don't know, but I do know he wouldn't have stood for it.' She patted Estelle's shoulder. 'We will find a way to help them, lovie. But I imagine the punishment will be severe if we're caught. We need to be careful and clever. We won't help anyone if we get ourselves into trouble.'

That night, Estelle made an excuse not to join her grandmother, Hans and Herr Fischer for their meagre dinner. The thought of being able to chew and swallow in front of men who represented the sort of behaviour she had seen in town that day was not something she would be capable of doing. She took a bowl of vegetable soup that her grandmother had made her and a cup of their ersatz tea to her bedroom. Estelle had just reached the top of the stairs when Herr Fischer walked out of his room and stopped in front of her, so she had to step past him to get to her bedroom door.

'You were in town earlier,' he said, pointedly, as she went to close her bedroom door. Estelle stiffened to think that yet again he had been watching her without her knowing. 'You must not try to assist those prisoners, Miss Le Maistre. There will be serious repercussions if you do.'

Unable to help herself, Estelle snapped back, 'You mean

the poor souls who were paraded through town and treated with such brutality?'

He studied her for a moment before giving a slight shrug. 'They are Russian slaves. They are nothing and you must not involve yourself in them being here.'

'But someone said they were prisoners from the Spanish Civil War. Political dissidents. I don't understand.'

'It is not for you to understand.' When she stared him down, he added, 'They are brought here from Spain, Holland and other European countries to work for Organisation Todt. They are nothing.'

She had no idea who the organisation was that he mentioned and was disgusted to hear him describe people as 'nothing'. He reached out suddenly and stroked her cheek with his right hand. Estelle recoiled in disgust before spinning round and slamming her bedroom door in his face.

The following morning, Estelle was sweeping the yard when she heard footsteps coming up behind her and turned to see Hans walking up to join her. He was frowning. 'You retired early last night. Are you well?'

She nodded. 'Quite well, thank you. I was a little tired last night, that's all.'

He stared at her until Estelle stopped what she was doing and stood up facing him. 'What?'

'There is more, I can tell.'

She looked around her and stepped to the side to see

past him. The last thing she needed was Herr Fischer creeping up on them and listening in to what she had to say.

'Estelle, please tell me,' he said, his voice encouraging and gentle. 'I will keep whatever you tell me between us, but I know something has happened to distress you and I wish to help you, if I am able to do so.'

Estelle picked a piece of straw from her pullover and twisted it around her forefinger as she thought back to what she had seen the day before and relayed her experience to Hans. He listened without speaking, waiting for her to finish patiently.

'It was horrific,' she said, her voice cracking with emotion at the memory. 'I don't understand how the soldiers on the street could simply stand there without stepping in. They just let those bullies whip and hit those poor people.'

'It sounds terrible. But the soldiers probably did not step in because the men with the dogs and whips were not from the Wehrmacht.'

Estelle didn't understand. 'But they had uniforms on.'

'Not really. Not like ours,' he countered.

'Then who are they and why are they here? I don't understand.' It didn't make any sense. Surely, the Wehrmacht were in charge of everyone on the island, so why would they put those guards in their place?

'Those guards are from the Organisation Todt.'

'Herr Fischer mentioned that name last night. What is it?'

Hans frowned. 'When did he speak to you last night?'

'When I went up to bed.' She shook her head. 'What is Organisation Todt?'

'The OT. I've heard it said that most of them are men who were refused by the Wehrmacht. They, and the prisoners you saw with them today have been brought to here to build fortifications across the islands.'

'You mean like down in St Ouen's bay, where the holiday camp used to be, near the Martello tower?'

He nodded. 'Yes and at other strategic points around the island. The Channel Islands are the closest place in Europe to England and they need to be defended should your military decide to come and take you back.'

'They won't do that,' Estelle said bitterly. 'They abandoned us.' Then again, she thought, even if they did decide to step in and defend them again, it would probably only end in bloodshed of unarmed locals, so maybe they were better off on their own.

'I am not supposed to say anything, but I trust you to keep this between yourself and Frau Woods. Anyway, you will soon see enough to work it out for yourselves.'

The thought of their beautiful island becoming a fortress for the Nazis was devastating. To think now that the very landscape she and the islanders had grown up on was being altered.

'We are not encouraged to stand in their way,' Hans continued. 'For any reason. I am sure you can imagine how difficult that is for many of us. Their brutality shocks most of us the way it does you, Estelle.'

'I believe you. But how these poor souls are treated is... it's inhumane!'

She might believe him, but she wasn't so certain that some of his brothers in arms would be as upset as Hans to see what she had done the previous day. Especially, Herr Fischer.

'Estelle, I–'

'Hauptmann Bauer?' When Hans didn't reply Herr Fischer shouted once more. 'Hauptmann Bauer? *Wo bist du?*'

Hans stared straight ahead and Estelle could see the muscle working in his jaw. 'I must go. Please, Estelle, promise me that you will not do anything. The punishment for anyone helping those prisoners is most severe.'

Estelle shook her head. 'I won't,' she said, trying to reassure him as best she could. She wondered if he knew that given half a chance she would break that promise in a heartbeat. How could she stand by and watch such suffering without doing anything?

THIRTY-TWO

Rosie

JULY 1942

I'm so excited, Essie. I've been pestering Aunt Muriel to let me cut my hair. After all, I'm now fourteen. Today, it finally happened. It's a lot curlier than I had expected, but it's just below my shoulders and she's shown me how best to arrange it. It's going to take me a little time to get it right I think, but I'm looking forward to trying. She had also been saving her coupons to buy me a summer dress because I've grown rather a lot and my other two were way too tight. It's not completely new but I'm finally feeling less like a little girl and more like a grown-up and I love it.

There's a boy I like. I haven't told Aunt Muriel because he's a Private in Pierre's unit. I've seen him around a few times when we've been out with Pierre and I think he might like me too because he blushed the other day when I spoke to him. I know Aunt Muriel won't let me out of her sight and can't see that I'll ever have any time alone with him, but it's the first time I've liked someone and I enjoy the fuzzy feeling in my tummy when I think of him. Maybe when you read this I will know more about him *and might even have had my first kiss. (I hope Aunt Muriel never reads this book because, if she does, I'll be for the high-jump).*

I'm not allowed out by myself when it's dark because of the blackout. Aunt Muriel worries about me being hit by a car but I've tried to tell her that I'd be careful. So, most evenings, we sit and listen to the BBC in case there's any official announcements, and we also enjoy listening to ITMA, *it's very funny and stands for* It's That Man Again *and the comedian is someone called Tommy Handley, but there are other people in the show, too. Almost everyone we know listens to it.*

I'm tired of rationing and queuing for things at shops but Aunt Muriel said that everyone has to do it, so why shouldn't we? I wonder if you and Gran have to queue at Mr Gibault's shop? I shouldn't really grumble. At least the bombs have stopped and it's not nearly as bad here now as it was during the Blitz.

THIRTY-THREE

Estelle

SEPTEMBER 1942

E stelle cycled into the yard and held tightly on to the handlebars careful not to let the bike fall. It had been a cool and rather duller summer than usual and it was the first time in a while that she had felt this warm. She had been fetching sea water from supplies kept in tanks for the islanders to collect.

'I'm back, Gran,' she sang, carrying the container into the kitchen.

Her grandmother looked up from where she sat scrubbing potatoes over a small bowl of muddy looking water. 'As soon as you've taken off your hat and coat, can you pour some into a pan and we'll boil it. I'm desperate for some salt to make our meals a little tastier.'

Estelle nodded and did as her grandmother requested. She could barely recall the taste of a roast lunch with all the trimmings. Her mouth watered at the thought and she promised herself that the first thing she would do after all this was over was to find something tasty to eat.

'What's on the menu tonight?' she asked, grinning at her grandmother playfully. 'Shall we have apple pie for pudding?'

'Very funny,' her grandmother said without smiling.

She sensed that something wasn't right with her grandmother. 'Has something happened while I was out?'

Her gran didn't look up. 'Like what?' she asked, picking up another potato.

'I'm not sure, but you're frowning, and I can tell you're concerned about something.'

Her grandmother gave a deep sigh and stopped what she was doing resting her hands on the table. 'You know they've been deporting British-born people off the island to Germany.'

Estelle nodded. She'd been too frightened to mention anything to Gran in case she might be one of those sent away. 'They haven't... that is... you haven't been summoned, have you?'

She shook her head. 'No. I lied on my Identity Card,' she said, whispering, although Estelle was sure they were alone in the house. 'I've been waiting anxiously in case someone turned me in or tipped them off about me being born in England and not actually being local but, so far, no one has.'

Estelle, needing to give her a cuddle, went over to stand behind her grandmother and wrapped her arms around her shoulders. 'Oh, I'm so relieved. I don't know how I'd cope if you were sent away.'

Gran murmured something Estelle missed. 'Sorry, what did you say?'

'There are those, a couple from Antoinette's street, who

have— have killed themselves rather than be taken away.'

Estelle's stomach clenched in fear. The thought of being so frightened that you could do something that drastic devastated her. She walked around her gran to the table and pulled out a seat and sat down. Estelle took her gran's closest hand to hers in her own, removed the sharp knife from her damp fingers and placed it on the table. Looking her in the eyes, she asked, 'I know we both hope that your true birthplace won't be discovered, but promise me that if they do come for you that you won't do that?'

Her grandmother didn't react for a while but stared down at the bowl of brown water. Then, looking Estelle direct in her eyes, she shook her head. 'I would never do that to you, or Rosie,' she said with such determination that Estelle believed her.

'I can't imagine life without you.'

Her gran sighed. 'Well, you will have to one day, but I can reassure you that it won't be at my own hand – and not by the Jerries, if I can help it.' She pulled her hand from Estelle's and picked up the knife, seeming a little more like her old self. 'Now, I need to get on with preparing our supper, otherwise we're going to go hungry tonight. Well, hungrier. I managed to buy some limpets from Violet's friend and you know they take two hours to boil before I can make them into a pie with a bit of swede.'

Estelle couldn't stand limpet pie. The limpets tasted similar to mussels but parts of them were very chewy and made her feel rather sick, but she knew her grandmother was trying her best to keep them fed so kept her thoughts to herself.

She was outside sweeping the yard, grateful for the rain to help clean the cobbles when a German car pulled up. She gave a cursory nod as Hans and Herr Fischer stepped out of the vehicle, but was surprised when the driver didn't leave. She couldn't help wondering what he was waiting for, but supposed the two officers must be changing to go out to dinner somewhere.

She pretended to keep busy, waiting for them both to leave, but was left surprised to see only Herr Fischer coming out of the house. He handed his bag to the driver and then Estelle groaned inwardly to see he was coming over to speak to her.

'Fräulein,' he said, his guttural tones irritating her as the sound of his voice always did.

'Herr Fischer, you are going somewhere?' she asked, hopefully.

'I am to move out from your farm today.'

'Oh, I see.' She did her best to keep any delight from her face. 'You've found somewhere else to live, then?'

He gave a nod. 'I am sorry to leave here. However, I am needed to the north of the island and have been billeted in a house several miles away.'

He stared at her and Estelle wondered if he was waiting for her to say something. Well, she had no intention of telling him that it had been fun having him at the farm, or that she would miss him.

He stared at her. 'Fräulein, I...' He reached out and took

her by her free hand. 'I know that you only pretend not to like me.'

Estelle's skin seemed to crawl underneath his touch and she tried to pull her hand away. 'Herr Fischer, I don't wish to insult you...'

'Silence.'

Seconds later, he pulled her forwards roughly and into his arms, pressing his mouth against hers. Estelle gave a muffled cry, but his arms pinned hers to her sides tightly so she couldn't fight him off her. She could barely breathe as he pressed himself hard against her. Her body was rigid with shock and she was helpless to defend herself. Tears filled her eyes and all she could do was try to forget what was happening.

'*Oberleutnant Fischer!*'

She heard Hans bark his name and, after one last push of his tongue into her mouth, the officer dropped his hold on her and spun on his heels, saluting Hans. 'Hauptmann Bauer.'

Estelle had no idea what Hans yelled at him, but he sounded furious and nodded to the car. Herr Fischer clicked his heels together and gave another salute to Hans before quickly turning to Estelle and whispering. 'Did you enjoy that as much as me, Fräulein?'

She shuddered at his words, still horribly aware of his rancid breath, but didn't answer. Hans shouted another order. The officer immediately marched over to the car, got in and was driven away, but not before giving Estelle a one last leer and wave as the car went down the drive.

Hans rushed over to her. 'Estelle, are you all right?' He

took her arm lightly and looked at her, full of concern. 'Please, accept my sincerest apologies. I am so very sorry. I have been trying for months to have him moved from here. I could see he was wanting to... wanting to do this. Now he has... and I shall make sure he pays severely for it.'

Estelle was shaking and cold, she could barely focus on Hans. She shook her head. 'Just make sure he doesn't come here again. I've been looking over my shoulder since he arrived. I'm sure... I'm sure I'll be... be fine.'

'You are certain?' Hans asked, looking distraught. 'I have let you down. I knew he wanted to get you alone, which is why I always tried to be with him whenever he was here. I hated leaving the island knowing he was sleeping in your home.'

She was grateful for all he'd done but mostly for him arranging another billet for Herr Fischer. 'I just don't want to ever have to see him again.'

His hand moved from her arm. 'I will do my best. Again, though as his senior officer and as your friend, please accept my deepest apologies for what has happened.'

'Please don't let my grandmother know what happened. I don't want her upset unnecessarily.'

'Of course. Come with me inside,' he said, his voice gentle as he led her to the warmth of the kitchen.

Too traumatised by what she had experienced, Estelle didn't reply. He pulled out her chair for her and she sat down.

'Please, will you wait one minute, I have something I wish to give you.'

She waited as he went upstairs.

Returning, Hans crouched down by Estelle so he was on her level and pressed a small, solid bar into her hands. She stared at it before turning her gaze to him. 'Is this what I think it is?'

'Yes. It is chocolate. I brought it with me for you from Germany.'

'You still have chocolate in Germany?'

He shook his head. 'It is something that is given to Luftwaffe pilots and I swapped it with a friend in exchange for a book of mine that he wanted.' He rested a hand lightly on hers. 'I had intended giving it to you on my return but thought it too risky with the Oberleutnant here. You must eat some of it now though. For the shock.'

Estelle unwrapped the bar in her hand and, barely able to recall the taste of chocolate, broke a piece off and ate it. The sweet, soft chocolate soothed her instantly. She looked up at Hans and smiled. 'Thank you, Hans.'

In the following weeks, the weather had turned nasty but there was not enough fuel for heating the house or hot water. But for Estelle, life was a little easier. Herr Fischer had gone and she started to feel stronger, to deal with his violation of her, but not before promising herself she would use the fire she felt at the injustice of it to make sure no one would ever do that to her again. She would make him pay. In some way. It was November again and cold and it felt like they had been living under the Occupation for far longer than just over two years.

Estelle was changing into her father's old overalls, she had taken in and taken up. She wore some of his woollen socks under her boots and two of his pullovers to keep warm and was glad now that they had thought to keep his clothes. Not only for the warmth but also the comfort of feeling something of his close to her. That awful day since she had last seen him felt so very long ago now. What would he think of everything? What would he think of her?

Some of his better woollen pullovers had been unravelled and Gran had spent many summer evenings, or afternoons knitting new tops for those in need and for themselves. The latest things she had created from one of her dad's older pullovers were new bed socks for them both to keep them warm at night – and, wanting to pay Hans back for being so thoughtful, she also made a pair for him.

Estelle was outside in the yard, breathing in the cold damp air, when she felt a drop of rain on her face and looked up at the heavy steel grey clouds. Wanting to put her bike away in the barn before it got soaked, she grabbed the handlebars and pushed it at a quick jog over to the barn. She pulled open the heavy wooden door, the dark red paint of which had faded over the years to a muted pink, and thought she heard a rustling noise. Stopping instantly, Estelle was on high alert, listening carefully for any further noises. Did she expect Herr Fischer to jump out at her from behind the hay bales? No. She was being ridiculous. Hans had promised he wouldn't come here again and she trusted him to keep Herr

Fischer away from the farm. But… but she couldn't forget the way he had forced himself on her and the determined look he'd had in his eyes as he left.

Trying to put those thoughts out of her mind, she pushed her bike under a tarpaulin and returned to the house. She hated these colder dark nights keeping them inside much earlier than they had done during the summer. She decided to pour herself a glass of water and have an early night. At least she could get slightly warm in her bed. Candles were scare now too so she couldn't afford to stay up drawing during the night.

Estelle had just turned off the tap at the kitchen sink when she was certain she heard a knock on the window. Her heart missed a beat. However, she reasoned that if Herr Fischer was going to come to the house, he wouldn't knock on the window, but on the door. Or would he even knock? He was not a man who asked for permission. There was another quieter tap on the glass, and Estelle's heart pounded heavily as she pulled the blackout blind slightly back to peer out, not knowing what to expect. It was before curfew, but she couldn't imagine any of her neighbours needing to come to the farm.

She couldn't see anything, initially, but then someone stood up and a pale, grey face with a haunted look in its deep-set eyes stared back at her. Estelle opened her mouth but didn't know what to say. The young man was trembling and she suspected it was due to fear as well as the freezing weather. He looked like one of the Todt slaves. Looking at the clock on the wall, she saw it was almost eight o'clock and knew Hans was due back at the farm soon. She pointed for the man to go to the barn. He seemed to understand, so Estelle replaced the blackout blind and ran upstairs to her grandmother's bedroom and knocked on the door.

'Gran, are you still dressed?'

The door opened and her grandmother waved her inside. 'Whatever's the matter?'

Estelle told her about the face at the window. 'It's one of the slaves, Gran. I think he's gone to the barn, but Hans is going to be back soon. How did he know to come here? Where's he come from? He was taking a chance, surely? What if we reported him?'

'You need to take a few deep breaths and calm down, my love' she said. 'He's come here because he will have been reassured we would help.'

'How would he know that?'

Her grandmother smiled. 'Because I know people.'

Estelle's mouth dropped open and she couldn't think of anything to say at first. 'Who?'

'That's for me to know, not you. The least you know, the better. Right, come on, now, we need to give him food and water and something to wash with. Then he needs something warm.'

Estelle knew her grandmother had changed her details on her Identity Card but had no idea the friends she would pop out to see had ulterior motives. 'Gran, you are a dark horse. And, an incredible lady.'

'Right now, I'm more concerned with the poor chap waiting for us in the barn.'

'What shall I do?'

'You fetch a bowl of water and two cloths. One for him

to wash with and a towel for him to dry himself. I'll take out some of your father's clothes for him.' She hurriedly slipped her feet out of her slippers and into her shoes. 'We must be quick and help him before Hans returns, otherwise he will be out in that barn all night until Hans leaves again in the morning. It's too dangerous to go out to him while Hans is here in the house. Right, move yourself. Oh, and make sure to leave Rebel in the house, I don't want him to frighten the poor man.'

Estelle wasn't so sure Hans would turn them in but knew she couldn't take the risk that she was wrong. She left her grandmother and ran down to the kitchen. Taking a deep bowl from one of the cupboards, she grabbed a cloth and a towel. Rebel got out of his bed and waited by the door ready to accompany her. 'No, boy. You have to stay indoors.' Without pulling on her own coat, she ran outside through the rain to the barn, careful not to spill any of the water. She closed the door behind her and waited for her eyes to get used to the dark.

'Hello? Are you there?' She could hear the tremble in her own voice, but her grandmother would be joining her soon, so it wasn't as if she had anything much to worry about. Anyway, she decided, this poor man must be far more frightened of her than she was of him.

She heard movement to her right and turned her head to see the man carefully stepping forward. He was barefoot and his feet were caked in dirt and mud. She didn't think she had ever seen anyone so thin or cold before.

'I'm Estelle. I've brought you something to wash with,'

she said, unsure if he understood her, so she mimicked using the water to wash herself.

'Thank you.'

His voice had an accent but she had no idea where he might be from. 'I'll leave this here and go and fetch you something to eat and drink. My grandmother will bring you clothes to change into very soon.'

He looked a little confused, but Estelle left the barn and ran back across the yard. She pulled open the front door and almost slammed into her grandmother.

'Sorry, Gran. Shall I take those from you?'

Her grandmother shook her head. 'No, just follow with whatever you can find for him to eat and bring a mug and a jug of water with you.' She stepped outside, before coming back in immediately after. 'I thought we should give him your dad's jacket, cap and boots. What do you think?'

Estelle couldn't think of a better person to hand them over to. 'Dad would be happy to think his clothes are helping someone so desperately in need of them.'

'Good girl. I know how difficult it is for you to part with them.' Her grandmother gave her a smile and patted her cheek. 'Right, hurry now, before Hans returns.'

Estelle took a mug out of the cupboard and put it on the draining board. Then she grabbed a jug and filled it three quarters of the way to the top. Then, taking one of her grandmother's smaller baskets, filled it with two carrots, an apple, and a bowl of potato, pea and beetroot soup. It was cold now but it tasted good. At least it was healthy, and looking at the skeletal man in the barn, he needed all the nutrients she could find. They had a little stale bread that he could dip into the soup, so Estelle popped that into the basket, too. She also grabbed a spoon from the cutlery drawer at the end of the pine kitchen table.

She took down her father's jacket, his cap still firmly folded into the pocket. She lifted it to her face and breathed in, hoping it still retained some of his smell. It did, but only very slightly. This would be the last time she saw it but knew her father would approve of her giving it to help someone. She slung the coat over her left shoulder and bent to retrieve the boots, then ran outside to the barn.

Her grandmother was helping the man, with a little difficulty. 'Here, you go,' Estelle said, taking everything she had over to them.

He looked at her with tears in his eyes.

'I think his name is Ivan,' her grandmother said. 'He's freezing so go and fetch a couple of blankets from the back of the linen cupboard. Hurry now. I don't think we have very long.'

Ten minutes later, with Ivan settled comfortably for the night, they returned to the house. It had been hard to leave the poor man there, in such a state, when they could come back to their farmhouse and beds. But they had done what they could and he was now in a better position than he was before.

They were sitting in the kitchen, in silence, each nursing a cup of mixed tea, both lost in their own thoughts, when her grandmother gasped and raised her hand to her chest.

'Look.' She pointed to the bare hook on the back door where Estelle's father's coat had hung until a short while earlier. 'We need to replace that with something else before Hans comes back. He'll definitely notice it missing.'

She was right. 'I've mentioned it was Daddy's to him, last winter,' Estelle recalled. 'He knows it means a lot to me and that we just wouldn't give it away.'

Her grandmother gave it some thought and then raised her right forefinger with a smile. 'Your father's suit. We'll bring down the jacket from that and hang it up. Bring an old scarf, too, we can try and mask it a bit.'

Estelle did as her grandmother asked. As she rifled through her father's clothes, which she had put away into an old trunk, she felt enormous relief that Ivan had come to the farm for their help *after* Herr Fischer's departure. She shuddered to think how brutal he might have been to the unfortunate man if he'd found him in the barn. She grabbed the suit jacket and went to her room to find an old scarf of hers just as she heard the sound of a car coming up the driveway.

'Estelle, hurry up.'

She could hear the fear in her grandmother's voice and ran as fast as she could down the stairs, tripping up on the final step and only just managing to save herself from falling by dropping the jacket and grabbing hold of the newel at the bottom of the handrail. She quickly bent to grab the jacket and hurried into the kitchen, only just managing to hang it – and the scarf – up before she heard Hans bidding his driver good night.

'Quick, sit down.' Gran waved frantically for Estelle to take a seat.

She pulled out her chair and her bottom landed on the wooden seat as the door handle turned and Hans walked in.

'Good evening, Frau Woods, Estelle.' He gave Estelle a strange look and she could feel her face reddening.

She would make a lousy spy, Estelle realised, hoping that Hans might think her pink cheeks were to do with seeing him again. It wasn't what she would normally want, but it was preferable to him suspecting anything was amiss at the farm. 'Did you have a good evening?' she asked, hoping to distract him.

'I did. Thank you. And you both, the same?'

'Yes,' her grandmother said. 'It's been quite a day. It's far too cold, though, don't you think?'

He agreed and began speaking about harsh winters at his parent's farm as he removed his cap and jacket.

Estelle noticed her grandmother's eyes widen. It was only slightly but enough for Estelle to note that something was amiss. Her gran nodded at something Hans said and stood up. She picked up Estelle's cup, which was still half full, and her own and carried them over to the sink. Estelle smiled at Hans and pretended to be listening to him. As he placed his cap on the table, she glanced over towards the sink and spotted the mug she'd meant to take out to Ivan. At that moment, Hans stopped talking and noticed it, too.

'Ah, you have had company today. One of your friends came for your tea, I think?'

There was nothing accusatory in his tone, but Estelle's

heart pounded so heavily that she worried he might hear it.

Both hesitated. Then Estelle replied, 'No,' at exactly the same time as her grandmother said, 'Yes.'

Hans frowned before raising his eyebrows in amusement. 'You did have a friend, or you didn't have a friend? I am confused.'

Estelle glanced at her grandmother, not wishing to make matters worse. Then, seeing that her grandmother was unsure what to say, she laughed, hoping it didn't sound to forced, and said, 'One of my Dad's old friends popped round briefly and we had a cup of our disgusting tea together. So I suppose it was a friend, while not being one of *our* friends.' She laughed again, willing him to believe her.

Hans looked from Estelle to her grandmother and shrugged. 'I think I might have had one too many glasses of wine tonight. I am happy that you have had a good day.' He picked up his cap. 'I shall bid you both a good night.'

Estelle noticed his line of vision resting on her dad's suit jacket. He stared at it for a while and then looked down at the space on the floor where the boots used to sit. 'You decided to part with your father's belongings, after all?'

His gaze seemed so penetrating that Estelle had to hold her nerve and not show how terrified she was at that moment. 'Yes,' she said, as calmly as she could manage, 'we discussed it and decided that it was about time.'

'The man who visited us today needed the coat to replace his old one,' her grandmother said. 'We thought Estelle's father would be happy to know that his things had been passed on to a friend of his who needed them.'

Estelle was impressed with her grandmother's quick

thinking. She noticed Hans's expression as he thought it through. 'A good idea. It is nice to hear that people stick together and look after their friends when they need them.'

They mumbled their agreement. Estelle didn't know how much more her nerves could stand but focused on acting calm despite her pulse racing.

'The jacket is for another friend, if they come?'

Estelle nodded. Did he suspect that they were trying to fool him? She just wanted him to hurry up and leave them in peace. 'If it's hanging there, it will remind us that we have it,' she said, aware she probably sounded a little confused, but not knowing what else to say in reply to his question.

Hans glanced at the jacket. 'It is a shame you do not have more boots.' He walked over to the kitchen door. '*Gute nacht.*'

Estelle didn't like to think that his reverting back to German might be a reminder to them not to forget why he was on the island. Did he suspect them of something? She hoped not but she couldn't be sure. His expression was inscrutable.

'Good night,' they said in unison as he left the room. Waiting until they heard his bedroom door close and his footsteps on the wooden floorboards overhead, they both sighed with relief.

'That was close,' Estelle whispered feeling, exhausted suddenly. 'What shall we do about—' She indicated the barn and waited for her grandmother to respond.

'We look after him for as long as we need to and hope for the best we don't get caught.'

THIRTY-FOUR

Estelle

A fter a restless night full of nightmares about Ivan
being discovered, Estelle woke to another freezing
cold day. She set about her chores making sure to go into
the barn as usual but not speaking to Ivan or even looking
in the direction of his hideaway until she was certain Hans
had left for the day. Once he had gone, she left it another
half an hour in case he returned to the farm for any reason
before checking on their secret guest.

She decided to take Rebel out with her to see Ivan this
time. He needed to meet Ivan and know he wasn't someone
to bark at, just in case he picked up his scent when Hans
was around. She felt anxious about introducing Rebel to
him having seen how vicious the OT guard dogs were but
hoped Ivan would trust her enough not to be unduly
frightened. Estelle took some bread wrapped in a napkin
and a mug of their carrot tea with her.

'Heel, Rebel,' she said firmly as they entered the barn.
'Stay here.' She left Rebel sitting obediently by the barn

door and walked up slowly to where Ivan was hiding. She placed the mug and bread on to one of the hay bales. 'It's me, Ivan. Estelle. I've brought my dog with me,' she said, aware he probably didn't understand her, but hoped that maybe he recognised the word. When Ivan didn't come out of his hiding place, she went back to Rebel and took hold of his collar. 'He won't hurt you, I promise.' She kept her tone as gentle as possible hoping it would help Ivan to trust her.

She was about to think he had left, or, she thought with rising panic, maybe died during the night, when she heard movement behind the hay bales. Slowly, Ivan's head appeared. His eyes widened in horror to see Rebel, but she stroked the dog's head and held her other hand up to Ivan. 'Please, don't worry. Then she bent down and hugged her fluffy pet, to show that he was a gentle dog.

Ivan's face relaxed and, seeing the mug and napkin, sat back, seeming now not to be too afraid.

She pointed to the carrot tea and bread and nodded to indicate he should take them. When he did and she was sure he seemed calm enough in Rebel's company, she slowly let go of the dog's collar.

'You slept well?' she asked by enacting her words. Ivan nodded. He already looked a little better after a wash and some food and she was relieved to see him looking warmer, too.

He nodded and appeared to smile, but his face was so drawn that it ended up being more of a grimace.

Estelle noticed a bad scar on his top lip that went up to his cheek and that he had several teeth missing. The scar didn't look very old because it was still pink and she assumed it must have been caused by one of the vicious OT guards. Estelle's heart went out to this man who she assumed had lived a normal life before this war began and he was brought here. Did he have a family who wondered where he might be? She wasn't even sure how old he could be because it was difficult to tell. She had been concerned at seeing someone else wearing her father's clothes, especially his cap and jacket expecting the sight to bring back memories. But looking at Ivan now, she knew there was no resemblance to her healthy, tanned father's face and this painfully thin man who had been so appallingly treated.

She called Rebel to walk slowly next to her as she went towards Ivan. The man watched her dog but didn't seem unduly alarmed so she didn't stop. When she reached where he was sitting on one of the hay bales she waited for Rebel to sniff the air. He stared at Ivan and then wagged his tail. Estelle smiled when Ivan moved slightly forward, reached out and Rebel walked towards him until Ivan's hand could touch his furry neck. She wasn't sure if it was Rebel's gentleness or Ivan's trust in her and the dog, but she could see that he was a man who loved dogs and the affection from Rebel meant a lot to him.

'I'll take this inside,' she said lifting the jug and the bowl of dirty water. 'I'll freshen this up for you and bring you back something more to eat and drink. Rebel, come.'

As Estelle walked across the yard, she tipped the dirty water down the drain and returned to the house, relieved that although Ivan might not understand what she was saying he appeared to trust her. What choice did he have?

she thought miserably. At least he now knew that Rebel wouldn't hurt him.

Her grandmother came into the kitchen just as Estelle closed the back door.

'How is he this morning?'

'Much better, I think,' Estelle was relieved to report. There was one moment during the night when she had worried that he might not last until morning he had appeared so ill and drained of most of his energy. 'I was wondering if I could give him our egg this morning?'

Her grandmother stroked Estelle's hair. 'I was going to suggest the very same thing. I can't imagine how long it must be since Ivan has tasted one. It will do him good.'

She took the egg with a tiny bit of their precious salt out to Ivan, together with another mug of tea. He took them from her and stared at the food before looking up at her with anguish in his dark eyes. Estelle wasn't sure if she had offended him and opened her mouth to offer him something else when she noticed tears running down his face. She had to swallow hard to stop herself from crying with him. Estelle cleared her throat and rested a hand on Ivan's bony shoulder.

'You eat this. I'll bring you some fresh water and new cloths so that you can wash. I'll leave you to eat now.'

He gave her one of his smiles and she smiled back before leaving the barn and Ivan in peace with his breakfast. As soon as Estelle was outside, she closed the barn door and walked a few steps to rest back against the wall of the barn, to gather herself before going back to see her grandmother in the kitchen. How could human beings treat others so wickedly, she thought, recalling the brutality of the OT guards she had seen in town and state of poor Ivan's body? How could anyone glean satisfaction out of making others feel such fear?

Apart from taking Ivan the fresh water and collecting his dirty plate and cutlery, Estelle left him alone to rest. Who knew what would happen to him next? She hoped that he would at least have time enough to recover some of his strength and maybe a little weight before having to move on. She wished she could invite him into the house to sleep on a proper bed. It was far too cold to sleep outside, but at least the barn was solid and weather-proof and, she guessed, far better than living in the manner he had been forced to do up until now.

That afternoon, as Estelle was outside working in the yard, she heard Rebel growl quietly and realised that a car was coming down the drive. She peered around the barn and the basket of vegetables she had been holding slipped out of her hand at the familiar sight of a Nazi vehicle drawing up to the back of the house. Hans never usually came back at this time of day. She hurriedly crouched down to collect all her vegetables and glanced at the barn desperate to warn Ivan to hide but there was no time unless she wanted to risk alerting whoever was here that someone was inside the barn. She wished she could call for her grandmother and hoped that both Ivan and her gran had heard the vehicle too.

Estelle scrambled around in the icy mud, trying to retrieve her vegetables and, hearing footsteps looked up to see Hans striding towards her. She opened her mouth to speak when he reached down and picked up a beetroot and a cauliflower that she hadn't noticed rolling down the slope towards the yard.

'Everything is all right?' he asked placing them into her basket and not seeming to mind that his leather gloves were now filthy. 'You dropped your basket.'

She forced a smile and rolled her eyes heavenward. 'It's colder out here than I had realised and I was too lazy to go back inside and fetch my gloves,' she lied hoping he believed her.

Hans reached out his hand to help her to her feet. 'Yes, your hands are very cold. You must be careful not to get...' he thought for a bit. 'No, I do not know the word in English.'

'Chilblains, maybe?'

He shrugged. 'Maybe.' Rebel came up to him and nudged his leg for some attention. 'Hello, boy,' Hans said, making a fuss of him.

'You're back early today, aren't you?' She prayed silently that he wasn't here because of Ivan.

His face fell. 'I am here because an OT prisoner has gone missing. Two, in fact. We need to find them.' His eyes filled with sadness. 'I know that you do not like what I have to do for my country, Estelle, but I must obey orders and help look for these men.'

She thought back to the execution of François Scornet, the young French lad, the previous year. 'No. It can be hard to imagine someone like you doing things like that,' she said quietly. 'Shall we go inside? I know I could do with one of Gran's strange teas.'

'Yes, but let me carry your basket. It looks very heavy.'

Estelle was perfectly capable of carrying the basket, but happy to allow him to be distracted, so handed it to him without argument.

As they walked down to the yard, she saw that the driver was standing by the car, waiting for orders. She didn't need him waiting outside or even worse going into the barn for some warmth.

'Is your driver waiting for you?'

'He is. I am collecting a coat because it is very cold, as you are aware today. I'll tell him to wait in the car.'

'No.' She hadn't meant to snap at him and, when he seemed surprised by her reaction, she quickly added, 'Why don't you invite the poor man inside. I'm sure he could do with some warm tea, too. It's only carrot but it's not nearly as bad as the parsnip coffee Gran sometimes makes.' She grimaced. 'Even if it does taste a little odd.'

Estelle went inside while Hans went to speak to his driver. She was glad to find her grandmother in the kitchen, already heating some water for their drinks. She must have heard them arrive and then listened to what Estelle had suggested. Estelle placed the basket on the drainer and took out four cups and saucers.

The men came inside. 'We are unable to stay for many minutes,' Hans explained. 'We have much to do today, but a warm drink for both of us is very welcome.'

'You gentlemen take a seat. These drinks will be ready in no time at all.'

Estelle sat at the table. 'Can you tell us about the prisoners, Captain Bauer?'

Hans seemed happy for her to act more formally in front of his driver. 'They went missing while working at a quarry some miles away to the north of the island early yesterday afternoon.'

'Where are you going to start your search for them?' her grandmother asked, placing their drinks in front of them on the table.

'The OT have been searching for them since yesterday afternoon and, to be honest, I wouldn't be surprised if they hadn't di...' his voice tailed off.

'Go on, please,' her grandmother urged, handing Estelle her cup and sitting down to join them.

Hans thanked her and, taking off his gloves, placed them neatly on the table, in such a way as to keep the mud on them from touching the table. Then seeing her grandmother look at his muddy gloves, quickly removed them from the table and rested them on his lap. 'Last night was very cold. They have little by way of clothing to protect them from the weather and we believe they might have perished during the night.'

'It wouldn't' be surprising,' her grandmother said. 'It has been particularly cold and the prisoners I've seen on the island seem to be extremely under-dressed and malnourished.'

Estelle watched Hans lower his gaze to his cup. She could see he was embarrassed – and so he should be! Although, she truly believed it wasn't his fault that the OT treated these people so appallingly. Hadn't he explained to her how he and the other Wehrmacht soldiers had very little say in how things were done and were even encouraged not to become involved.

'Where will you be conducting your search?' Estelle asked, willing him to say somewhere out in St Mary, or St John, or one of the other parishes away from St Ouen. They needed time to move Ivan to another safe place. She didn't even know who had suggested he come here, if anyone. She heard Hans say something and tried to focus on his words. 'I'm sorry, what was that?'

'We will begin in St Mary. We don't know of course that they are coming this way, but other search parties are working from where they were last seen towards Trinity and to the east.'

Hans drank his tea in silence and a short while later placed his hands on the table. 'We need to leave. Please do not make food for me this evening, Frau Woods. I am unsure what time I will finish tonight.'

Estelle struggled to hide her relief as she listened to her grandmother reminding Hans not to forget to fetch his coat from his room.

As soon as the soldiers left, Estelle sat with her grandmother at the table and rubbed her eyes. She was so tired although probably more from worry than lack of sleep. 'What are we going to do?'

'I don't know. My friend is in town at the moment so I think the best course of action would be for you to go to the shop and pass a message on to Mr Gibault.'

'Mr Gibault? Why?' She thought of the kindly shopkeeper who looked after his bedridden mother so well.

'He will know who to speak to. Go now and make sure no one overhears you. If there is someone else there say you've forgotten your purse and return later. Do you understand?' Estelle nodded and went to pull on her coat and hat. 'Remember your gloves this time. You'll draw attention to yourself if you're not dressed accordingly. We don't want any soldiers to pick up that that your mind is elsewhere. Remember they will be watching us even more now that two slaves have gone missing. If they don't find them, and we know that they won't find Ivan if we have anything to do with it, then they will know he's being sheltered and we'll all be under suspicion.'

Estelle shivered at the thought. She wound her scarf around her neck, picked up her gloves and grabbed her purse slipping it into her basket and covering it with a handkerchief. 'I'll be back as soon as I can.'

She walked as fast as she could to the shop telling herself over and over to remain calm and not show how terrified she was of being caught. She joined the back of the queue and decided to stay there unless anyone else came in after her. She had to wait for Mr Gibault to serve several customers before they were the only ones in the shop, then began to explain to him what had happened. Estelle could see by the expression on his face that he understood the urgency of the situation.

'I don't know how quickly I can arrange for someone to come for him,' he said keeping his voice low.

The shop door opened and she knew without turning around by Mr Gibault's change of expression and the heavy sound of jackboots that a soldier had just entered. Estelle knew she had to say what she needed to know, while she still had the chance. Who knew what would happen if she didn't arrange something now?

'I will prepare for tonight,' she said in Jèrriais, keeping her voice level, knowing the German soldier would not understand the local patois.

Mr Gibault smiled at her looking more relaxed. 'Yes, return to your grandmother and prepare for tonight. We'll do what we can. Right, you'd better give me your ration book so that I can sell you this butter.'

Estelle took her ration book from her basket. The soldier walked up to the counter and leant against it, smiling at Estelle. '*Guten tag*, Fräulein.'

She smiled at him, enjoying the fact that she and the shopkeeper had made arrangements right under his nose. Mr Gibault handed her the butter and her ration book and told her how much she owed in English. As soon as the exchange had been made, she thanked him using Jèrriais once again and left.

Back at the farm, Estelle hurried out to the barn to do her best to explain to Ivan that he would be moved tonight. She also gave him a bag with two apples and bread inside should he need it during the night.

Estelle thought that he understood the gist of what she was saying. Then she bid him farewell and returned to the house to wait. Before she left, his frail hand reached out to touch her arm and as she turned to him he placed his hand together as if in prayer.

'We should go to bed,' her grandmother said. 'We don't want to be caught up when Hans returns. I don't want to find out whether he would arrest Ivan – or us. I'd rather not know.'

Estelle agreed. She would have liked to check on their secret guest once more but couldn't go outside without breaking curfew. She took Rebel to sleep in her bedroom so she could quieten him and stop him from barking if he was alerted to anyone coming for Ivan.

She heard Hans return just after midnight. Had they caught the other prisoner? Any questions would have to wait until morning. At about two-thirty, Rebel's grumbling woke her. Something was going on outside.

'Shush, Rebel,' she whispered, stroking his head and creeping over to her window to peek outside. She pulled the blackout blind back slightly but the temperature was so low her breath frosted up the window. She wiped the glass with the back of her sleeve and held her breath while she peeked outside once again. Nothing moved in the yard. Rebel made another sound. 'Quiet, boy,' she whispered. 'Lie down.'

Estelle turned back to look outside again and squinted as she tried to make out if anything was happening. The moon was full so the timing couldn't have been worse. The barn door opened slightly and she watched as a shadowy person disappeared inside before closing it. Moments later, the door opened again. A man who she didn't recognise, probably because he had a hat pulled low over his face and a scarf wrapped high around his chin, glanced up at the windows. Estelle gasped and stepped back. She didn't want to unnerve them. But either he hadn't seen her or knew she was friendly because, seconds later, he led Ivan out of the barn. They scampered around to the back of the barn and she presumed they would go from there across the fields to someone else's home.

'Stay safe, Ivan,' she whispered, before moving back from the window and returning to her bed. She lay down under her covers her heart pounding rapidly as she listened as hard as she could for any movement from Hans's bedroom. There was none. Had Ivan been whisked away without him noticing? She hoped so, very much.

THIRTY-FIVE

Estelle

MARCH 1943

E stelle was sweeping out the barn a few months later when she moved several hay bales near the back by the tractor they had stored away at the beginning of the war. As she lifted one of the bales, she spotted a spoon and thought back to when Ivan had rested in their barn for a couple of days. He had never been caught, at least not as far as she or Gran were aware. They had been upset to learn though that the other man who escaped with him had been found dead the day after Ivan left the farm. She had asked Hans how the search had gone, anxious in case he gave her bad news about Ivan. Any joy she felt at him not being found was masked by her sadness that the other man had perished in the freezing November weather.

She hoped Ivan was well wherever he might be. Estelle wondered if she would ever come across him again and if she did whether she would recognise him after months of better treatment and a reasonable amount of food. 'The less you know the better,' her grandmother had insisted.

'You are sad today, Estelle?' Hans asked covering the solid ground underfoot with his large strides as he came up to join her by the barn. She quickly hid the spoon in her pocket and turned round to him to give him a weak smile.

'I was thinking of my sister Rosie and how much I miss her. It's almost three years now since I've been able to hug her.'

After a few seconds of indecision, Hans carefully stepped forward and pulled her into a hug. Estelle stiffened slightly, she didn't know how she felt about being comforted by him. She put her hands against his chest to push him away.

'I know how it feels to miss someone. I'm sure you will see your sister again.'

Estelle listened to Hans's deep voice, so full of caring. She was exhausted. It had been so long since she had been held like this and without fully realising she allowed herself to relax into his arms for a fraction of a second.

Then, frightened that someone might see them together like this, she pushed him gently away from her, thinking of Gerard and how he would feel if anyone ever told him they had seen her in the arms of a German soldier. How could she be so disloyal? She was no better than a Jerry bag, she thought bitterly.

'Thank you,' she said as she moved away from him. 'I know you mean well and, if the circumstances were different, I think we could be good friends.'

His face fell and his arms dropped to his sides. 'You do not think of me as your friend now?'

How could he not understand how complicated

this was?

She clasped her hands together. 'What I mean is that I do think of you fondly. You are a good and kind person. I know that to be true. But you must also know that there has to be some sort of divide between us.' When his expression didn't soften, she added. 'For appearances sake, if nothing more.'

Hans nodded slowly and Estelle relaxed a little.

They looked at each other for a moment. Estelle wondered if she might ever meet up with Hans after this was all over. What would it be like to see him in his own world with his family and going about his business just like any ordinary man?

'Why do you smile?' he asked, looking a little confused.

'I hadn't realised I was,' she admitted. 'But it's probably because I was trying to picture you in your life before the war.'

He gave her a wistful sigh. 'I enjoyed my life very much then. Although of course there were signs that this might happen for a long time before the war began. It used to worry me that I would be forced to leave my home and my job.'

'And now, do you long to return to that life?'

He cleared his throat. 'I can't speak of such things. This is the way things are. I cannot be disloyal to the Reich and so I must continue to do my work as an officer for as long as it is expected of me.'

And there was the soldier again. Obeying orders. 'We all have a role to play in this, don't we?'

He nodded sadly. 'Yes, we do.'

THIRTY-SIX

Rosie
7 AUGUST 1943

*I*t's been a while since I wrote in my diary. I have to admit that for a few months now it's made me miserable thinking about writing something for you to read when we don't really know if we will ever meet again. The longer the war goes on, the more it feels like it will never be over. I hid this note pad from myself in the lower shelf of my chest of drawers under my winter pullovers. I thought it was better if I forgot about you and Gran for a while and tried to make the best of this strange new life.

Something has happened now that I can't share with Aunt Muriel and I don't think Queenie would want to listen to me going on about, so I thought the best thing to do is write it down. Aunt Muriel's friend, Pierre and his infantry division have been sent away. Well, his unit has been sent away. She hasn't heard from him for over a month. Although she insists she's fine whenever I ask, the other day I turned on the radio and Vera Lynn began singing 'We'll Meet Again'. Aunt Muriel shouted at me to turn it off and get on with my homework. I was upset at first *because she never snaps at me, but then I realised how worried she really was about Pierre.*

We popped in to visit her friend, Lynne earlier today and I heard them whispering a siege in Sicily, where she thinks he must be and I know she's frightened for him that he might be killed if he hasn't been already. More and more deaths are reported in the newspapers every day. Oh, Estelle, I wish you were here so I could speak to you about this. I don't know to say Aunt Muriel or how to make her feel better. So many men aren't coming back.

I miss you so much, Essie.

THIRTY-SEVEN

Estelle

JUNE 1943

E stelle wasn't sure if she was being ridiculous but the summers seemed hotter and the winters much colder since the island had been under occupation. It had been so hot for the past couple of days that the last thing she had felt like doing was to traipse to Violet's house on an errand for her grandmother. But she wasn't going to let their lovely neighbour down simply because she was feeling lazy and all she wanted to do was lie in a bath filled with cold water. Ideally she would have preferred to walk with her costume and towel under her arm down the hill to Greve de Lecq and swim in the sea. She closed her eyes and tried to recall the joy of diving into the cool water. Of course, even if she did have time, the beaches were still blockaded with barbed wire and covered in mines.

Estelle had spent far too long at Violet's helping her with chores around the house and she had been heading home dangerously close to curfew when her bicycle got a puncture. She knew a patrol would be along any minute and these days the soldiers, weary from the lack of food on the island and the long years away from home, were becoming even more severe with locals caught breaking the regulations. She also couldn't risk being a woman out alone at night with bored and homesick soldiers roving the deserted lanes.

Hiding her bike on the side of the road, she ducked and entered the nearest field. She needed to keep off the road if she didn't want to be seen.

She climbed through the hedge, breathless but knowing that she would soon be safely inside the farmhouse as she could run across the two fields that separated them and their neighbour. She ran the length of the field. Soil seeped into her shoes between her toes, it was cool and felt rather comforting. She would have liked to take off her shoes and run barefoot but didn't dare waste the time. It wasn't long before she could see the lights of the farmhouse in the distance turning out one by one as her grandmother went through the house putting up the blackout blinds.

'Almost there,' she whispered, pushing herself to keep running. She spotted what she thought was a bird but realised it must be a bat. Then another. They swooped past her and Estelle ducked but her next step landed at an angle and her knee twisted to the side sending a shooting pain through her leg. She fell to the ground. 'No, please,' she hissed, trying to stand but unable to put any pressure on to her leg. She had to reach the house in the next seven minutes or she would be breaking curfew. She tried to hop, but it was no use in the soft ground. Trying once more, she fell again, frustration coursing through her.

She glanced at her watch. 'Three minutes.' She had to find a way to get back to the house. If she couldn't run or hop, then she would simply have to crawl, she decided. Seconds later, she realised that was a stupid idea when she tried to put pressure on her knee. 'Idiot.'

Tears of frustration ran down her face. Estelle grabbed hold of a branch in the hedge and pulled herself to her feet. She would just have to hop. It might take longer but if she was lucky the patrol would come a little later and not find her in the field. Why, she thought had she worn her yellow summer dress? The moon was waning but still bright and if anyone was to pass she would stick out like some sort of beacon.

The next moment, she spotted a torchlight scanning the surrounding field and someone coming closer. She dropped to the ground hoping if it was a soldier on patrol he hadn't seen her yet. Her heart pounded so loudly that she was sure it could be heard and would give her away.

'Estelle. Estelle, it's me.' A whisper cut through the silence.

Estelle peered at the figure coming towards her. 'Oh, thank goodness. Hans, I'm here. I can't walk.'

He reached her. 'You are hurt?'

'Only my knee.'

He bent down. 'Put your arms around my neck.'

'What?' she asked, embarrassed. 'Why?'

'Estelle we do not have time for coyness. I need to lift you and you will help me by doing as I say.'

Mortified, she did as he asked amazed at how easily he

then scooped her up into his arms. She held on tightly to him, her emotions fighting with each other.

'You have broken curfew,' he said through gritted teeth as he made short work of covering the remainder of the distance to the edge of the field. He stopped at one of the granite pillars either side of the field entrance and listened. 'Do not speak.'

She did as he asked aware that if they were going to be seen from the road then it would most likely be now as they made their way from behind the barn across the yard to the back door. She held her breath as he crossed to the house. As if by magic the door opened as they neared it and closed as soon as they were inside.

'Where the hell have you been?' her grandmother snapped as she locked the back door.

Hans lowered Estelle on to one of the kitchen chairs and stood back, hands on his hips breathless. She looked up at the two of them.

'I'm so sorry. I was at Violet's, helping her, and forgot the time. The evenings are so light. Then my bike got a puncture and I had to leave it behind.'

'You have broken curfew.' Hans glared at her. 'I should report you for this.'

Estelle glanced at her grandmother still standing by the door, looking serious. 'I know and I'm truly sorry.' She gazed at him, unsure what he would do next. 'Will you report me, though?'

He stared at her for a while before shaking his head slowly. 'Not this time. But I can't keep doing this for you, Estelle.'

She had to concentrate on not smiling with relief. 'Thank you.'

He turned to leave the room. 'I will go to my room now.'

As he went to pass her chair, Estelle grabbed his hand. 'Hans, I really am sorry for putting you in this position,' she admitted.

He looked down at her, his expression softening. 'Would you like me to carry you to your room?' he asked gently.

Estelle went to stand and winced in pain. 'Yes, I think I do.' She looked at Hans, picturing the width of their stairway. 'You're not going be able to carry me up the usual way though, are you?'

He smiled at her for the first time. 'No. You will be going over my shoulder this time.'

Estelle sighed. 'You're going to enjoy carrying me upstairs like a sack of spuds, aren't you?'

He laughed. 'Yes, I am.'

THIRTY-EIGHT

Rosie

DECEMBER 1943

Another Christmas away from you, Essie. That's the fourth one now. Aunt Muriel says that now things are moving in the Allies' favour that this could be the last time I have to spend Christmas away from everyone in Jersey. I'm crossing my fingers with my other hand as I write this.

Aunt Muriel has finally heard from Pierre. He was badly injured in Sicily but is now back in England convalescing at a hospital in the Midlands somewhere. He's invited her up there to visit him. At first, she said she couldn't go and leave me behind, but I spoke to Queenie on the quiet and she's invited me to stay at her flat for the two days Aunt Muriel will be away. I'm looking forward to it very much. Queenie is always great fun and I think she's looking forward to me staying with her, too.

Pierre has promised Aunt Muriel that he is on the mend now and it won't be long before he can come to visit us. She's worried that he will be sent back to Canada and she won't be able to see him until after the war, but I think she will be more frightened if he joins his division again.

Oh, Estelle when is this horrid war going to end? Aunt Muriel is getting tired of me asking her when she thinks this will all be over and I don't mean to get on her nerves but I miss the farm so much, even Rebel who's always frightened me a little.

I do wonder if Pierre will ask Aunt Muriel to marry him, but don't think it will happen until he's feeling back to his old self. That's what I heard Queenie saying to her the other day anyway, when they were making plans for me to go and stay with her. If they do marry and she goes to live in Canada, do you think she might ask me to be bridesmaid?

THIRTY-NINE

Estelle

FEBRUARY 1944

Estelle heard her grandmother groan in the washhouse. She had heard her moaning during the night but when she had asked if everything was all right her grandmother insisted she was fine. She had been quiet for a couple of days, but when Estelle tried to comfort her she shooed her away.

Estelle couldn't understand why her grandmother was being so distant over the past few days and suspected she was pretending to feel better than she actually was so as not to concern her. She was tired of arguing and was determined to be more forceful with her this time. She left the barn and crossed the yard to the washhouse.

'Oh, Gran,' she said, stepping into the room only to be distracted by the cold in the brick outbuilding. 'It's freezing in here. Please, let me finish this washing.'

Gran shook her head slowly, flinching in pain. 'Don't start that fussing again, Estelle. You know how I hate it.'

Estelle was too worried about her grandmother's health to care if she annoyed her this time. 'Whether you will admit it or not I can see by the grey pallor to your skin that you're not well. You have to let me call the doctor to come and see you.'

'Why?' She scowled at Estelle. 'I don't see the point in paying for a visit when we both know he has nothing in the way of medicines to give me. Even poor Mrs Le Blancq from the village is now having to cope without her rheumatism medication and she's in a dreadful way. Supplies just aren't getting through to us. They're struggling terribly at the hospital.'

Estelle didn't add that it would reassure her a little if the doctor checked her, just to know Gran was healthier than she looked or sounded. 'Fine. Then if you won't see him, at least let me finish this and get yourself indoors. It's too cold for you to be out here.'

Her grandmother slammed the sheet down on to the mangle. 'It's hardly much warmer inside, though, is it?'

Estelle puffed out her cheeks. 'You're ill, whether you want to admit it, or not.'

'I'm only a little worse today,' she argued, not looking Estelle in the eye.

'I disagree. But you leaving me to finish this and going indoors to change into dry clothes makes a lot of sense to me right now. It should do to you, too.' She indicated her grandmother's wet clothes. 'Well?'

Her grandmother groaned, irritated no doubt to be beaten in this difference of opinion. 'I'll go inside then, but no doctor.'

'Fine. No doctor.' Estelle was happy to agree to anything if it meant her grandmother taking things easy for a while. 'Why don't you make a hot drink and sit down and put your feet up for a while. Please.'

The old lady nodded and walked out of the washhouse. Estelle watched her go. She was much slower than usual and despite her irritation at being told what to do she seemed lethargic and fragile. She was going to have to watch her closely over the next few days and probably weeks.

Estelle carried on with the washing, putting the wet sheets through the mangle and then folded them to take them inside to hand on the wrack that came down from the kitchen ceiling. She didn't think there was any point hanging them outside, not with it being so cold.

Later that afternoon, Estelle heard a car. She peered down into the yard from the field and saw it stop and Hans step out. It must be later than she had realised. Just then her grandmother opened the back door and stepped out carrying a basket. She spotted Estelle and raised the basket weakly opening her mouth to say something when she collapsed on to the ground.

'*Gran!*' Estelle ran down the slope into the yard. By the time she reached her grandmother, Hans was kneeling over her, his left arm under her head and the back of his right hand resting on her forehead.

He looked up at Estelle gravely. 'She is very ill. I have

seen this before. There is an outbreak in town of diphtheria and many of our soldiers have been taken ill with it.'

Estelle's heart pounded with fright. 'What can we do?' She asked, her voice cracking with emotion, furious with herself for not insisting on going to fetch the doctor earlier.

'Bring me a blanket. My driver and I will take her to the hospital immediately.'

Estelle ran inside, grabbed a crocheted blanket from the back of her grandmother's chair and rushed back outside. 'Here,' she said, holding it out for him to take. Hans was crouched in the vehicle, talking in a soothing voice to her unconscious grandmother. He took the blanket from Estelle and covered her grandmother, then shouted an order she didn't understand to the driver who seemed reluctant to get back into the car.

'May I come with you?'

He shook his head and took her by the shoulders. 'There is no room. I'm sorry. We will take her to the hospital and I will return and let you know what the doctors say. Please, try not to worry.'

Estelle stood back, wishing desperately that she could accompany them but aware that to argue would only delay her grandmother reaching medical help.

He got into the car without another word and she watched them drive away.

Estelle spent several frantic hours doing her best to keep busy. Finally, just before seven in the evening, she heard the car pull up outside the house and was opening the back door in the kitchen just as he closed the car door and began striding towards her.

'Come inside,' he said his expression stony. 'It is too cold outside.' He ushered her into the kitchen and closed the door.

'What did the doctor say? Will she be all right?' She was so tired with worry and close to tears.

Hans took off his cap and coat and hung them up over her father's jacket on the hook. She wondered if he was giving himself a little time to try to decide what to say to her. The thought made her even more anxious. He turned back to face her.

'Please,' she pleaded. 'Tell me. I'd rather know. How bad is it?'

'She is very sick, Estelle,' he said his expression solemn. 'Frau Woods has diphtheria, as I suspected.'

Estelle gasped and covered her mouth with her hands briefly. 'Can I go and see her?'

He shook his head. 'It is highly contagious.' He rested his right hand on her arm. 'You will need to be careful in case you've also contracted it.'

Estelle thought about Hans and how he had rushed her grandmother in his car to the hospital. 'But what about you and your driver? You could have caught it from her, too?'

'We will see. She was unconscious the whole way to the hospital and the doctor told me that the disease is passed by coughing and sneezing.'

She thought of what he had told her earlier. 'You said

that there had been an outbreak on the island. How are they going to deal with something infectious if there's no medicine getting through?' She thought everyone must be suffering from a lack of food, especially fruit, and must have little defence against illnesses like this one that she knew could be deadly. 'I couldn't bear losing Gran too, Hans,' she suddenly cried out. 'I'll have no one left to face all this with.'

He looked down at the floor and Estelle could tell he was battling with whether or not to tell her something.

'What? There's something you're not telling me?'

He pressed the tips of his fingers against his eyelids and exhaled sharply.

'Hans. Tell me, please.'

He lowered his hands and, after a second's hesitation, said, 'Your grandmother will be fine. I made one of the nurses on the German ward give me a phial of the diphtheria antitoxin. I took it to the doctor treating Frau Woods and he assured me he would give it to her. So, please try not to worry.'

'You did that for her?'

'And for you.'

Estelle stared at him unsure what to say. 'I'll never be able to repay you if you've saved her life, Hans. Never.'

He stared into her eyes looking sadder than she had ever seen him look before. 'You have no need to repay me, Estelle. I am happy to do this for you.'

'But could you get into trouble for doing this?'

He waved his hand. 'It is of no matter.'

'Can't the German doctors share their medicines with

the local ones to help the islanders?' she asked. Surely, as a doctor, they must wish to help all people who come into the hospital suffering from a sickness.

'There is very little in their stocks, too, I'm told.' His voice was quiet and Estelle could tell just what a chance he had taken helping her grandmother like he had.

She sensed he wanted to move away from talking about it. 'If there's no medicine then how are the staff at the hospital going to be able to stop the disease spreading?'

'I am told that they isolate the sick from the healthy until the virus runs its course. Which is why –' he gave her arm a gentle squeeze – 'you are unable to visit your grandmother at the hospital until she is well again.'

'I have to see her, though. What if she needs me for something?'

He shook his head. 'There is no option, I'm afraid. She will be well looked after by your nurses and doctor. They are used to coping with disease. You have to put your trust in them, Estelle, and hope she recovers soon.'

Estelle thought of the nurses and doctor working tirelessly to care for the locals. She had heard that their wards were below the ones for the German soldiers who were now cared for by German nurses brought over from Germany to relieve the local nurses to care for the islanders.

'It appears I have no choice, then.' She felt like crying. What if she had seen her grandmother for the last time and their final conversation had been one where she had irritated her? Why hadn't she called for an ambulance when she knew her to be ill? She voiced her angst to Hans and lowered her head into her hands.

'Even if you had called for an ambulance, you know as well as I do that the horse-drawn vehicle would not have arrived here and been able to deliver your grandmother back to the hospital quicker than my driver did.'

He was right. 'I just feel so hopeless. I'm not sure what to do?'

'It is hard, but you must carry on looking after the farm. If you need me to, I will help you.'

She smiled at him. 'Thank you. Yes, I suppose staying busy will help keep my mind from worrying. How will I know how she's doing though?'

'Will it make you happy if I make it my duty to visit the hospital each day and ask after Frau Woods for you? I can then report back to you on my return each evening?'

Estelle didn't think she could be more grateful to anyone at that moment. Without thinking, she twisted in her seat and put her arms around him. 'Thank you,' she said. 'I don't know what I would have done without you today.' Her throat tightened and she tried to push back the threatening tears. 'If my grandmother survives this then it will be down to your selflessness.' Unable to hold back any longer, Estelle began to cry. 'And your bravery and quick reactions,' she sobbed. She turned away, embarrassed.

'Estelle?' Hans whispered. She couldn't speak as she tried to gather herself. 'Estelle, your grandmother will be fine, I am sure of it.' He took her by her upper arms and gently turned her around to face him. Estelle looked up at him his blue eyes filled with emotion as he gazed at her. She was so full of gratitude and relief that her grandmother now had a chance because of him.

Hans slowly went to move away from her. Without thinking, she slipped her arms around his neck and kissed him. Gratitude merged into something else, into desire and longing. His arms circled her, pulling her tightly against him as he kissed her back. She had never been kissed like this before.

Rebel growled, bringing them both back to reality, but Estelle opened her eyes and wished more than anything she could stay exactly where she was. She let herself feel everything she had been holding back from. She loved Hans, deeply.

He looked stunned and his hands fell away from her. 'I'm sorry,' he said, pushing her away from him carefully. 'I do not know what I was thinking.'

She hated to see him so ashamed by what he'd done. She wanted to reassure him then thought of Gerard locked in a prisoner-of-war camp while she was kissing an enemy officer, and guilt coursed through her. She had crossed a dreadful line.

He cleared his throat. 'This is wrong. We must not do this again.'

Estelle nodded. 'I'm – I'm sorry.' If anything more were to happen between them, it would only lead to misery – for them both.

Shaken by what had just happened, Estelle watched him leave the kitchen. She had loved Gerard since she was fourteen. She knew she loved him. But she knew now that what she felt for Gerard was a gentle, sweet love and might not be the all-encompassing passion she had just experienced. But how could she betray him in such a way?

And how could someone as kind and willing to put his own freedom at risk be her enemy? Hans was a good man. Hadn't he proved that today?

That wasn't the point, though. Their countries were at war. It simply couldn't be.

FORTY

Estelle

E stelle was desperate to see her grandmother again. It was nearly eight weeks since she had been taken ill and today she was being brought home to complete her recuperation at the farm. Estelle was determined to be much stricter with her. It would be a relief to have Gran back home again. Disease was rife on the island. Countless islanders and Germans had died from diphtheria and illness because there were no medicines getting through to the island. Her grandmother had been very fortunate.

Since their kiss, Hans had made excuses to be out for much of the time, only returning late when he assumed she would be in bed. At least that was how it seemed to Estelle. She missed his company but was relieved not to have to see him too much in case she inadvertently showed her feelings for him again. She had to find a way to forget him. There was no other way.

It has been lonely on the farm with only Rebel to speak to.

Now, though, the weather was getting warmer, the spuds were ready to be harvested and Hans had promised to help her and the three farmhands work the fields in his free time. It seemed that as long as they were in different parts of the field he was happy to help.

Estelle wanted everything to be ready for her grandmother's return and spent the morning cleaning and dusting and making up her bed with fresh bed linen. She had placed a small tray with a jug of fresh water and a glass in case her gran was thirsty when Estelle was out working on the fields and a vase of wildflowers she had picked earlier from the garden sat on her grandmother's dressing table to brighten the room. She left a pan of thick vegetable soup on the side of the range to be eaten with a small fresh loaf of wholemeal bread she had brought earlier that day from Mr Gibault.

'Here, love,' he said, popping out to the back of his shop and returning with a small fillet of fish. 'Give this to your gran for her supper, it'll do her good.'

Violet had come to the house earlier with a bunch of wildflowers, which Estelle had placed in Gran's favourite vase and set on the kitchen table. It would be one of the first things she would see when she arrived home.

It occurred to Estelle that her gran might want a picture of her husband by her bed. There was one in the living room on the mantelpiece, but she thought it might be nice for her to have one closer to her. She ran up the stairs to take a quick look though Gran's drawers to see if she could find one. Recalling her gran mentioning keeping something in an old suitcase, she looked towards the top of the wardrobe where she knew it had once been, but it wasn't there. Maybe it's under the bed? she thought bending down to have a look.

She smiled to see the old suitcase lying there and then noticed her father's shotgun sticking out from behind the case. So that's where it went? They were lucky not to have been searched. She opened the suitcase to look inside and noticed an envelope addressed to Esther Woods inside.

'Esther?' she said aloud to herself. Her grandmother's name was Marnie, at least that's what her father and Violet had always called her.

'You didn't know?' Hans asked from the bedroom doorway.

She dropped the envelope, in shock to hear his voice so unexpectedly. Quickly, she closed the lid of the case and pushed it back under the bed to ensure he didn't see the shotgun. She hadn't heard him come back and wished she'd thought to close the bedroom door. 'Know what?' she asked standing.

'That your grandmother is Jewish.'

'What? Don't be ridiculous. What on earth makes you say that?' But as she asked the question, Estelle began to recall the strange and distracted way her grandmother had been acting, especially when the orders for Jewish islanders to register had come into force.

She had been so anxious. Wait, not anxious, Estelle thought. Terrified.

'Her name is not Marnie. She is Esther Woods.'

How did she not know? Her grandmother had been hiding such an enormous, terrible secret all this time. Living with the fear that any moment the Germans could have knocked down their door and dragged them away?

'*You knew?*' She stared at him in disbelief. 'You knew and you didn't report her?'

'Yes.'

'I don't understand. How did you find out when I didn't even know?' How oblivious must she be not to know this about the person closest in the world to her?

'I have suspected she was hiding something for a long time but it was when her friend Mrs Green was taken away and I happened to come across her burning papers early one morning. She told me everything but she didn't beg me not to report her. All she did was ask that I made sure you would be all right. Her first thought was for your safety.'

Estelle folded her arms across her chest. 'For my sake? Why?'

'Estelle, if your grandparent is Jewish, then so are you. She wasn't afraid for herself but trying to protect you.'

'But you haven't reported her. You kept her secret for her.'

'I was honoured to. Your grandmother is a fine woman. Generous and kind. Brave. I only wish I could have helped more people in her situation.' He shook his head sadly. 'I am loyal to the Fatherland, to my people, *but* my country is not my country any more.'

Later that day, Estelle sat at the end of her grandmother's bed. She was still stunned by her earlier discovery and now that her grandmother was settled she needed to speak to her about it. She hadn't been this happy for weeks, she realised, pushing aside her guilty memory of how blissful it had felt to kiss Hans.

Her grandmother gazed at the flowers on her dressing table and then looked at Estelle and smiled. 'It's so good to be back home again, my love. I've missed you and this place.'

Estelle took her grandmother's hand in hers. 'I can't tell you how much I've missed having you here. Now, you are going to do as I tell you and take things easy. Agreed?'

Her grandmother grinned. 'Yes. I've learnt my lesson. Probably.' She laughed. Then patting Estelle's hand asked, 'How has it been with just you and Hans living in the house alone?'

Estelle couldn't meet her grandmother's eye. 'It was a little awkward at first, but he's been very busy and out most of the time.'

'I don't like to think of you alone here for long periods of time.' She frowned, a thoughtful expression on her thin face which Estelle noticed for the first time seemed to have many more lines than she had ever noticed before.

She took a deep breath. 'We need to talk and I think you know what about.'

Her grandmother stared at her silently for a few seconds before patting Estelle's hand. 'About me lying on my Identity Card when I've always insisted that liars are beneath contempt.'

'I think it's a little more than that, don't you?' she said. 'Why did you never trust me enough to be honest with me?'

'To protect you, Estelle. I didn't want you to have to worry about what I'd done.'

'You took such a risk. How did you think you could get away with keeping this to yourself?'

Her grandmother smiled. 'I almost did.' When Estelle raised an eyebrow in irritation, the older woman continued, 'I grew up attending the synagogue in London but I haven't been practicing my faith since coming to live in Jersey, so apart from my friend Rachel Green.' She shook her head slowly. 'Poor Rachel. I can't bear to thing what they did to her.' She collected herself and continued. 'No one apart from your father, of course, knew that I was Jewish. I thought that if I kept it to myself there was little chance of anyone ever finding out.'

Her grandmother turned her head to stare out of the window, thoughtfully. 'I've kept abreast of the increased harassment of Jews across Europe for years now, heard stories from friends and cousins living on the continent. So when the war began I knew I had to hide my identity. I had to take a chance when the Germans ordered all Jews on the island to register and withhold the truth because if I was honest then you would also be sent to a camp and I couldn't bear for that to happen.

'Because I'm from the mainland, another fact also withheld, the Germans had no way of checking my religion because there are no records of me here. I felt I had nothing to lose by lying about my background when registering for my Identity Card. I admit I did feel rather guilty at first for lying to you but your welfare is more important to me than anything else and for that I have no regrets.'

'But Hans knows,' Estelle said.

'He's a good man, Estelle.' Her grandmother gave her a solemn look. 'One of very few that I've come across. I'll be forever grateful to him.'

'As will I,' she said, honestly.

'And you understand my reasons behind my decision?'

'I do.'

Her grandmother smiled and gave Estelle's hand a gentle squeeze. 'Thank you. I hoped that when you found out what I'd done that you'd know I did it for the best.'

She put her arms around her grandmother and gave her a kiss on the cheek. 'Always.'

A week or so later, Estelle and her grandmother saw first-hand just how much of a risk they were taking. Estelle had been to Mr Gibault's to hear that he didn't have any of the items she needed and that she should try Louisa Gould's shop on the other side of the village. It was a longer walk but today Estelle didn't mind.

Several German cars sped along the road and Estelle stepped back to avoid them. Something was amiss. She had no idea what was going on but her instincts told her to turn around and go home. If she was wrong then she could go shopping again tomorrow. But what if she was right?

She was on her way into the house when Violet stepped out of the back door.

'You're leaving?' she asked, surprised when Violet

didn't return her smile. 'Is something the matter, Mrs Le Marrec?'

'I'll leave your gran to tell you everything. But something dreadful has happened, Estelle.' She lowered her voice to a whisper. 'Those bastards have arrested Louisa Gould and her maid.'

Estelle was shocked. She'd never heard Violet speak in such a way before. 'When?'

'Just now. And I believe her sister, Ivy, was arrested, too, but at her house, and her brother and someone else. I don't know the whole story yet, but I do know it's bad.' She clasped her handbag to her chest. 'I'd better get home. To think it was only down the road from us.' She shook her head. 'Poor women. I do hope they let them off, but I can't see that happening, not after what they did.'

'What on earth did they do?' Estelle couldn't imagine the kindly lady who had lost one of her sons at the beginning of the war being capable of doing anything too drastic to the Nazis.

Estelle ran inside. 'Gran? Gran, where are you?'

'I'm here,' she said walking into the hall.

'Violet just said...'

'I know. Come.'

Estelle listened to her grandmother and shuddered. 'She housed a prisoner? But Gran, that means... Ivan?' Her words trailed off as her grandmother shook her head and the seriousness of what they had done for the poor man in the past sank in. 'But what's going to happen to them? If it wasn't Ivan, did they find the man she was sheltering?'

'Violet says not. Apparently, someone warned Louisa in

time for him to escape out the back but in the rush he left something behind, a book I think, and now the Germans have the evidence that she was sheltering a Russian.' She placed a hand on her chest. 'What is the world coming to when we are persecuted for helping others less fortunate than ourselves?'

'Who told on her, that's what I'd like to know?' Estelle said, furious that someone Mrs Gould knew could have told the Germans about her sheltering an escaped slave. How else would they have known he was there?

FORTY-ONE

Estelle

7 JUNE 1944

E stelle helped her grandmother deadhead her roses in the front garden as another distant boom sounded. She couldn't believe that what they were hearing was coming from across the water in Normandy. They'd heard on the wireless that it was Allies advancing. D-Day everyone was calling it. 'Do you think they'll come to the Channel Islands next, Gran?'

'Everyone thinks so and I hope they're right.' She carried her wicker trug filled with the cut flowers she was collecting to brighten the house on to the next border. 'I always have to remember to be careful not to disturb the carrots and mange tout we're growing among these flowers. I look forward to a time when my flower borders aren't part vegetable garden.'

'We're lucky we have our veg garden, Gran,' Estelle grinned. 'If this was our only growing space we'd have had to forgo all our flowers these past few years.'

She heard her grandmother mumble something under her breath before saying, 'Never mind that. Four years has been more than long enough.' She lifted a pink rose to her nose and breathed in the rich scent. 'I hardly dare believe it though.'

Estelle knew what she meant. She dared to let herself hope that liberation might soon be coming to their small group of islands.

Her gran put down her trug, walked over to Estelle and held the rose up to her nose to smell it. 'This to me smells of happiness,' she said. 'It won't be long now, my girl. Who knows maybe Rosie will be home with us in a few short weeks? Then we can spend the rest of the summer enjoying the garden and slowly rebuilding all that we've gone without. This island will come back from this, you mark my words. We might be a little battle sore but we're tougher than we appear.'

Estelle gasped. 'Do you really think so?'

'I'm hoping so and, what's more, you never know.'

Another louder boom. They stood in the garden staring over in the direction of the bombs. Estelle smiled. Never mind Gran's smell of happiness being the scent of tea roses, to her the sound of freedom was what she was hearing now. Or at least she hoped it was.

It was a glorious day made even more fun by a visit from Antoinette who came from town with Louis to relax with them in the garden for a couple of hours.

Estelle sat with Antoinette and her grandmother watching as the little boy threw Rebel's ball and giggled excitedly each time Rebel fetched it and brought it back to him dropping it at the boy's feet.

Another boom made Antoinette flinch.

'You all right?' Estelle asked.

She leant forward in her chair resting her elbows on her knees as she watched her son. 'I know the sounds of those bombs is good news for us, but I can't help worrying what's happening to Paul each time I hear one go off.'

Estelle experienced a rush of guilt towards Gerard. Why hadn't she thought of that too? Gerard deserved so much better. Did she still love as she once had, or was it that he just belonged to another life, the one they'd shared before the war?

'We'll most likely be free from this hell soon,' Antoinette said, thoughtfully. 'But what about Paul and Gerard and all the other people who've been deported from the island? How soon will they be home, do you think?'

Estelle had no idea and said so.

Her grandmother caught her eye and motioned to the other side of the house. Estelle wasn't sure what she was trying to tell her at first but then heard the familiar sound of the car dropping Hans off. She didn't think Antoinette had met him yet and didn't want her friend to see how relaxed he was with them and get the wrong idea.

Antoinette began speaking again but Estelle was too busy listening out for the unmistakable sound of Hans's footsteps. Rebel ran past Louie and the little boy screamed in excitement. Seconds later, Estelle heard Hans running around the side of the house, no doubt to see what was wrong in the garden. Antoinette saw him and, leaping out of her chair, ran towards Louis in panic.

Estelle glanced back at the house coming face to face with Hans as he came around the corner. He was ashen and not his usually collected self. In fact, she thought, he was in a bit of a state. He stopped suddenly when he saw the three women.

'I thought…' He noticed Antoinette and gave her a curt nod. 'I apologise. I heard the child and was worried something had happened.'

Antoinette clasped Louis tightly to her. Louis burst into noisy tears, his eyes wide with fright at the sudden change in his mother's mood.

'It's fine, Captain Bauer,' Estelle said, noticing his surprise at the formal use of his name before he managed to correct himself. 'There's nothing to be concerned about. This is my friend Antoinette and her son, Louis.' She smiled, hoping to lighten the change in atmosphere. 'He was playing with Rebel's ball and got a little excited, bless him.'

'I see.'

There was another distant boom, slightly louder than the last and Estelle saw something cross his face. Was it fear? The end to this occupation that would bring such joy to her meant defeat for Hans. She gazed at his handsome face and recalled how his kiss had made her feel and all the kind things he had done for her and her grandmother, but try as she might, she couldn't feel sympathy for his countrymen. He was a good man but the Nazis had no right taking over the Channel Islands when they were at their weakest and she longed to see the back of them and a return to her previous life.

Gran gestured at Antoinette, and Estelle realised she hadn't introduced Hans to her yet. 'This is our friend Antoinette Hubert,' her grandmother said. 'Antoinette, please meet Captain Bauer. He is the officer Estelle must have told you about. He has been billeted here at Beau Bois Farm since early in the war.' Gran smiled at Hans. 'He has been a gentlemanly house guest, but I'm sure he will be as pleased as us when this is all over and he can return to his life back in Germany.' She looked at him. 'Won't you?'

He appeared to have to think before answering her question. 'We have not lost the war just yet, Frau Woods.'

'By the sounds of those explosions, it won't be long, I shouldn't wonder.' Antoinette loosened her grip on her son and watched as he picked up Rebel's ball and gave it another throw.

'I will wish you all a good day. I have a report to write in my room. It was good to meet you, Frau Hubert.' He gave a nod to Estelle and her grandmother. 'Frau Woods, Miss Le Maistre,' he said before turning and retracing his steps.

They sat and chatted with Antoinette for another hour, their conversation a little stilted at first, but Antoinette soon relaxed and seemed to forget about Hans being at the farm. It really was such a glorious day, Estelle thought, resting back in her seat and closing her eyes listening to her friend's laughter as she played ball with her son.

From the sound of the distant explosions, they would

soon be able to enjoy their freedom again, she mused. Rosie would come back and they would all be together again. Her heart ached to think that her father wouldn't be with them when their lives returned to normal again. Later in the month, it would be the fourth anniversary since his murder. She had certainly tried to do her best for the farm, but still missed him very much.

How different it would have been if Papa was still alive. He would have run things much better than her, but she doubted he would have found it easy having a German Officer living in their home. Either way, Hans would soon be gone and everything would have to find a way back to normal. She couldn't bring herself to contemplate what it would be like without his presence in the house so instead she focused on the thoughts of her resuming once more.

During that evening's supper – or what they could call supper – Estelle and Gran found it difficult to suppress their excitement. They could hear how close to the islands the Allied Forces were. It was only a matter of time now before they were liberated. Days maybe.

'You haven't eaten much of your supper, Hans,' Gran said. 'I'm sorry it's mainly vegetables again and only a little fish, but that was all Estelle could buy for us at the shop this morning.'

He moved the food around his plate absent-mindedly. 'I am sorry, Frau Woods. I do not wish to be ungrateful but my appetite is not what it should be today.'

Estelle could feel her gran's eyes on her but refused to look at her. They both knew exactly why he had lost his appetite. If the situation was reversed they would surely feel the same way. He looked so downcast. Maybe the thought of the mighty Third Reich losing the war after all the certainty the soldiers had possessed these past four years was worse than knowing he was able to return home? Maybe he felt humiliated on behalf of his country, whose soldiers had marched on to their island from their troop ships with their chests puffed out and heads held high. But hadn't he said his country was not his country any more? She knew he didn't condone the brutality and inhumanity of the Nazis. He wasn't one of them.

'I must admit,' he said eventually, placing his knife and fork down on to his plate, 'I will always be grateful to have spent my war here on this island with you both.'

A week later, the islander's euphoria that they would soon be rescued by the Allied Forces had all but vanished.

'Why do you think they've abandoned us, Gran?' Estelle asked, frustration brimming over one morning just after Hans had left for the day. 'They were so close and it doesn't make any sense to come so far and then pass us by.'

Gran pulled her into a hug, her bony arms holding tightly around her. 'I've no idea, my love. We have to trust they've done so for the best reasons, not that I can work out what they might be.'

'I thought it would all be over by now,' she said.

Gran sighed heavily. 'So, did I, my love, so did I.' She held on to Estelle and then after a short while let her go and took her face in her hands.

'Now,' her grandmother said pointing to the back door, 'you need to get back out to the fields and carry on with harvesting those remaining Royals. We can't allow any to go to waste.'

Estelle nodded and slipped her feet into her dusty boots. She was being helped by several of the local women during the day and their sons or nephews came to the farm after they had finished school each day to lend a hand with the harvesting. Hans had helped her each evening or when he wasn't on duty and slowly they were making their way across the top field. It was backbreaking work but Estelle was happy to keep her mind busy and focused on something useful like food.

She had been working for a few hours when she heard the sound of a plane and looked up. 'It's British!' Estelle exclaimed delighted to see an RAF plane flying over St Ouen. She pointed towards the plane and the others looked up and several of the boys cheered.

'Is it a Spitfire?' Elise Hamon asked.

'No. That is a Hawker Typhoon,' she heard Hans say.

How unnerving must it be for him to see a British plane over the parish? Seconds later, she heard anti-aircraft fire fill the air quickly followed by a shriek from one of the women. Estelle looked up and to her horror saw that the aircraft had been struck.

'It's on fire,' someone cried out.

Estelle dropped the potatoes she was holding and clenched her fists willing the pilot to bale out not knowing if it was even possible for him to do so. All of them stood staring upwards at the plane as it plummeted downwards.

Estelle gasped at the sound of the explosion that followed. 'No! that poor, poor man. I hope he manages to survive.'

'I don't think he will have done,' Hans said quietly from two rows away.

Estelle shuddered. Would there ever again be anything to make them smile?

FORTY-TWO

Rosie

JULY 1944

I t's very frustrating not being able to share my news with you in person especially when so much has happened recently. I'm fine, but if I'm honest with you, I almost wasn't.

We're now living with Queenie in her flat that for her alone was probably big but with me and Aunt Muriel and one of Queenie's nieces it's a little cramped. Not that Aunt Muriel and I have anything much any more since a couple of days ago. We were out, thankfully, walking to Ravenscourt Park to meet Lynne and Billy for a bit of a picnic when we all heard a doodlebug and looked up. You have to watch to see when the engine cuts out and hope that when it does that you're nowhere near it because they drop like explosive boulders and obliterate everything around it. And that's what it did to our lovely little flat. The whole house in fact, and the ones either side.

We didn't realise of course until we arrived back home, but we knew it was somewhere near to where we lived, so the picnic was forgotten as we rushed back and that's when we saw the devastation. Oh Essie, it was such a mess. Everything apart from the clothes I was wearing and my handbag with my hairbrush and papers have all gone. We all clung to each other and cried.

But now we're living with Queenie. She's very kindly found us other clothes that some of her stallholder friends have donated to us, which was wonderfully generous of them. Aunt Muriel said that we might have lost our possessions but we still have our lives and each other and that, quite rightly, is what matters.

More news! I've joined the Women's Voluntary Service with Aunt Muriel and doing things like serving hot drinks to soldiers arriving home at the railway station. I've also helped out at the clothing centres where people, like us, who have lost everything can go to be given a change of clothes. To be honest, it was her who suggested I join because I was too nervous to be left each time she went to work. So, now I'm sixteen, I can finally feel like I'm almost a grown up and that I'm doing my bit to help the war effort.

I wish I could hear all your news, Essie. I think about you and Gran and pray for you a lot. We thought you would be rescued after D-Day last month, but Aunt Muriel said that the British Forces were probably too frightened about any repercussions towards the Channel Islanders if they tried to liberate you. I pray this will all end soon.

FORTY-THREE

Estelle

7 SEPTEMBER 1944

The summer dragged on and instead of the Allied Forces making an appearance like she and Gran had hoped everything got worse. Much worse.

'What do you mean there's nothing today?' she asked Mr Gibault having queued outside his shop for an hour before opening time to ensure she was able to buy something.

'You know I'd tell you if I had something, Estelle,' he said looking much thinner, and worn out, than he had done at the beginning of the war. 'But what can I do. Since the supply lines were cut by the allies on the sixth of June, the Jerries have been unable to bring in the meagre rations they had been sending over here for us all.' He pushed her ration book back to her. 'We're not the only ones starving either. The Jerries are suffering as much as we are with this lack of food.'

'But what are we supposed to do?' she asked trying not to panic. 'I've been foraging each day for berries and whatever I can find, but there's so little around now that everyone's doing the same thing.'

He bent forward and lowered his voice. 'If you still have that chicken of yours I'd take her inside at night-time, just to be sure no one steals her.'

'We already do, Mr Gibault,' Estelle said. 'Gran is beside herself ever since last week when someone came and stole our pig. She's terrified they'll come back and take Clara, too, that's the chicken. Or even Rebel, so she won't let him out at night or even in the daytime by himself any more.'

'She's a sensible woman that grandmother of yours. You'll do well to pay good attention to her.'

'I do, Mr Gibault,' Estelle reassured him.

'I wonder if the RAF will drop more of those paper bombs we've been getting since the end of August?'

Estelle thought of the thousands of papers that had been dropped over the island for almost two weeks. She recalled her excitement when seeing the papers floating down on to the farm on the first day, running to grab one but frustrated when she realised it was in German and she couldn't understand it. She had shown it to Hans later that day and watched him read it silently, a scowl on his face.

'I asked him what it said,' she explained to the shopkeeper. 'And he told me that the allies were ordering them to surrender.'

'I bet he didn't take kindly to that?' Mr Gibault smiled. It was the first time Estelle had seen him do so for months and it cheered her slightly.

She pictured Hans as he screwed up the leaflet and marched into the farmhouse without saying another word.

'Do you think they'll surrender, Mr Gibault?' Estelle asked hopefully.

He raised his hands, then dropped them to his sides. 'I would like to think so, but I can't see it happening, and I have a horrible feeling that the allies intend keeping us under siege until we either starve to death or the Jerries do give up and wave their white flags. Somehow, I can't see that happening for a long while yet. Can you?'

Estelle shook her head miserably. 'It's more frightening than ever now that they seem to feel as under siege as we do.'

———————

Estelle heard the commotion in the yard as she neared the farm. Breaking into a run she heard Hans's deep voice shouting at someone. She reached the yard breathless to see him holding a young boy by the collar.

'Hans? What's happened?'

Then she spotted Hans's other hand. He was holding Clara the chicken and it was clear that she was dead. Estelle cried out, dropping her basket, and ran to take her chicken's lifeless body from him.

'Did you do this?' she shouted at the boy through her tears.

'Tell her!' Hans glared at the boy who Estelle could see was clearly terrified.

'I... My mum... W... we...'

Estelle looked at the skinny boy, who she recognised as being Chantal's oldest son. 'Your mum sent you to do this, didn't she?' Estelle asked, aware that as much as she might be hungry the thought of killing Clara to eat her was something she would never have been able to do. 'It's all right,' she said, motioning for Hans to let the boy go. 'He's only doing what his mum has told him to do.'

'I was only going to take the bird,' he sobbed. 'I didn't mean to kill it, but I fell over when he came back and chased me.' He glared at Hans. 'It's your fault the bird is dead, you Jerry b—'

'*That's enough!*' Estelle shouted. She could see by the expression on Hans's face that the boy was speaking the truth. She thought of the times he had helped her feed the chickens and clean them out and knew he would be as upset as her about Clara's demise. 'I've got some blackberries and apples that you can take home to your mum, but you need to leave the chicken here.'

Hans let go of the boy's collar and the boy nodded. 'Thanks, Miss. I daren't go home empty-handed. She'll go barmy if I do that.'

'You won't have to. Tell her we were here so you were unable to take the chicken. You can say you found the fruit on the way home. All right?'

He nodded slowly. 'I'm sorry, Miss.'

'I don't want to see you here again. Do you understand?'

'Yes, Miss.'

'We have nothing left for you to steal, so there's really no point in coming back.'

Hans took a deep breath. 'And I will be watching out for you next time.'

The boy gave him a sideways glance. 'Don't worry. I'm not coming here again.'

Estelle told the boy to follow her. She collected her basket and took it inside. Then finding an old tin scooped several handfuls into it. There were a few apples in a fruit bowl on the kitchen table waiting for stewing that evening. 'Take these. Now, get going before my grandmother discovers what you've done, or there'll be hell to pay.'

'All right, I'm goin'.' He reached the kitchen door and turned back to face Estelle. 'Thanks for these, Miss. Me mum will have given me a cuff around the ear if I'd gone home with nothin'.'

She wasn't surprised to hear it. Estelle couldn't imagine any mother being harsh with their children especially over something like this. Although it must be terrifying not having enough to feed your children, she thought trying to see things from Chantal's point of view. None of them could do much about the scarcity of the food on the island, especially not a young boy. 'Right, off you go.'

He had only been gone a few seconds when her grandmother rushed into the room. 'What's all the racket outside? Are those blackberries?' she grinned, picking one up and popping it into her mouth. She closed her eyes and Estelle could see how delighted she was to taste the sweet fruit.

Estelle watched her eat another few blackberries. Let her enjoy them while she can, she thought miserably. How was she going to break the news about Clara?

FORTY-FOUR

Rosie

W*e're very worried about you and Gran, Essie. Aunt Muriel has heard that there is no food reaching the island since D-Day. I know you're clever and will have thought of something, but I can't think what. We don't have much here, but Aunt Muriel insists we have a lot more than everyone in the Channel Islands. How are you surviving? What will you do when the food runs out? I know you'll hate to eat the chickens, but Aunt Muriel said that you will have no choice and that having been brought up on a farm you will understand that. I tried to tell her that our farm was mostly crops but she didn't seem to understand there was a difference, which I found odd.*

Every time I don't like something Aunt Muriel has cooked for me or the dinners at school I make myself eat them knowing that you would be grateful to have the chance to do so. Oh, Essie, please, please think of something. I know this will all be over soon. It has to be, surely? It can't be too much longer. Aunt Muriel says that it's like running a cross country race where you are so exhausted near the end that you think you've run out of energy but you have to dig deep and find it somehow.

Dig deep, Essie. I know you can't hear me but maybe if I wish or pray hard enough you'll know that I'm willing you to keep going. I can't bear the thought of not seeing you and Gran again. I know that I will and I know that one day we'll be able to go down to Greve de Lecq with our swimsuits and lie on the warm golden sand with our toes in the sea and share a picnic and share all our experiences while we've been apart. Please keep fighting, Essie. For me.

FORTY-FIVE

Estelle

DECEMBER 1944

E stelle stood in front of her grandmother's pantry with one hand on the open door and the other resting on her bony hip. It was pouring with rain outside, yet again. In fact, Estelle thought miserably it hadn't seemed to stop raining for the past three months. In November, the Germans had come to the farm and inspected it, making a list of their food and meagre stocks. It hadn't taken long and a week ago they had returned and taken all the potatoes and vegetables she and Gran had left. Estelle was relieved they didn't still have her father's cows from before the war when she heard that the Jerries had started slaughtering all the cattle to feed their troops.

The pantry shelves offered no solace. They were completely bare. Nothing was left. They had long ago used all the tins of food that had been sitting at the back of the shelves gathering dust because no one fancied eating whatever was in them. At least in September they had been able to eat fruit and other foods that Estelle had foraged for, but now the weather was very cold and miserable and all she could think about was how her hunger seemed to gnaw at her stomach. She was starving, they all were – ever since the food supplies had been cut off after D-Day, the Jerries hadn't been able to bring anything through France and into the island. She had always been slim but hated catching sight of herself in the bathroom mirror and seeing how gaunt she looked. She had no idea how long her grandmother's health would keep up if this carried on for much longer. Why did the British Forces not do something? Didn't they know how much they were all suffering? Wasn't it bad enough to live under siege without being starved, too?

Estelle had heard rumours that the Red Cross would come and help them, but she had also listened to the same people insisting that the islands would be liberated back in June and that hadn't happened. It was difficult to keep her spirits up. There was no point sitting up in the darker evenings, so she and Gran took to their beds much earlier than they did earlier in the war. They may as well be warm, it wasn't as if they had anything to eat, or candles to be able to read books by. Estelle was beginning to think that they had been forgotten and that this was it for them all.

Hans had initially tried to bring back small amounts of food for them in the summer but that had soon run out and even he had lost weight. He rarely smiled now, too, and she wanted to comfort him but didn't dare let herself, fearful of what it would lead to and her previous disloyalty.

The thing that frightened her most, apart from not having enough to eat, was being able to find enough food to feed Rebel. She had heard other rumours of Germans stealing people's pets, what few remained, and eating them.

Christmas came and went and Estelle and Gran decided that it wasn't worth celebrating.

'What's the point,' her grandmother said. 'It's not as if we have any food or presents. Let's just leave it this year. I'd rather pretend it was an ordinary day. It will be less upsetting that way.'

Estelle readily agreed. She had no wish to try to make something of a day that just made them more miserable when they compared it to past Christmases when they were together as a family and their beautiful Christmas tree standing above carefully chosen and wrapped presents. No. This year was different. It was also the fifth Christmas without Rosie and her father. There was nothing to be thankful for this year.

Someone banged heavily on the back door. '*Estelle!*' The sound of Mr Gibault's voice coming from outside made her heart race.

She ran to the door and pulled it open waving for him to get inside. 'You're soaking wet. Are you all right?'

'Yes,' he said breathlessly. 'Something wonderful has happened. I'm going to all the neighbours' houses to let them know.'

'What is it?' she asked barely able to breathe.

'A Canadian Red Cross ship, the SS *Vega* has docked in St Helier. They've come from Lisbon, or so I'm told, and were in Guernsey before here. One of my customers told me a short while ago. He says they're carrying food parcels.'

Estelle knew her mouth had dropped open but it took a

few seconds for her to gain enough control to be able to close it again. Did he say food? 'Food parcels? For us? You're certain?'

'Yes. I'm told there's chocolate, biscuits, soap and marmalade. Estelle, you have to get down to Patriotic Street tomorrow. They'll be distributing them from there. You can collect a box for you and your grandmother.' He turned to leave. 'I have to get on and let more people know. He placed his hand on the door handle and turned his head to her smiling. 'Isn't this the best news? Well, almost the best news.'

'It is,' Estelle said barely able to conceal her emotion. 'Thank you so much for letting us know. I'll be there first thing tomorrow.'

She watched him leave and closed the door, leaning heavily against it. So, they hadn't been forgotten after all. She couldn't stop her tears from flowing for a couple of minutes. Then, wanting to let her grandmother know the good news as quickly as possible, she ran upstairs. It had been several days since Gran had bothered to get out of bed and the amount of time she lay dozing was worrying Estelle.

'*Gran! Gran!*' she shouted, bursting into her grandmother's bedroom.

Her grandmother rubbed her eyes and scowled at her. 'What's all the fuss about?'

Estelle pulled open the bedroom curtains and helped her grandmother to sit up in bed, fluffing up her pillows. Once she was comfortable, Estelle sat at the edge of the bed and told her about Mr Gibault's visit.

'What do you think of that then? This time tomorrow, we'll have food and even soap.' She was hoping this wasn't a dream, or that she might be going a little mad. 'I'll go down on my bike and bring back our two boxes.'

Her grandmother stared at her without saying anything.

'Did you hear what I said, Gran?' she asked taking the wrinkled hands in her own. 'The Red Cross have arrived at the harbour and they've brought us food.'

'I heard you, my girl.' She gave Estelle a tight smile. It was the first time Estelle had seen her smile for months and it was almost as if she had forgotten how to do it. 'Tomorrow is the thirty-first. Now that's what I call the perfect end to a rotten year. Maybe this bodes well for nineteen forty-five. I do hope so.'

So did Estelle. 'We're going to survive this. I just know we are.'

Her gran pulled one of her hands from Estelle's and rested it on her right cheek. 'I think you could be right, my love. If I'm honest, I was beginning to wonder how long I could manage to keep going. This has been such a long, exhausting battle.'

She moved forward and put her arms around her grandmother, hugging her bony body tightly. 'I was worried you might be giving up hope. I think this has come at just the right time for all of us.'

Her gran went to pour herself a glass of water from the small jug on her bedside table, but when Estelle saw how shaky her hand was, she took over.

It was the right time for everyone on the island, even the Germans. Many of the men were finding it especially difficult being stuck on the island when they learnt of how their own families were suffering in Germany. Several had committed suicide at the thought of being sent to the Eastern Front, a brutal war where Hans had lost his brothers and many friends. Estelle's feelings towards them were complicated. Men like Herr Fischer and the Operation Todt guards deserved everything they got.

But this was the first time in months that something had happened to give her hope and Estelle was going to enjoy every minute, and morsel, of it.

FORTY-SIX

Estelle

MARCH 1945

The islanders were feeling a little more positive and finally Estelle had the soap she had desperately craved. She luxuriated in the small bar that had come from the red cross and treated it like it was her most valuable possession. That, and the nutritious food brought to them on the three trips to the island by the SS *Vega* since December was the only good thing in their lives currently. The underlying tension caused by mounting resentment and the low morale of their occupiers was increasing to a frightening level and they were all extremely anxious wondering where it could all lead.

She understood the soldiers were starving and had to contend with the knowledge that they had pretty much lost the war, but did that necessitate them terrifying the islanders? She didn't think so. She thought back to cycling to see Antoinette a few weeks before. She had passed several buildings with swastikas painted on them in what looked like black paint, or possibly tar. If that wasn't bad enough three days before someone had retaliated by setting fire to the Palace Hotel, where German officers were living.

They had tried to stop the fire spreading but in doing so had ended up setting fire to a nearby ammunition store which gutted the hotel and several houses, killing and injuring soldiers and islanders. It was as if the relief in receiving the food was unable to balance out the horror of the increasing trouble.

Estelle had listened to accounts on her hidden crystal set over about mounting violence and knew she had no way of protecting her and Gran should someone come to the farm to do them harm. Then again, she thought, recalling her father's shotgun under Gran's bed, she did have that, and she knew she would use it to defend them. They were so close to liberation, she could feel it and no one was going to take that away from them after what they'd been through.

'I don't want you going into town any more,' Gran insisted one morning in March after reports of local women being assaulted and widespread looting. For almost six weeks, Estelle did as she asked, only venturing as far as the village. Things were getting tougher and Estelle felt her father's loss much more now than ever before. He would have protected them and made them feel safe. Would she be able to rely on Hans to do the same against his own men?

FORTY-SEVEN

Rosie

15 APRIL 1944

W*ell, it looks like it's all happening at the moment doesn't it Essie? So much nervous excitement going on I can almost taste it. Everyone is desperate to survive especially as we've come this far. If we hadn't thought the doodlebugs were bad enough we've been having to contend with V2s since late last year and I have to admit that the slightest sound in the distance has me trembling and scanning the skies. Surely, it can't be long now, can it?*

So much seems to be happening according to the news. I was sad though to read that President Roosevelt had died of a stroke and so close to what surely must now be the end of this interminable war. Thank heavens for the Red Cross. I don't know what we would have done without replies to our telegrams and you're probably thinking the same now that they're bringing food and supplies to the Channel Islands.

I so want to be able to hug you Essie. I try to picture everything. The farm and how it looks now. How you wear your hair and if you and Gran are thin, which I imagine you must be after so many months on what must have been a starvation diet. I can't wait for you to see me. I've grown several inches but I still don't think I'll be as tall as you are. My hair is a little darker I think, but that's from not being out in the sun as much as I was at home. I look more grown up now that Aunt Muriel helps me style it a little, but she won't let me wear lipstick yet because she said it makes me look older than I am. She says that's a bad thing because I don't yet have the maturity to look after myself if I receive any unwanted attention, whatever that means.

Essie, I just know if we can get through the next bit of the war that we will see each other soon and you'll finally be able to read all my notes in this diary I've kept for you. I dare hardly hope that sometime soon we could be lying in the long grass among the wildflowers in the top meadow and telling each other all about our different wars.

So much has changed in the past five years since I last saw you. So much death and destruction, but Aunt Muriel keeps insisting we'll get through this and I do believe her, although there have been times when I've doubted her.

Much love, Essie. I wonder how we'll look back on this time apart? Or will we simply want to forget it ever happened? You know, I don't think we will want to forget because whatever we've gone through, these experiences, for good or bad, have made us who we are.

FORTY-EIGHT

Estelle

4 MAY 1945

'D id you see last night's *Evening Post*?' Mr Gibault asked when she went to his shop.

Estelle shook her head, anxious about what bad news he might have for her. 'No, why?'

'I'll show you,' he said, grinning and reaching under his counter for something. He lifted a copy of the local newspaper and slapped it on to his wooden counter. 'Look,' he said, pointing to the headline. 'Read that out loud to me, young Estelle. I want to hear it as well as see it for myself.'

Estelle read it once to herself and gasped in disbelief. 'Really?'

'Go on then, read what it says.' He rested his hands on his hips. 'Loudly.'

Estelle giggled. 'ADOLF HITLER FALLS AT HIS POST.' Could it really be true? Was that monster dead? 'Does that mean this is over, do you think?'

'I think it definitely soon will be.'

She could barely believe it. 'I'll buy a copy please. Gran

needs to see this.'

He rolled up the newspaper and handed it to Estelle. 'No, it's my gift to your gran.' He stared at Estelle for a moment. 'How is she coping?'

Estelle gave his question some thought. Her grandmother was definitely looking healthier and a little stronger since the Vega had begun delivering food parcels for them. Estelle was certain it was due to the realisation that the outside world hadn't forgotten them. And tasting decent food after so many months eating nettle soup and bramble leaf tea wasn't harming her either. She knew that after this war she would never eat another turnip, the very thought made her feel sick, but the tasteless vegetables had helped keep them going.

'She's hanging on in there, Mr Gibault. I can tell she's putting on a brave face so that I don't worry about her too much, but I know her well enough to see through it.' She sighed. 'She's exhausted from everything we've gone through. It's as simple as that. Her spirits are low and I don't know if it was the diphtheria that sapped most of her strength, or the shortages.' She realised she was worrying him. 'That's why I want to show her this headline. It'll give her the boost to keep going that she desperately needs. It certainly gives me hope.'

'As it does me, Estelle.'

The following few days were a mixture of excitement and frustration. 'I don't know why the Bailiff said we can't raise our British flags,' Estelle grumbled on 8 May as she climbed down the attic ladder holding some tatty bunting and two flags that her father must have put up there at some point before the war. She shook the Jersey flag and the Union Flag that her father had hung from the upstairs windows whenever there had been a Royal visit to the island. She sneezed. 'They're really dusty. We should have put them away in an old suitcase for the duration of the war.'

'It's a bit late now to worry about a speck of dust.' Gran took one from her and the two of them went outside to the yard and gave them a good shake. 'Anyway, you know it makes sense not to raise the flags just yet. We don't want to get this far and antagonise the Jerries. Who knows what they might do?'

She had a point, Estelle thought, giving her flag an extra shake and watching the dust fly into the air. It was good enough just to be able to bring these outside in preparation of the celebrations they now felt certain would soon arrive.

They hadn't seen much of Hans and she wasn't sure what was going to happen to him. She supposed he would return to Germany and then at some point be allowed to go back to his family and carry on with his life. She hoped so.

Realising it was almost three o'clock, Estelle nudged her grandmother gently. 'Give me that flag and let's go inside and turn on the set. I can't miss what Mr Churchill has to say today.'

She hung the two flags and bunting over the back of one of the kitchen chairs and sat down at the table opposite her grandmother. Estelle turned on her crystal set and waited. At exactly three o'clock, Winston Churchill's voice crackled through the set. Estelle reached for her grandmother's nearest hand and held on to it.

'Hostilities will end officially at one minute after midnight tonight,' he said, his familiar voice ensuring that neither of them dared barely breathe as he spoke. 'But in the interests of saving lives, the ceasefire began yesterday, to be sounded all along the Front, and our dear Channel Islands are also to be freed today.'

Estelle couldn't speak. She wished she could hear him repeat what he had just said, just to be certain that she hadn't imagined the words.

Her grandmother cleared her throat. 'Estelle you do realise that this means we're free?' she whispered.

Estelle could barely move. All these years hoping and wishing for this to happen, she had always imagined she would be jumping up and down cheering and shrieking. All she could manage to do was sit and stare at the crystal set as her mind slowly absorbed that this was really happening.

She bit her lower lip and looked at her grandmother. 'You're crying, Gran,' she said, wondering why her grandmother didn't wipe away her tears.

'So are you, my love.'

Later that evening, as Estelle was making her way along the hedgerow along the back field, she spotted Hans. His hands were in his uniform trouser pockets and he was staring up at the blue sky, deep in thought. She decided not to disturb him. After so long of him being here, of the unexpected strength and comfort he gave her, he would be leaving in the next day or so.

'Good evening, Estelle,' Hans said, noticing her and waving.

'Hello, Hans. Rebel and I were going for a walk.'

'Making plans for the farm now that the war is over?'

'Yes. I can't say that I'm not. To have our freedom again.'

'You can turn your clocks back to the proper time, too,' he said in a half-hearted attempt at a joke.

'Oh, Gran has already done that,' she said. 'But don't report us, will you?'

Hans shrugged. 'No one could do anything about it now, anyway.' He stood in front of her and reached down to stroke Rebel's head. 'I'll miss you, boy.'

'He'll miss you, too,' Estelle said realising it for the first time. The dog had spent a lot of time with him. It dawned on her that Hans hadn't just been standing staring at the sky. 'You're leaving now, aren't you?'

'Yes, I've been called to the barracks. You are to have your island back, Estelle. I am pleased for you.'

She couldn't untangle her emotions, so complicated but so strong too. 'I'm glad that if we had to have any officer billeted with us that it was you.'

His lips drew back into a slight smile. 'Thank you. I am happy to hear you say this. But of course you will be happier when I am gone and your little sister returns from England.'

Estelle nodded. 'Yes, I can't wait to see her again. It's been a long five years.'

He patted Rebel's head. 'It has.'

'Do you know what will happen to you?' She couldn't shake how desperately sad she felt at the thought of never seeing him again. Or her worry for what would happen to him as the loser in this terrible war.

'No, not yet.' He gazed at her for a few seconds. 'I hope to be able to return home to see my mother soon though and, one day, I like to think that I will return to this pretty island and see what it is like in peace time. Would you mind me doing that?'

Estelle's heart broke. 'No, I wouldn't mind. But I think you should wait a good few years before then, don't you?'

Hans smiled. 'I agree.' He bowed his head slightly and took her hands in his. 'Goodbye, Estelle. I'm grateful I was lucky enough to spend my war on your farm. Please say my goodbyes to Frau Woods. I believe she might have gone to visit one of her friends.' He leant forward and gave her a lingering kiss on her cheek that she leaned into before letting her hands go.

'Goodbye, Hans,' she said, her voice barely above a whisper, still able to feel the pressure of his fingers on her own. The imprint of his kiss.

She watched him walk away, turning once as he reached the side of the barn to give her a brief smile. She felt as if a hand was squeezing her heart and wondered how different things could have been between them if they had met in peace time.

She crouched down and hugged Rebel. 'It's finally over, boy.' But despite her joy at the war finally ending, Estelle buried her head in the Alsatian's fur and cried.

FORTY-NINE

Estelle

9 MAY 1945 – LIBERATION DAY

E stelle woke early and dressed. She could still barely dare to believe that they were to be officially liberated today. She had hung both her dad's Jersey flag and his Union Flag from the windows feeling as she did so that she was taking ownership back from the Germans and knew her father would approve of her doing so.

She hurried downstairs eager to step outside into the warm May day and breathe in deeply. Before she reached the back door someone banged on it several times.

'Miss. Miss.'

She opened the door and smiled at the boy who had caused such upset when trying to steal their chicken. 'Hello, what are you doing here?'

'Me mum said I should let you know about the boat.'

'What boat?'

'The HMS *Beagle*, it's called. It arrived at St Helier Harbour this morning with British soldiers. We're going to town soon to join in the celebrations. It's going to be fun.

The Red Cross boat is there, too, with more food parcels for us all. Mum said I can have half a bar of chocolate today from it to celebrate.'

She thanked him, surprised to hear that Chantal was being so thoughtful, and went to find her grandmother, who was in her garden sitting on a sun chair, her eyes closed. Estelle watched her relieved to see how relaxed she seemed. It made a pleasant change.

'Gran, we have to go to town. Everyone's going to be at the Pomme d'Or at two o'clock and we can't miss it.'

'No, lovey, I'm quite happy sitting here thinking about what it's going to be like when Rosie's back here with us.'

Estelle couldn't hide her disappointment. 'But, Gran, we went through this together and I was hoping to be in front of the Pomme d'Or with you when they hoist the Union Flag. Don't you want to be there? We're going to look back on this day and won't want to have missed anything.'

Her grandmother reached out and rested her hand on Estelle's cheek. 'You go for both of us. For me, it's enough that we came through this and to know that, apart from your dear father, the rest of us survived.'

Estelle thought of Gerard and Antoinette's husband Paul and hoped it wouldn't be too long until they discovered when both men would be able to come home. Gerard deserved to come home. To come back to his life. Did he deserve to come back to her, though? After what she had done?

'Would you rather I stay here with you?' she asked her grandmother. 'I'm not sure you should be here alone on such a historic day.'

'Estelle. Go. Take it all in and then come back and tell me everything that happened. I'm sure Violet will make her way here this afternoon, so I doubt I'll be alone anyway.'

Gran was right, Estelle realised. Violet would want to celebrate with her oldest friend and would probably come to the farm. 'Right, I'll go, then.' She bent down and kissed her grandmother on the forehead. 'I'll see you later.'

'Enjoy yourself.'

Estelle cycled into town happier than she could recall being in such a long time. Her bike wobbled and she giggled despite almost falling off as the RAF made flypasts overhead. She could hear the crowds before she reached them and spotted the red cross on the SS *Vega*, which was docked in the harbour. Excitement bubbled through her as she tried to think where to leave her bike. Determined not to miss a single thing, she left it with hundreds of others hoping she would be able to find it again, but not caring overly if she didn't. As she reached the edge of the crowds she joined in with the singing and dancing, her heart filling with joy.

She spotted Antoinette waving at her and beamed happily to her friend as she made her way towards her. 'I've been hoping to find you,' Antoinette shouted over the happy voices all around them.

It was two-thirty before she saw the first British soldiers marching towards the Pomme d'Or Hotel. Estelle laughed watching the beaming men being kissed and hugged as they neared the hotel building.

Finally, she watched the swastika flag being lowered and the Union Flag being hung from a balcony on the hotel and joyful tears streamed down her face while Antoinette and others cheered. If only Dad was here with her right now. She wondered if he was looking down on her. Her gaze drifted across to the harbour where he had been killed. So much had changed since then. She had changed and she knew she would never be the same person again.

They were free, finally.

Epilogue

'Gran, Rosie, please hurry up.' Estelle finished washing the dishes and dried her hands on her pinny before untying it and hanging it on the back of the kitchen door. She stared at the place where once her father's jacket had hung and recalled that day three years before when she had been so fearful that Hans would notice that the old jacket had gone missing. She wondered where Ivan, the escaped slave she had helped, was now and prayed he was safe with his family once more.

The sound of Gerard's lorry coming up the driveway snapped her back to the present and she ran to the bottom of the stairs and called up to her grandmother and little sister. 'Gerard's here. Come along, or we'll miss the celebrations.'

Then, buttoning her jacket, Estelle quickly checked that her hair was still neat and her hat at the perfect angle. She was looking forward to joining the crowds at People's Park to celebrate the first anniversary since the island had been liberated. She knew Gran was hoping to get there early enough to find a decent spot so she wouldn't miss the march past, or the speeches. Rosie's heels stamped noisily down the stairs followed by Gran's quieter shoes.

'I thought you were never going to be ready.' Estelle studied her sister who in the time she had been in London had grown from a bubbly twelve-year-old girl into a stylish young woman. Sometimes it threw her to see the change in Rosie. She pulled Rosie into a hug. It concerned Estelle that she might never be rid of the momentary fear each morning as she woke that Rosie's return to the farm had been nothing but a cruel dream. 'Did I tell you how wonderful it is to have you back home with us?'

'Only every day.' Rosie grinned.

Gran entered the kitchen, red in the face and flustered. 'Hurry up you two, Gerard's waiting.'

Estelle and Rosie glanced at each other and smiled, then followed Gran out of the house.

Rebel raised his head as Estelle reached the back door hopeful of an invitation to join them. 'Sorry, Rebel,' Estelle said. 'You're going to have to stay here and guard the farm for us.'

She walked outside enjoying the thought that there was no need for anyone to watch over the farm now that they were free and the island was safe once more.

Gerard stood at the back of his lorry smiling at them. 'What do you think then?' he asked, arm outstretched to show off his display of bunting. It flapped gently in the breeze from where he had tied it around the back of the lorry where his passengers were sitting waiting for Estelle, Rosie and Gran to join them.

'I thought you could sit in the cabin with me, Mrs Woods. It's more comfortable in there.'

'Why would I want to do that?' Gran snapped. 'Give me a hand so I can sit up on the back with everyone else. After all we've been through I'm not missing out on any fun. Hello, Violet, dear. Good to see you're feeling well enough to join us.'

Estelle took one of Gran's hands, while Gerard took the other, and soon Gran was sitting on one of the benches between Rosie and Violet. He helped Estelle onboard. She glanced at Gerard's new girlfriend, Bernadette, who was laughing at something Rosie was saying. Estelle was glad that she and Gerard had been honest with each other about their feelings and that he had now moved on and was happy. He was a good man. Always kind and sweet and Estelle was happy that he had been her first love. Too much had happened to each of them since the beginning of the war for them to go back to how things had once been.

She caught his eye and Gerard beamed at her. 'All set?'

A chorus of cheers rang out and Gerard returned to the cabin and started the lorry.

As everyone around her sang and chattered, Estelle put her hand in her pocket and felt the crumpled letter that she received from Hans a few days ago. She had read it over and over again, the relief that he had survived causing silent tears to slide down her cheek. She knew the words off by heart now.

Dear Fräulein Le Maistre, Estelle,

I am writing to you in the hope I do not offend you by making contact in this way. The day we said goodbye feels like a lifetime ago but I want to apologise for my presence being imposed upon you and your grandmother for those years. However, I must admit that I am not sorry to have made your acquaintance. It cannot have been easy for either of you to have a German officer living under your roof, but I hope that not all your memories of my stay at the farm are negative ones. I am grateful to have spent my time in Jersey at your farm. With you.

Much has changed here in Germany and I am now home with my family and together we are rebuilding our lives. I am sure you and your grandmother are doing the same and I hope you have been reunited with your sister and your fiancé.

I would like to be able to return to your beautiful island one day and see for myself what it is like to drive down the pretty lanes and swim on one of the beaches in peacetime. It is far too soon of course but one day I hope to meet you under more pleasant circumstances and I like to think we would spend time together because you choose it and not because it is something that is forced upon you.

For now, Estelle, I would like to wish you a free and happy life. If I do not hear from you, I will understand, of course, but words cannot express how much it would mean to me to only know that you are well.

Your friend,

Hans Bauer

That evening after a long, emotional day celebrating with her family and friends, Estelle sat at her dressing table. She read Hans's letter once more and set it down onto the polished wood, smoothing it flat with the palm of her hand. Then, taking a piece of writing paper from her drawer, she picked up her pen, and after a little thought began writing.

Dear Hans,

It was a welcome surprise to receive your letter and just in time for the first anniversary of our liberation. I am happy to learn that you are well and have returned to your family and the life you enjoyed so much before the war.

My sister, Rosie, returned to Jersey soon after the island was liberated and it is a joy to have her back with us once again. Gran and I are well and we're slowly, with Rosie's help, building the farm back up to how it was before my father's death. My aunt Muriel is now married to a Canadian soldier she met earlier in the war and Gran, Rosie and I are very much looking forward to them coming to stay with us for a few weeks this summer. Gerard is back on the island, too. He is well, although, I feel I need to tell you we are now just good friends and no longer engaged to be married. We are both very happy. We aren't the same people we were before the war.

The island is starting to feel like it was before the war. Though the bunkers remain as silent, dark reminders of what happened. They remind me of what we survived.

All that is left to say is that I look forward to showing you my island in peace time – as a man, not a soldier.

For now, with my good wishes,

Estelle

A Note from the Author

Dear Reader,

Firstly, thank you for choosing to read *An Island at War*. As someone who was born and lived her entire life in Jersey, apart from eighteen months travelling when I was twenty-one, this book is very dear to my heart.

Living in Jersey I come across reminders of the five-year Occupation of this island during World War Two every day. There's a long stretch of Hitler's Atlantic Wall, the coastal defences and fortifications built by Nazi Germany as a defence against Allied invasion, running across most of St Ouen's Bay where I walk my dogs, as well as many other concrete bunkers dotted around the island. Louisa Gould, the shopkeeper who took in a Russian forced labourer, was arrested and deported to Ravensbrück concentration camp where she died in a gas chamber in 1945, lived and ran her shop down the road from where I live. And I've grown up listening to neighbours and other islanders talking about what it was like to live on the island under Nazi rule.

My paternal great-grandmother, Marguerite Wood, remained on the island despite originally being from Scotland. I discovered her Occupation Registration Card and was shocked to find that she lied about where she was born, as well as her maiden name. I'm not sure why she chose to do this but I'm sure she had her reasons. Nazi officers were billeted next door to where she lived on St Aubin's Road. I've based Mrs Woods, Estelle and Rosie's gran, loosely on my great-grandmother, especially her quiet determination to ensure her family's safety. My maternal grandmother, Muriel, who lived through the Blitz inspired Aunt Muriel in the book.

My father was four when he was evacuated on the last boat out of the island with his mother, brother, and cousin. They lived in London for most of the war and he was evacuated twice more from there to safer places during the Blitz. My late mother-in-law, Margaret Carr, was also evacuated. She was from Guernsey and was heartbroken to leave the island and her cat with her mother when she was fourteen. She dreamt of being a dress designer and it was her drawings that I now have displayed in my home that inspired me a little with Estelle and her own dreams.

Being a Jersey girl, I wanted to write a book to honour islanders who lived through those long, difficult five years and who somehow had the strength and drive to survive all that they faced. I wrote this book during the Covid-19 pandemic's first lockdown and although I thankfully have never experienced oppression, starvation and the fear that the islanders must have faced, I didn't know, as they didn't, how long I myself would be separated from my grown-up children who both lived overseas. I was able to use my fear for their safety and dread about how long it would be until I could see them again as I wrote this book.

I hope I've done my fellow Channel Islanders justice and that you, my readers, have enjoyed discovering a little more about this small island fifteen miles off the coast of France. If you ever visit you must go to the Jersey War Tunnels, maybe have a stroll around some of the bunkers you come across along St Ouen's Bay and Noirmont and maybe if one or two are open during your stay, go inside and see for yourself what the forced labourers, brought to the island during the Occupation, had to build.

Thank you, once again, for choosing to read *An Island at War*. If you've enjoyed it please consider leaving a short review on Amazon as reviews help other readers discover authors' books.

Stay safe and best wishes,

Deborah

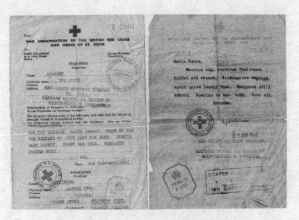

*Above: examples of Red Cross telegrams sent to the
author's family during the Occupation.*

Above: a family member's Identity Card from Guernsey.

Above: one of the author's mother-in-law's dress designs.

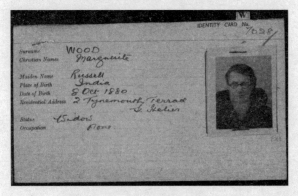

*Above: the author's great-grandmother's Identity Card
courtesy of Jersey Heritage.*

Acknowledgments

Thank you to my amazing publisher and editor at One More Chapter, Charlotte Ledger, whose own family comes from Jersey and whose idea it was to write this book. I was at first unsure about whether I could do my fellow islanders justice in writing a novel set during Jersey's dark years of the Occupation, but ultimately felt that I should give it my best shot and here it is.

Also thank you to Lucy Bennett for her amazing book cover for *An Island at War*. I love that it shows Marine Peilstand 3, the MP3 tower at Battery Moltke at Les Landes, where I often walk my dogs.

To my father for his stories about being evacuated with his mother and for the stories he recalls his grandmother sharing with him from her years living in Jersey during the Occupation.

My late mother-in-law, Margaret, for the Red Cross telegrams she and her mother received from their relatives in Guernsey, with her mother's replies on the back sent months later, as well as Identity Cards from the Occupation and her own dress designs that she worked on as an evacuee.

To everyone who helps keep the history alive from that time including my Auntie Monica and Uncle Alan Le Feuvre, who were both children during the Occupation. To all at Jersey Heritage, especially Senior Archivist, Stuart Nicolle for his help once again, and everyone at the Jersey War Tunnels, the Jersey branch of the Channel Islands Occupation Society and the Channel Islands Military Museum as well as everyone who remembers and tells people's stories from the Occupation so that others, like me, can discover, to an extent at least, what it must have been like to live in Jersey and the other Channel Islands during that time.

To the Red Cross for all that they did for the islanders during the Occupation from arranging telegrams to delivering desperately needed food parcels and medicines.

Mèrcie bien.

YOUR NUMBER ONE STOP

ONE MORE CHAPTER

FOR PAGETURNING BOOKS

One More Chapter is an
award-winning global
division of HarperCollins.

Sign up to our newsletter to get our
latest eBook deals and stay up to date
with our weekly Book Club!
<u>Subscribe here.</u>

Meet the team at
<u>www.onemorechapter.com</u>

Follow us!
 <u>@OneMoreChapter_</u>
 <u>@OneMoreChapter</u>
 <u>@onemorechapterhc</u>

Do you write unputdownable fiction?
We love to hear from new voices.
Find out how to submit your novel at
<u>www.onemorechapter.com/submissions</u>